The Geek who Saved Christmas

ANNABETH ALBERT

Copyright © 2021 by Annabeth Albert

All rights reserved.

No part of this book may be reproduced in any form or by any electronic or mechanical means, including information storage and retrieval systems, without written permission from the author, except for the use of brief quotations in a book review.

Cover Credit: Cate Ashwood Designs, Illustration by Lauren Dombrowski

For all the readers who love this season as much as me & also for my mom who makes every holiday so special!

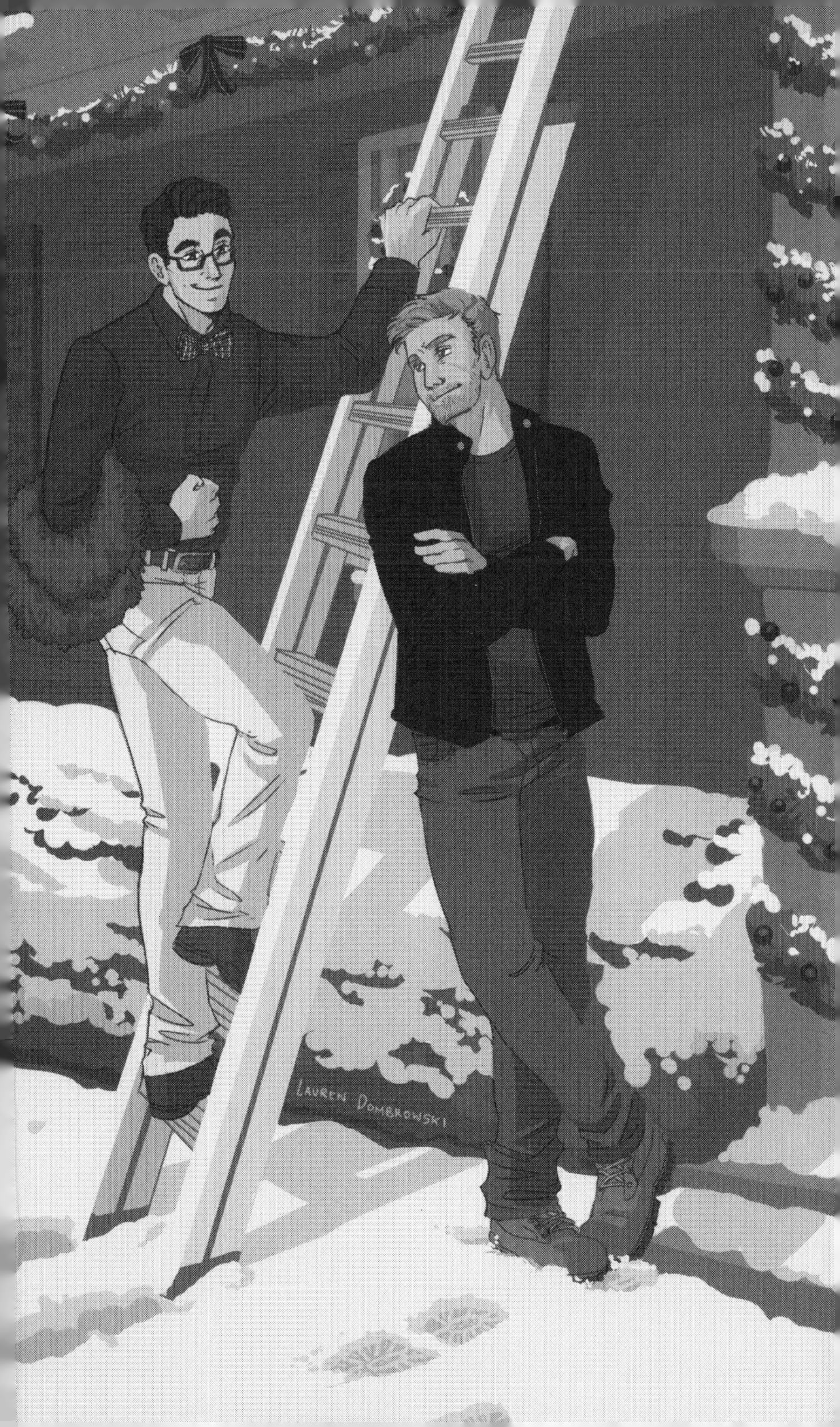
LAUREN DOMBROWSKI

Chapter One
GIDEON

'Tis that time of year again, neighbors! The annual holiday lights charity fundraiser is coming! It's time to get serious about those decorations, folks! ~Cheryl Bridges posted to the What's Up Neighbor app

"See the blazing Yule before us," I sang happily. I was running late, but that didn't stop me from summoning some early seasonal spirit on my way into the tiny Evergreen Park community center at the heart of our historic neighborhood. I'd been looking forward to this meeting for weeks now, the moment when my grand plans would all be revealed. I did love a good plan, and I had the schematics to prove it.

Deck the halls, indeed. If I had my way, the whole neighborhood would be transformed into a perfect—

"Watch it." A voice I knew a little too well had me looking up in the nick of time to avoid crashing into my next-door neighbor. My very hot, very grumpy, very not-into-community-meetings neighbor.

"Paul!" I faked some cheer in the hopes that maybe his

grinchy heart had thawed this year, and he'd finally join us in decorating. "You here for the meeting?"

"Yep." Typically monosyllabic, his stony face revealed nothing about his intentions.

"Does this mean you're going to put up some lights this year?" I asked brightly. My voice had the same embarrassingly breathless quality it always took on around Paul Frost. Something about all those muscles and silver-fox looks combined to fluster me every darn interaction. We were both over forty, but he wore it so much hotter. "I'll be going over guidelines and helpful hints."

"I don't need hints." It really was a darn shame, the way the man totally lacked an appetite for fun and community togetherness. But maybe when one filled out a leather jacket like he did, a personality was strictly optional.

"Still, everyone is looking forward to hearing my plans." Everyone other than *him* went without saying. And if he was there to object, he could save it. I'd worked too hard on my plans to turn back now. "I'd better get in there."

"Sure." Paul held the door for us both. "Nice tie."

"Um. Thanks." I had no idea what to make of the half-smile that teased the edges of his mouth as he indicted my bow tie, which featured cheerful and seasonally appropriate turkeys.

Mr. Leather Jacket had an endless wardrobe of plain black T-shirts and wasn't the type to appreciate my fashionable whimsy, making me even more suspicious of his motives for coming to the meeting. However, before I could question him further, Cheryl, our longtime leader, frantically motioned me over to the coffee table. I headed toward her and most certainly did not sneak a look at the flex of Paul's muscles as he found a seat near the back of the community center.

Liar. Okay, a tiny peek. It wasn't my fault the man was riveting. Even frowning, he added something to the otherwise drab space. The multipurpose room consisted of a low stage at the front and folding chairs, which could be stowed for senior citizen fitness classes, kid art classes, and other community activities.

"See something you like?" Cheryl raised an eyebrow as I reached her. Oops. Maybe I hadn't been as subtle as I thought.

"Your new sweater. Love the rose shade on you," I said smoothly.

"Gideon." Her pragmatic tone was just this side of scolding. "Paul Frost is a tree you can't climb."

"Not planning on trying," I lied. I'd blaze his Yule in a heartbeat if I thought he was interested, but he was most decidedly not. Every neighborhood interaction tended to turn *frosty* in a hurry. Which was a shame because we were both single men of a certain age.

According to Cheryl, who had an unparalleled talent for getting details, he'd never been married and didn't have kids. What he did have was a discreet rainbow on his truck and business logo. And over-forty, unattached homeowners who were possibly into guys didn't come along all that often in our sleepy suburb. So, understandably, I'd initially been gleeful when he'd moved in, but four years of terse interactions said that short, geeky, snappy dressers didn't float his particular boat.

Or maybe it was my relentless optimism. Maybe he was allergic to smiles and needed someone similarly dour to hang with, not that I'd seen him date. No hookups escaping late at night or early morning either. And yes, I was a nosy enough neighbor that I'd know.

"Well, he's not the only new face tonight. This crowd is an excellent omen." Cheryl patted me on the sleeve as I removed my stack of handouts from my leather messenger bag.

"The big turnout is great, but we may need more snacks." I gestured at the table, which was already running short on cookies and coffee cups.

"I'm on it." Smiling deviously, she retrieved an extra platter of turkey-shaped cookies from under the table. "Think Paul will actually decorate this year?"

"That would be a pleasant change." This was my third year as holiday chair, and if I'd learned anything, it was that Paul Frost didn't do seasonal celebrations and quite possibly went into hibernation each December. No parties. No appearance at Cheryl's big New Year's Eve celebration. No neighborly food offerings. And nary as much as a wreath or single strand of lights.

"I suppose we should get started." After setting out the fresh platter of cookies, Cheryl clapped her hands with all the authority of a woman who'd raised four sons to adulthood. "Now, I'm sure you're all here for Gideon's decorating plans, but before we get to that, we have some housekeeping. The first snow is coming soon, and you'll want to remember our shared sidewalk obligations."

Cheryl had a number of such reminders before moving on to new business. "The Morrisons have raised the issue of the high schoolers. Again."

This got a murmur from the crowd. Paul straightened up from his earlier lazy sprawl. Ah. Maybe he wasn't here about my decorating after all. And undoubtedly, he sided with the only residents who were possibly bigger scrooges than him. The Morrisons lived to complain. This time it was about the increasing number of young people who were cutting through the park to reach the high school on the other side and trudging across the shared green space maintained by the neighborhood association. The lack of a formal path meant they left muddy footprints and trash in their wake.

"We need to fence off the area." Mr. Morrison went right to his preferred solution for everything. "Close access. Post signs. Big signs."

"Yes, that's one idea." Cheryl's tone was way nicer than he deserved. "Proper signage is always a good first step."

"This is a problem. We can't keep letting them strut on through like they own the place." Morrison's rant got several nods from the crowd.

"Sure we can," Paul spoke clearly from his spot, not bothering to stand or raise his hand, but he had the sort of voice that when he spoke, people tended to listen. Deep. Gravelly. Working-class Philly with a little hint of Jersey. His sort of blunt directness always impressed me, the way a tell-it-like-it-is person could cut through a lot of game playing and posturing.

And this was a stunning turn of events. My head whipped toward Morrison, eager to see how he'd respond. Paul taking the side of the high schoolers caused wide eyes all around the room and more than one swift intake of breath. High drama for a Tuesday night around here.

"Let them continue to cut through?" Morrison's skin was getting all splotchy pink and a sheen of sweat appeared on his forehead. "We can't make it that easy on them."

"They're kids." Paul shrugged, completely unmoved by Morrison's bluster. "They're trying to get to the school fast, often in bad weather. Let them cut through. But let's make it even easier."

"Easier? Why would we do that?"

"Now, Ernest, let's hear Paul's idea." Cheryl made a sit-down motion with her hand that Morrison ignored.

"What you need is a path. A real path. Add a trash can at each end to handle the litter issue."

"Paths cost money." Cheryl spoke before Morrison or someone else could. The community center itself was held together with love and a lot of rusty screws, many years removed from its humble midcentury origins. The greater township never had enough spare budget for parks and rec for the neighborhoods.

"Yup. Any sort of landscaping is going to have costs. But so do fences." Paul had a sharp look for Morrison. "And it would be a short path. Quick project. My guys can do it, on us. It's a slow enough time of year for our crew that we can do it between other jobs. If we hurry, we can get it in before it gets too cold to pour concrete."

Even Cheryl's experienced eyes went wide at that. Grumpy Mr. Frost had a heart? For late-running high school students, no less? I'd known he was a contractor from his large truck emblazoned with his Frost Construction & Landscaping logo, but this was unexpected generosity from a guy who glared if my trash cans were a few inches out of line on our shared driveway.

"You'd donate a path?" Cheryl clarified.

"Yep. That's what I said." Paul rubbed his neck as if maybe public speaking wasn't his favorite activity. "It's work for my crew, keeps us busy. And it will look better than a fence, which the kids would likely jump anyway."

This got a murmur of agreement from a large portion of the audience.

"Well, I suppose it's worth bringing to the improvements committee for a vote. Maybe something can be scared up for materials expenses." Cheryl gave a decisive nod. Her stamp of approval meant the project was likely a done deal. Apparently none too happy about this turn of events, Morrison went harumphing his way toward the exit, his long-suffering wife trailing after him.

"Wait!" Cheryl called after him. "Gideon Holiday was about to speak. Don't you want to hear the neighborhood decorating plans?"

"Don't need to." Older with saggy jowls, his scowl was a lot less interesting than Paul's. And they were the only neighbors as uninclined toward the holidays, what with their house's lone spindly reindeer lawn ornament and same ancient wreath each year. Morrison was also one to loudly rant about others' displays, complaining excessive lights and decor were eyesores. And he had endless things to say about the traffic it brought to the neighborhood.

Paul, on the other hand, wasn't a complainer. Somehow his lack of participation didn't feel as mean-spirited. More like he simply wasn't interested, but this year, I had a plan for that. And after discovering that he had a bigger heart than I'd originally thought, I was even more optimistic that my efforts might be successful at long last.

Knowing he had something of a soft spot for younger people, I looked right at Paul when it was my turn to speak. The specifics of the lighting schedule could wait. Instead, I waxed poetic about the children's programming here at the center we were collecting donations for from visitors who would come to see our displays. We'd also collect food and unwrapped new toys for needy families.

I was super passionate about obtaining more support for the community center's efforts, but meeting Paul's sharp hazel eyes as I delivered my appeal was a mistake. There was a reason I tried not to look too hard or too long at the guy. All that stubbly gray hotness had a tendency to make me fumble my words and tried my careful composure.

"The box will go in the toys." I blinked at my bungling of the point. "Er. Toys. In the box."

Get a grip, Gideon. I had to look away from Paul and fast. He already thought I was the nutty Holiday guy. I didn't need him thinking locking gazes with him was enough to trip me up like a high schooler with a crush. Even if it was.

"The kids need our help, and by working together, we can ensure our display makes all the best of the area lists. More visitors equals more donations. The charitable giving committee says requests for help are way up this year, and they need all the assistance we can give them." There. I finished strong, but Paul didn't seem particularly moved, glancing down at his phone and shifting in his seat. Maybe he was simply too polite to follow Morrison out the door.

His disinterest didn't faze me. I had a plan B, C, and D where Paul Frost was concerned, and I wasn't giving up quite yet.

Chapter Two
PAUL

Have you seen the muddy mess of footprints in the open space? I spotted two girls cutting through it again this morning. Something must be done before the snow starts. ~Ernest Morrison posted to the What's Up Neighbor app

I'd said what I'd come to say. Neighbors worried about a little mud and some footprints needed to chill out. These meetings were hardly my usual style, but as a contractor, I also wasn't unused to planning commissions and zoning boards. I could have left my objections at how ugly and unnecessary additional fencing would be, but I'd known Cheryl wouldn't be able to resist the free labor offer.

Standing next to her on the stage at the front of the room, Gideon Holiday's expression had gone all amazed. Felt good to startle him a little. He was such a bundle of contradictions. He never failed to sport a pristine appearance with a perfectly pressed shirt, ridiculous bow tie, and poofy haircut that probably cost more than my last pair of boots. But for all he could be cultured and charming to others, he was always skittish around me. His fumbling for words and nervous gestures made it seem like he expected me to whip out a tire iron any moment.

I understood his wariness. I was too blue-collar for a lot of these longtime residents, many of whom were associated with the nearby college. Stanton Anthony had been an exclusive women's school before finally integrating a few years back. Gideon did something suitably techy and important over there. But even with all his polish, the guy still managed to get rattled by my existence as if I was about to make off with the silver any minute. He sure was enthusiastic about these seasonal lights though.

"The theme this year is Magical Wonderland, which you all should know from the memo I sent a few weeks back." Gideon had moved on to talking specifics for the neighborhood decorating efforts. I wanted to leave, but after Morrison's rudeness, it felt like staying was the least I could do, especially if I wanted the committee to approve the path project. Always with the committees around here.

And whatever the neighborhood crisis, Gideon had a memo, a spreadsheet, or a rule book at the ready. But he was wrong. There was nothing inherently magical about December. These days it was just another month on the calendar for me and not worth all this fuss. Not that I'd tell the guy who was currently gushing over silver-and-gold lighting schemes and rotation of the donation collection duties. I let the signup sheet for that slide on by me.

Finally, Gideon finished, and after yet more reminders about proper snow removal techniques and prompt stowing of trash cans, the meeting was dismissed. About time. Now I could make my escape and head home before Jim got too restless without me.

"Paul! Wait up!" Gideon called right as I reached the door. I narrowly suppressed a groan as I slowed my strides.

"Yeah?" I turned toward him. His smile could reach almost blinding levels. No guy our age should have such deep dimples or such an impish grin. Seemed like his eyes were always sparkling behind his pricey-looking horned-rimmed glasses. He made an adorable hipster, but as much fun as he was to look at, I still dreaded whatever he had to say.

"I'll walk back with you. I wanted to say thank you for sticking up for the kids. That was very…unexpected of you." Gideon coupled his dramatic pause with raised eyebrows as if I was more likely to run the kids off with a pitchfork.

"No problem." I continued my trek out of the building. I didn't question how Gideon knew I'd walked rather than drove. He was one of those highly observant folks who probably didn't mean to be nosy but simply couldn't help noticing every little detail. Reminded me of my brother, which caused my tone to be a little gruffer than I'd intended.

"It was very charitable, and I'd like to help in any way I can." Gideon was nothing if not earnest. I couldn't see him pouring cement or leveling a trail in his fancy clothes. Even his jacket was a fashionable wool number, and his jogging clothes were always color-coordinated. Not that I snooped, but Gideon was kind of hard to miss.

"Thanks." The evening had turned crisp and chilly. It wouldn't be long at all until snow arrived. I hoped the improvements committee approved the path quickly. I needed some more hours for the crew before Thanksgiving, a reason to make sure my people had enough in their checks to get by. Man, how I hated the slow months.

"I, for one, like having more kids in the neighborhood." Unbothered by my lack of conversation, Gideon continued his cheery rambling. Leaving the park, we waited at the gates for a car to pass. "The younger families moving in is a good thing, despite some of the grumbles."

"Honestly, it's less about the kids and more about Jim," I admitted before he could go erecting a statue in my honor.

"Jim?" Gideon's mouth pursed like he'd said a curse word.

"My dog." Letting Gideon think I'd meant a human companion might have been funny, but it would have undoubtedly led to more prying. I'd spare us both the questioning.

"Ah, yes," he said with all the enthusiasm of a non-dog person. "I've seen you with it. It's a rather striking creature."

"Yeah, well, in the mornings, I walk her through the green space, let her run a little if no one else is around yet." Jim was a big, shaggy Bernese Mountain dog and would have preened at even Gideon's faint praise. I'd seen Gideon's little tortoiseshell cat lurking in his windows, and I'd bet that his fussy manners extended to daily pet hair removal. No way could he put up with all the floof of a dog like Jim, not to mention her talent for finding mud in the green space. "If they fenced off the area, we'd likely have to tramp all the way through the park to reach the open area, putting me way behind schedule."

"Ah." Gideon made a thoughtful noise. Undoubtedly, revealing my practicality took some of the shine off that statue he'd been so ready to toss up. Rounding the corner for Tinsel Avenue, we passed the Morrisons' large house. "Still, your help will make a difference to a lot of people. That counts for something in my book."

"Thanks." Finally on our own block, this walk needed

to be done soon before Gideon revived my sainthood application.

"And speaking of making a difference—"

"Why do I have the feeling I'm not going to like this?" I cut him off because I'd been expecting this the whole walk, the hard sell on some sort of civic engagement, likely involving costumes and crowds knowing Gideon.

"Let me finish. I have a proposition for you."

"Oh?" Stopping on my heel near a street lamp, I turned to give him a very deliberate once-over. I might be ridiculously out of practice, but I hadn't forgotten how to put some heat behind my gaze. Not that I had to work that hard with Gideon. For all his fussy ways that got on my nerves, I sure did enjoy looking at him.

"Not..." Gideon coughed, turning pink. He tugged his coat more securely around him. He didn't need to worry. His virtue was safe with me. Even if I was the sort to play the hookup game, I wouldn't fish in the neighborhood pond. I'd noticed the rainbow bumper sticker on his little import the day I moved into my place, but Gideon also seemed like the type to smudge easily, too fussy even if he weren't next door. But somehow, all my lectures on his lack of suitability didn't stop my body from reacting to his blush.

He coughed again before he took a big breath. "*Anyway*, the more houses we have decorated for the season, the more likely people are to come see the lights. More people mean more donations, and like your path, the donations make a huge difference to a lot of people in our area."

Damn it. I'd really walked right into this one, hadn't I? Groaning, I resumed walking. The faster I reached my door, the better. "I'm not really the decorating type."

"I know that. I get it." He gave an exaggerated nod as

if someone who changed his porch decor for each major holiday could truly understand. "This season simply isn't your thing. But that's where my proposition comes in."

"You're going to bribe me to decorate?" Almost to my house, I had to stop again. I'd turn him down, but I was still far more curious than I had any right to be about what he might offer. Thanks to those blushes and his nearness, my sex-deprived brain was more than happy to supply a few suggestions involving his ridiculous bow tie hitting the floor.

"No, no, of course not." Gideon quickly squashed my feverish fantasies, which was for the best. "I'm offering to do it for you. All the work. Lights, some tasteful decor, all set up and then later stowed for you, hassle-free."

"You want to string lights on my house for me?" I blinked. And blinked again. Gideon scampering around my roof would be a sight indeed. Not happening, but the image was almost enough to make me smile.

"Exactly." Gideon practically danced the rest of the way to our shared driveway. "And I can work with whatever preferences you might have—colors, secular, wintery without being holiday, or a nod to any traditions you might have. The Levy family has a gorgeous menorah."

"I've seen." The thing was probably eight feet and glowed like a landing pad, but it was memorable. Farther down the block, the Reeds always put up Happy Solstice messages and the Jordans on the other side of the street went with a Kwanza theme each year. The neighborhood's enthusiasm for the season was inclusive of all beliefs, but it wasn't religion holding me back. "I'm not Jewish. I just don't celebrate anything."

"And this way, you don't have to." Gideon grinned like he'd cornered me. And he had. Despite being steps from my door, escape seemed futile as he continued to hype this harebrained plan. "You can support the neighborhood efforts by simply loaning me your house."

"That easy?"

"Yes. I can put everything on timers. And with the newer LED lights, you'll scarcely notice a power bill impact."

"You sure have thought of everything." I whistled low because, in several years of living here, this was the most sentences Gideon had strung together around me without tripping over his words and definitely the most enthusiastic I'd seen the guy. Talking about lights, he practically glowed himself, radiating warmth and energy in the dark, damp November night.

"Yes, I have." He beamed at me.

"Look. Gideon. No offense, but I'm not sure I'm up for the hassle." When he opened his mouth, no doubt to tell me it wasn't a hassle, I held up a hand and used some of my rusty manners. "And I wouldn't want to impose."

"Oh, it's not an imposition." Predictably, Gideon didn't take the hint. One truly had to admire his dedication to the cause. "It would be fun! Since you're not into any specific celebrations, we can go with snowflakes and snowpeople. Yes, that's it. Cheerful snowpeople."

Lord save us. If I didn't put a stop to the runaway Gideon express, I was likely to have a lawn full of those inflatable glowing snowpeople with their serial killer grins and silly top hats. "I'm not sure—"

"Why don't you think about it?" Gideon gave me another winning smile right as Jim barked from my front window. She wasn't usually loud, but I also didn't usually dally in the driveway. "No need to give me an answer right now. Your furry friend seems eager for you to go in."

"It's dinner time." At last, escape seemed in reach. I meant myself, though, as I'd been late leaving a worksite, but I'd never make Jim wait. By the time I finally got my own dinner, she'd have conveniently forgotten her hasty supper and turned those big brown eyes my way, much like Gideon and his pleading. He was a tough guy to say no to.

"Of course. I wouldn't want to keep you." Gideon made a shooing motion like I'd been the one drawing the conversation out. "Think about my offer. I can draw up some plans to show you."

"That's not necessary." Why I couldn't manage a firm no was beyond me. Maybe it was his enthusiasm for his idea. Maybe it was his commitment to neighborhood causes. He might be a hammer short of a toolbox, but his wackiness sprang from good intentions.

He means well, my mom would have said.

"Maybe not necessary. But it sure will be fun." He stamped his feet, either from cold or excitement. With him, it was hard to tell. I liked a good blueprint myself, but I'd never had the prospect make me boogie.

"Uh-huh." Again, I couldn't seem to say no, shut him down. Sometime between now and when he inevitably flagged me down for further discussion, I'd have to find some backbone. I didn't want my front lawn to become a holiday circus, didn't need Gideon underscoring everything I disliked about this blasted time of year.

"Night, Paul. Thanks again." Giving a last smile, Gideon strode away before I could tell him he could save the thanks. I hadn't agreed to anything, and I wasn't about to let Gideon Holiday have his way on this. I knew better. Somehow, I needed to convince him to let me have my seasonal funk in peace.

Chapter Three
GIDEON

❧❦❧

Who needs a place for Thanksgiving? Always room for one more!
~Cheryl Bridges
    Us too! We've got a full house and twenty pounds of turkey!
~Frisk Family
    People! Please pay attention to where your guests are parking. Common courtesy goes a long way. ~Ernest Morrison posted to the What's Up Neighbor app

KNEELING UP ON MY ROOF WAS A RELIEF, NOT THAT I'D ever admit it aloud. But "I have to work on my decorating" was such a nice excuse to leave Friendsgiving before the tipsy shenanigans we were all getting too old for anyway started. Each year our group shrunk a little more as people coupled and throupled up, adopted, reconciled with biological families, and otherwise found new connections with more compelling invites.

    I'd had no shortage of other invitations myself, of course. My ex and her wife. Cheryl and her brood. The Jordans down the street. Peggy from work. But being the fun, single guest was exhausting. I'd had years where I'd attended multiple events, and as much as I loved people, dealing with my lights was a far better distraction from my sorry single state than all those happy clans.

Thus, here I was, Thanksgiving evening with the light fading over a neighborhood filled with family gatherings in full swing. But I was alone on the roof with thousands of LED bulbs, plastic hanger hooks, and all my timers. Bliss really, getting everything hooked to my new app for managing all the timers, setting the decorations just so, and reminding myself how much joy strangers were going to take in visiting our neighborhood. If I could light up one person's dark day, then all the work was worth it. Humming softly, this time a show tune that refused to leave my brain, I finished the front half of my roof and turned back to my ladder. Except...

No ladder.

"What the hell?" I said to the empty night. I'd left it against the same eave as always, the side porch the best and safest access point. But no ladder. I peered down and—

"Fuck." Sometimes there was no better word because there my ladder was, laying lazily across the driveway. "Fuck."

Not only was I blocking the driveway, a neighborly no-no, but more pressing, I had no way down. I wasn't some nimble skinny teen able to shimmy down the drainpipe. And all my upstairs windows were locked, a fact I verified. Butterscotch sat in his cat tree in the spare bedroom window, unmoved by my plight. I'd probably have to break a window, and wasn't that going to be a mess? I had my phone, but who would I call? Everyone I knew was either with family or in no shape to drive. Maybe if I yelled, Paul would hear. Embarrassing as hell, but rescue beat the alternative.

But no, Paul's truck was missing from its usual spot by his garage. He too was probably out at a gathering. Breaking a window seemed my only alternative. I removed my scarf to wrap my hand and was giving myself the requisite pep talk when a decidedly grouchy sigh cut through the night air.

"Holiday, what are you doing?" Paul called up. Damn it. The rescue I'd wanted, with a side of the humiliation I'd hoped to avoid.

"Lights," I answered brightly. "December first is right around the corner."

"Your ladder is blocking the drive." His frown was severe enough I had no problem spotting it from my vantage point. Tone all impatient, he held a shopping bag in one hand. "I had to circle three times to find a spot for street parking."

"Sorry about that." I tried to sound contrite. "If it wouldn't be too much trouble, could you prop it back against my porch?"

"You trapped up there?" The frown deepened.

"Not entirely." No way was I admitting to him how bleak I'd been feeling. "I was going to break a window."

Paul muttered something under his breath. "Why didn't you call someone?"

"Didn't want to be a bother." I went with the truth, but I kept it light and breezy.

"Better a bother than turning into an icicle or breaking a leg." His tone was all pragmatic as he set down his bag and hefted my ladder like it was little more than a sack of potatoes. Damn. I did like watching those muscles work. "Here you go."

Naturally, Paul didn't simply set up my ladder and

leave, instead he braced it with his meaty hands and staying there as I climbed down.

"Many thanks." My words came out all breathy because he was right there, much too close, much too spicy smelling. He smelled classic, the same scent as the first boy I'd ever kissed, and damn, that was *not* the memory to have right now.

"You shouldn't be doing this alone." His scolding tone was enough to drive my rogue kissing thoughts away.

"I was fine. This was my first disaster in years of scaling my roof in pursuit of the perfect lighting scheme." I smiled, but he didn't return the grin.

"Only takes one slip. I never let my crew work a roof alone." Paul shook his head like I was some foolish kid. Fair enough, as that was often how I felt around him, despite the similarity in our ages. "Would have figured you'd be gone tonight anyway. Family dinner."

"I wish." My voice came out a little too wistful, which wouldn't do. I forced a laugh. "My family's scattered to the winds. Mom in Phoenix. Dad in Florida. Both were only children, but there are a few second cousins here and there all across the Eastern Seaboard. None I'm particularly close to. But it's all right. I had a lovely Friendsgiving for lunch. How about you?"

"Me?" He twisted his mouth.

"Big family?"

"No." His face shuttered, dark curtain pulled tight, no admittance to whatever private thoughts he was having. "Just me and Jim and some football. Speaking of, I should get back to the late game."

Reaching down, he picked up his bag. I spied two cans of dog food, a carton of vanilla ice cream, and a frozen turkey dinner. *Oh, Paul.* My own fridge was stocked with leftovers from Friendsgiving and the pie Cheryl had dropped off earlier because they "accidentally" had too many at her house. No way could I enjoy my bounty knowing he had a microwaved Thanksgiving dinner.

"Thanks again for the rescue. Would you like to come in for some cherry pie? I've also got turkey and ham. More than enough to share."

"Let's not talk about your lighting schemes right now." He rubbed the bridge of his nose with his free hand. Him immediately assuming I had an ulterior motive had me bristling. I had tried to talk decorating plans for his place several times recently, but he'd put me off each time. In this case, however, I'd simply figured that maybe we didn't have to both eat alone.

"I wasn't—"

"Not tonight. Please." There was a weariness to him that wasn't usually there, a certain slump to his shoulders. I wanted to rub his tense muscles, an impulse that would likely get me summarily pushed away. And I also wanted to press, see if sharing some food chased some of those clouds in his eyes away, but before I could, a muffled bark sounded from Paul's house. "I better get in there. Try to keep the driveway clear of all those extension cords. I want to move the truck back in."

"Sure thing. No problem." Keeping my decorations out of the way was easy. Trying not to care about whatever was making Paul so lonely was far harder.

Chapter Four
PAUL

Who has an extra heavy-duty extension cord? We're getting our decorating on bright and early tomorrow! ~ Jordan Family

Anyone need turkey bones for soup? ~Molly Reed posted to the What's Up Neighbor app

I SHOULD HAVE SAID YES TO PIE. I DID LOVE A GOOD cherry pie. But there was nothing I hated more than pity, and Gideon had sympathetic eyes and an almost too-kind voice. I shut him down, same as I had invitations from a couple of crew members to join their family celebrations.

I was terrible company, anyway, and when my phone buzzed partway through eating my microwaved dinner, I almost didn't answer until I saw Brandon's number flash on the screen.

"Little bro!" I forced a hearty tone. "Figured you'd be too busy today for a call."

Brandon had texted the day before to wish me a good Thanksgiving and to tell me that they'd reached Elaine's parents place safely, so I'd figured it would be a couple of days before I heard more, what the social whirlwind he always seemed to get caught up in when he visited his girlfriend's folks in Newport Beach.

"It was a hectic day today, but I snuck away for a little air outside. Glad I could catch you. Did you have a good dinner?"

"It was fine," I lied, praying he didn't ask where I'd gone.

"Great. I caught the tail end of the Eagles game and thought of you."

"Hell of a final down. Good game." Football was always a safe topic for us, even if I was far more a fan than Brandon, who was more into the stats than the competition. "Greene is gonna set a rushing record."

"Yeah. Made me miss Philly." He sounded the same kind of homesick he had when he'd first landed at Cal Tech, and same as then, I made myself laugh again.

"Ha. You're out there soaking up all the sunshine and solving mysteries of the universe while we're expecting snow next week."

"The weather is pretty great." His tone brightened considerably. "You'll see if you come for graduation in May."

"Wouldn't miss it." May was one of our absolute busiest months, and leaving for even a couple of days was going to require all sorts of juggling, but no way was I letting Brandon down. "You still on track for that big research battle?"

"Dissertation defense," he corrected me. Damn it. I didn't speak PhD as fluently as him and his crowd. "Yes. Everything's set. And Elaine is on track too. We'll both be on the job market in the spring. That should be fun, trying to find positions close enough geographically that we can be together."

"I'm sure you'll find something." My pulse sped up. Maybe something on this coast even, not that I'd ask. Elaine was a California girl through and through, and Brandon would follow her to whichever fancy college she ended up at.

"Yeah, and I have a plan about making sure she's stuck with me no matter where she finds a professorship too. That's part of why I'm calling, actually."

"Oh?"

"I'm coming for Christmas." He sounded all giddy, and there was a crunching sound like he was bouncing on his heels, exactly how he'd done as a kid. "Well, we both are. Elaine's coming too."

"But you and Elaine always go to her folks." I pushed my half-eaten dinner away. Last several years, I'd become used to the pattern of Brandon saying he missed me and Philly but heading to Elaine's family for every major holiday anyway. I'd be thrilled to see him, no question, but I'd stopped holding my breath a long time ago.

"They're going to be in Melbourne for an extended work trip, and Elaine doesn't want to travel that many hours for what's likely to be a short vacation with so much for us to do at school." There was always a ton for Brandon to do at his university, courses to teach, research to check on, committees to be on. I made a sympathetic noise as he continued, "Besides, did you know she's never actually had a white Christmas? They've been to Aspen and Jackson Hole for skiing, of course, but never for Christmas."

"Of course." Elaine's parents were the sort of wealthy I had trouble wrapping my head around, her mom a top executive at some tech company and her dad a big Hollywood lawyer type.

"So, since her folks are going away, I asked her to come

home with me. I can't guarantee her a white Christmas, but I can show her your neighborhood all lit up, the Evergreen downtown shops, and go into the city, show her all the holiday sights."

"You always did like that." I tried not to dwell on those memories of taking him to see the lights he'd loved so much, but I could see where he'd want to take Elaine to Franklin Square and other spots he remembered fondly. We'd both grown up in Philadelphia, and further, unlike Elaine and her West Coast ties, we'd come from decidedly working-class neighborhoods. I had no idea what someone who'd grown up in a literal mansion would make of my place, but I supposed we'd muddle through.

"Exactly. And then, Christmas morning, right in front of the tree, I'm going to propose. With any luck, there will be snow outside, and it will be perfect."

"You're sure you want to propose?" I stood up from the table, earning a look from Jim as I paced across the kitchen. *Tree.* I didn't have any such thing. Didn't even have a guest room set up, and now, Brandon wanted perfection.

"Well, I've been dreaming about this for the last year, saving up for the ring and trying to pick the right place to pop the question. I was thinking flash mob—"

"Don't do that." Public displays always made me queasy, right along with the people who popped the question on the jumbotron at halftime at a big game.

"Yeah, yeah, bad idea." He had our mom's laugh, high and tinkly. "I kept thinking of these glitzy ideas because, you know, her parents…"

"I know." They sure did set the bar high. Brandon seemed to like them fine, but I got where he'd feel some pressure.

"But that's not really Elaine. Or me. Then, yesterday,

her parents announced their plans, and I dreamed last night about your place. A big tree. Remember me telling you that corner of your new living room would be perfect for one?"

A knot formed right in the center of my chest, making it hard to speak. "I remember."

"A real Christmas. Like we used to do, not the catered stuff her parents do these days. Everything all decorated will make great photos—"

"That's important?" God, Brandon might be a bona fide genius, but I had no idea what past he was remembering or what personality transplant he assumed I'd had. Decorated? I did sanded, leveled, varnished, tiled, and more, but holiday decorations? Ones worthy of a proposal backdrop? No way.

"Oh yeah. Elaine's huge on social media. Mainly particle physics memes, but she's going to want to share pictures of the big moment. Assuming she says yes."

"She'll say yes." If nothing else, I could say that. Elaine seemed head-over-heels for my brother, beaming in every selfie they took and delighting in their shared research. She did little things, like remind Brandon to eat, and they'd been living together for a couple of years now, so I figured a yes was a pretty safe bet.

"Hope you're right. I picked out the ring online at an exclusive place in downtown Philly that specializes in rare alloys. It won't be ready until the twenty-third, but that should work out. I hope. And see, that's why this plan is so good. You always calm me down."

"I try." And I did, but I had to find a way to tell him that my place was hardly Christmas ready. No tree. And he wanted to see a lit-up neighborhood. *Fuck.* They were both going to notice my lack of lights. I better fess up right now though. "My house—"

"Brandon! We're about to watch a movie in the theater room." Elaine's voice sounded off in the distance.

"Oops. Gotta go." Brandon's voice took on the same sort of lovesick tone he got whenever Elaine was nearby. "I'll text you the flight details when I have them."

"Okay." I was still more than a little dazed by this turn of events. "But I should warn you, the place…"

"Paul. You're such a perfectionist." Brandon laughed, then laughed again, higher-pitched like Elaine had tickled him or something. Their easy intimacy made my jaw tighten.

"It's not that—"

"Whatever renovation you're in the middle of, it'll be fine. And you're the neatest guy I know. Don't worry about the mess."

Oh, this was a mess all right, just not the kind he was assuming. "Mess isn't the—"

"Brandon, come on." Elaine interrupted again.

"We'll talk soon," Brandon hurriedly assured me. "It'll all be fine. You're going to love Elaine."

I didn't doubt that. Whether she loved visiting Philadelphia, now that was the real question. And she better damn well say yes. Brandon deserved a yes. Hell, I'd all but guaranteed him one. But how was he supposed to pull off the perfect Christmas proposal *here*?

Chapter Five
PAUL

Emergency! Our air compressor bought the farm. Anyone have one we can borrow for all these Christmas inflatables? ~Jeff Reed posted to the What's Up Neighbor app

Returning to my kitchen table, I sat for a long time, trying to make sense of the conversation with Brandon. I couldn't tell him not to come. But fuck it all, I was unprepared for this, and if there was one thing I hated even more than pity, it was being unprepared.

I needed a damn drink, but there was nothing stronger than beer in the house. And naturally, the universe chose that moment to make my doorbell sound. Jim at my heels, I padded to the front door. And somehow, I knew exactly who it was even before I looked through the curved window on the top of the door.

Gideon.

Fuck. I did not want to talk to anyone, him especially, but I couldn't exactly pretend to not be home. And I had lectured him about being up on that roof alone. What if he needed help? I couldn't turn him away only to have him risking his neck again.

"Yes?" I opened the door to find him standing there holding a plastic container. The air had a decided bite to it, but he had only a fleece pullover on.

"Hi." His smile was winning as ever, but I couldn't find the energy to return it. Best I could do was a nod. "I wanted to say thank you again for the rescue."

"No problem."

"And I know you said no to sharing my pie, but Cheryl brought a giant one over with her famous butter crust." He held the container out. "No way can I do it justice. So I brought you a piece. You can freeze it if you'd rather."

"Okay." I accepted the container, suddenly tired all the way down to my toenails. I shook my head, trying to clear it. I was being rude. Ruder than usual, at least. Fuck. "Sorry. Thanks. Appreciate it."

"Are you feeling all right?" Gideon narrowed his eyes right as Jim pressed up against my leg. Taking a step back, Gideon continued to study me. "You're pale."

"Me? Sure. I'm great." Earlier, I'd managed a hearty tone for Brandon, but here it came out all strained. Jim thrust her shaggy head past the doorframe, making Gideon look further alarmed. I made a shooing motion. "Jim, go lie down."

"You don't look great." Naturally, Gideon didn't seem inclined to drop his questioning and head back to his warm house. As seemed his custom, almost every light was on over there, unlike the dark living room behind me. "Forgive me if I'm overstepping, but if you need anything—"

"I don't."

He smiled sadly, like he'd expected my quick refusal. "Well, I'm here. If you need a favor or someone to listen…"

"What I need is a decorator," I said without thinking. I definitely didn't need help. Or to talk. Fuck that. I wasn't a complainer. I only needed to figure out this Brandon problem and I'd be golden.

Blinking, Gideon tilted his head. "Pardon?"

Damn it. Now I'd have to explain before he assumed I was high. "I need the perfect proposal backdrop."

"You're proposing to someone?" His expression grew more puzzled, eyes drawing together, mouth frowning, and nose wrinkling like he didn't much care for the notion of me marrying. *As if.*

"Not me. My kid brother. Just found out he's bringing his girlfriend here for Christmas. And he wants to pop the question." There. That was way more explanation than I'd intended to give.

"Congrats to them." Gideon's face lost some of its mulishness.

"Yeah, well, he's wanting some sort of ideal setting to do it." Apparently, I did need to talk because I couldn't seem to shut up and get on with sending Gideon back to his house. "Tree. Decorations. Whatever. I don't have a clue."

"And you're…not prepared for guests?" Wrapping his arms around himself, he shuffled his feet. I couldn't exactly let the guy freeze any more than I could have left him on his roof, so I opened the door farther to usher him in.

"You could say that." Flipping on the light, I revealed the living room, which had gleaming hardwoods and built-ins, but a decided lack of furniture other than one of Jim's beds. My old couch had had too many miles on it to move, and then I'd put off replacing it while I refinished the floors and woodwork. And then put it off again to paint. And then there had been little point because it wasn't like I had a lot of guests. Gideon and his pie were a rarity on multiple levels.

"You see?" I gestured at the open space. "Furniture hasn't been a priority. My guest room has a table saw in the middle of it."

"Ah." Behind his glasses, Gideon's perfect eyebrows flirted with his poofy hairline. "Maybe your brother could stay with another friend or relative?"

"No. It's just us." And no way was I sending Brandon to a hotel. I might not have some fancy guest suite like Elaine's folks, but I had my pride.

"Oh." Gideon nodded, more of that sympathy I hated so much in his brown eyes. He'd said earlier how he didn't have much family either, which had surprised me, a person like him home on Thanksgiving. He was so damn cheerful that I'd assumed a life packed with family and other obligations.

"I'll just have to do something with the room upstairs," I muttered, looking away from Gideon. Over on her bed, Jim glanced up, ever hopeful that I might give permission for her to come inspect Gideon. "Keep meaning to finally paint in there, but other projects came first."

"I know how that goes. But now you have an excuse to get that done." He smiled widely. He was the type to see the bright side of a piece of charcoal. There probably wasn't a disaster that he couldn't spin to some sort of positive. Had to admire that mindset even if I knew better myself.

"Yeah. I'll get it done. Buy a bed. And see about a tree." I started a mental list then quickly got overwhelmed in a way I hadn't been in years, too many things competing for my attention, everything with an ASAP label, and not enough time, money, or me to go around. "Fuck, I don't even know where to start."

"I do." Gideon's smile hadn't dimmed in the slightest despite my admission. "You need help."

Only he would see this as a good thing. "I don't think—"

"You do. You need help. And luckily, I've got a plan for that."

Chapter Six
GIDEON

Are those lights I spy? Congrats to the Levy Family for being the first to flip the switch this year. Let the season begin! ~ Cheryl Bridges posted to the What's Up Neighbor app

I HAD WAITED YEARS FOR PAUL FROST TO NEED SOMETHING. A cup of sugar. A spare fan. An extra chair. He probably had me beat in the tool department, but I did have a drill I was rather fond of. And I would have let him use it. But this, this was even better. He needed something I was good at, and finally getting the chance to impress him with something other than my knack for forgetting the trash cans had me all bouncy.

"I happen to be excellent at decorating," I said with no trace of humility.

"I can't ask—"

"You didn't. I'm offering. You need the perfect holiday proposal. And I'm Mr. Holiday." I gave a flourish with my hand, like a magician revealing a trick.

"I'm aware." That Paul didn't share my enthusiasm for

the situation went without saying, but he also seemed decidedly less pale than he had when he'd opened the door.

"I've even helped several friends propose." Such was the consequence of getting older. I'd orchestrated proposals, consoled public breakups, officiated second weddings, and watched most of my crowd happily pair up. Luckily, I did love a good excuse to dress up. "There was this one flash mob—"

"Please, no flash mobs." He rubbed the bridge of his nose. "I just need a tree."

"And a place to sit in front of it." I strode around the living room, getting a sense of the space. A good size, it had the sort of built-ins along one wall this era was known for, all refinished and every last shelf completely bare. The walls were a gorgeous cream shade, which was going to look so lovely festooned with holiday colors. The corner by the large front window practically cried out for a lush tree, but the spectacle would need seating for guests to be complete.

"That too," Paul groaned.

"And a dining set." I made my way into the adjacent dining room, which was similarly gorgeous yet barren. French doors. White wainscoting. Not one but two built-in china closets. Floors so shiny, my inner eight-year-old longed to slide around in socks. "Is that chandelier original?"

"Picked it up at a reclamation place." Paul scrubbed at his hair. "The one here was beyond repair. Walls were so grimy with peeling wallpaper, I wasn't sure I'd ever reach the wallboard. And I should probably start a list of what's needed. Kitchen table's too tiny to work in here."

"Don't bother trying to find a piece of paper for a list. I'll just use my phone." I whipped out my oversized smartphone that functioned as a small tablet as well. "I've even got a stylus in my pocket." Paul's eyes went wide like I'd revealed I marched around with a sex toy at the ready. "What? I write faster with a good stylus."

I started a new list entitled "Paul's Perfect Holiday Project," smiling at my alliteration and pun both. I had a feeling we were on a budget, so I added a column for cheap fixes. Luckily for Paul, my contacts list was bulging with people with cluttered houses and kind hearts. Like with networking schematics at work, I functioned best with a clear color code, so I started a legend at the top for essential, ideal, and optional projects.

"Why are you doing this?" Paul asked as I clicked around the screen, humming softly. I couldn't help it. This was simply too exciting.

"Taking notes?" I asked absently as I guestimated the length and width of the dining room. "I'm going with red for the projects that absolutely must be done in time."

"Helping. Why are you helping?" He sounded both bewildered and frustrated. Understandable. I did have a tendency to take over.

"Sorry. I'm getting ahead of myself. I do love a good challenge."

"Making me a list is a mental exercise?" Paul pursed his mouth like he didn't quite believe me. And oh, how cute that he thought I'd leave him with a list and no help executing it.

"That, and I have a feeling I'm getting something out of it." My voice was all light from picturing the perfect oval table to play off the room's unusual angles.

"Oh?" Paul went all suspicious, and too late, I remembered his reaction to my last proposition. Even with him looking edible in an Eagles sweatshirt, worn jeans, and silver-haired scruff, I'd been distracted by the scope of his dilemma, not as tongue-tied with sexy thoughts as usual. Definitely not picturing trading any sort of X-rated favors either, but now that he'd made my brain go there…

Don't do it. I made an effort to slow my suddenly galloping heart rate. Heading down that mental path would be a mistake. I couldn't have him thinking I wanted in his jeans or that I was harboring some sort of crush. Guys our age didn't crush. I appreciated his aesthetic appeal. That was all. I would offer this same help to anyone. *Yeah right.* Okay, maybe I didn't entirely believe my own logic, but I still managed a dismissive laugh.

"Lights, Paul. I'm getting lights for the neighborhood display out of this. I assume your brother already knows you don't do holidays, but your future sister-in-law will notice if you're the only dark house in our magical wonderland."

"Brandon doesn't," he mumbled. "I used to make more of an effort when he was around."

"So you have some decorations?" I sensed a story there, but his rigid body language said I wasn't getting it, at least not then. And if this was the brother's first homecoming in a long while, Paul needed my help even more. A good impression could go a long way.

"I've got a box in the attic. Somewhere." He gestured vaguely toward the stairs.

"Okay. We can work with that. And I'll handle the outside decorating, same as I told you I would. Luckily, I still have those plans I drew up."

Which he'd have known if he'd responded to any of my overtures to get him to talk lights the last couple of weeks.

"You actually did make plans?" Rubbing his neck, he glanced sheepishly at me. "I'm sorry I put you off."

An apology was more than I'd expected, and my chest went warm and tight. "It was nothing. Doodles."

"You did work." His voice was firm, commanding enough to make me shiver despite my fleece pullover. "And you're offering to do more work here. I can pay—"

"Don't be ridiculous." No way was I taking his money. We might not be friends, but I did this sort of thing for my crowd all the time. Need a master bedroom refresh? Call Gideon. Need a birthday party planned? Gideon will help. I was nothing if not good at throwing together random bargain finds to bring together a theme. "You're already donating a path to the neighborhood, and this is the sort of thing I enjoy. You're practically doing me a favor, letting me play around with your decorating."

Eyes narrowed, he shook his head. "I would have figured your December would be too packed to worry about someone else's issues."

Actually, he would be surprised how empty parts of the month could be for me and how hard I worked to keep busy. But we weren't here to talk about me. "I've got the usual obligations, but I can work this in, no problem."

"I'm not sure…" He was waffling. I was sure of it. He needed me, but he had the sort of stubborn pride I'd seen before. Admirable, but unnecessary.

"Don't worry. I intend to put you to work too." His sort always responded well to feeling useful, like when I'd ask a stuffy professor to hold a cable for me or press restart back when I did more hands-on IT work. "I'll come up with a plan, but you can help with the executing."

"Generous of you." Paul quirked his mouth as if he was thinking of smiling. Oops. Maybe he wasn't the same as someone at work feeling overwhelmed by technology and wanting my expertise. I *was* being a bit bossy.

Again.

I really did need to work on that. "Sorry. I do like to lead, but I can get carried away sometimes."

"So I see." His mouth still wasn't smiling, but his voice was warmer, more amused. At least he wasn't entirely put off by my steamroller act. That was something.

"But it's your project," I assured him. The big dog had stayed in the living room in its bed but now ambled toward us, making me speak faster. "We'll work to your taste and vision."

"I don't have a vision." He went right back to scowling even as he held out a hand for the dog, petting her furry head. She might be the size of a small donkey, but she did seem tame enough.

"Sure you do." I tried to focus on the issue at hand rather than my own weird nerves around large dogs. "What was your vision when you bought the place?"

His expression immediately clouded. "Flip the place and move on."

Well, okay then. He clearly hadn't, instead staying, and I was desperate to know more, but his posture had gone ice sculpture stiff again.

"We'll keep an eye to resale value then," I said brightly, not about to press him. "And what will make a good impression on your future sister-in-law. Any idea as to her tastes?"

"Expensive." His tone was clipped enough that even the dog sat up straighter.

"Oh dear." That was going to be a challenge. There was no escaping that this was a humble midcentury house with gorgeous bones, but glitzy was going to be a tall order. "Maybe if we stick to a classic scheme..."

"Wait. That's not entirely true." Paul pulled out his phone, thumbed it open. "Elaine's parents are the ones who are loaded. Her condo with Brandon is modern, but she has pictures all over. Like she does these little displays. Brandon sent me some to brag on her."

He held out the phone, and I stepped closer so I could see the pictures he was scrolling. As usual, he smelled so good that I had to make myself look at the phone and not do something embarrassing like sigh dreamily. The photos showed a loft-style condo, very open but with a lived-in feel. And lots of personal photos on the wall, arranged like something off a lifestyle blog. "Our First Date" in flowy script, surrounded by pics of some museum exhibit, complete with ticket stubs. Another grouping announced, "Life's a Beach," and had sand and seashells along with smiling faces. Most of the pictures on the walls featured a younger, nerdier guy with enough Paul in him to have to be Brandon and a slim, dark-haired twenty-something woman gazing adoringly at the guy.

"Oh, that is darling," I enthused as Paul flipped through photos. The style was a little too magazine-perfect for me, but I appreciated the care Elaine had put into her displays. "Yes, yes, I can work with this vibe. She's the sentimental type, even if she does appreciate quality."

"Sentiment is overrated, but I guess I'll leave it to you." Sighing, he pocketed the phone again.

"You do that." I jotted down some more ideas inspired by the pictures. This was a young woman who was absolutely going to want photos of the proposal, so the backdrop mattered. I didn't know her, but Paul's brother clearly mattered to him, and if Paul wanted a perfect holiday for them, then that was exactly what they were going to get.

"Do we have to do it all tonight?" Paul asked, looking over at my shoulder at my rapidly growing list of notes. The same weariness he'd had when he'd opened the door was back. Whatever was going on, there were some big emotions behind it.

"No, of course not. This is a lot. I get it." Turning, I touched his sleeve, but he quickly stepped away.

"It's not too much." He was a terrible liar, but I also knew when not to press on a sore spot.

"Fair enough. These things are always best handled in stages though." I clicked over to my calendar app. "Tomorrow, I have to finish my own decorating in the morning, then I'm helping a few other residents in the afternoon. In the evening, I'm going to work on this list for you. How about Saturday, I return with a plan, and we can see more of what we're working with here?"

"You sure do seem to have it all figured out."

I really didn't. And if anything, Paul Frost was even more of an intriguing mystery than he had been before, but if he wanted to view me as someone who had the answers he needed, I'd take it. I'd simply have to ensure I didn't disappoint.

Chapter Seven
PAUL

※

Thank you, Gideon, for helping solve our extension cord dilemma! Now we're ready for December! ~ The Clarks posted to the What's Up Neighbor app

GIDEON WAS A MAN WITH A PLAN, AND THAT WORRIED ME. Especially when he turned up with a thick stack of printout pages, a legal pad, and, lord help us, fabric samples.

"These are simply to get a feel for colors," he said breezily as he sauntered into my house. Other people walked. Gideon sauntered. No bow tie today, but he didn't need it. He managed to look fresh and crisp in a polo with the college's logo and pressed khakis. Again, my urge to rumple him up was strong. But it was the determined attitude that truly scared me.

"The tree will go there." He pointed to the same spot Brandon had liked. A cozy corner, it would be visible from the front window without blocking the window seat or the built-ins. "And the couch will go opposite with some side chairs…"

"Gideon," I interrupted, feeling a bit like I was about to pop a balloon. "No offense, but can we talk budget for a sec? How much is this gonna cost me?"

The business did well enough, but this was the time of year my crew came first. Limited hours meant limited paychecks, and making sure they had enough to get by was my priority, not buying out the furniture store.

"Oh, that." Gideon waved a hand. "I'm pleased to report a minimum outlay per room will be required."

"Simple words, please." I ran my own business. I could talk construction estimates with the best of them, but it had taken several years of community college classes at night to get a basic sense of business lingo. Gideon already had me unsettled, and that was before he trotted out the big vocabulary.

"Tell me a number. I think I can work with whatever you need."

I told him one I'd arrived at earlier after looking over my personal, non-business finances.

"Oh, we're not even going to need close to that." He laughed, holding up one of the papers, which had careful columns and even line drawings of various furniture items. "I've covered most of the large furniture pieces already."

"You've what?" I blinked, both at his organization and his moxie both. "I don't do charity."

"This isn't you accepting charity. It's you doing a service. More than one service, in fact. Services. Plural." He made a swooping gesture with his stack of papers.

"Explain." My neck prickled. This still seemed awfully like him arranging charity on my behalf.

"Well, for instance, the dining room." He pointed at the empty room beyond the living room. "My ex has been itching for a new set. Hers is from when we were together. Her new wife would also love a change, but they keep dithering over 'what will we do with the old one.' So, I gave them the excuse they needed. And I might have mentioned I had access to a truck and could handle the removal with my…neighbor."

Gideon paused near the end of his speech like he was about to say *friend* and thought the better of it. We weren't friends, even if the neighbor part was starting to get damn complicated.

"You volunteered my truck?" I wasn't sure which part of Gideon's nerve was the most shocking.

"Yes." Gideon at least had the grace to look sheepish, glancing down at his papers. "I obligated you, but I figured you'd rather do a fair trade than have me arrange a favor from a different friend with a truck. My ex was delighted at the prospect of free, reliable labor to haul the old set away."

"Yeah," I said faintly, grasping for some way to make sense of the warp speed with which his mind moved. "You were married?"

"Yes. Right out of college. Married my best friend. She's still my best friend, but about ten years ago, she came out in love with her other best friend. I didn't want her to feel bad, so I came out too."

It was such a Gideon thing to do. Brave, slightly misguided, and full speed ahead. My back tensed, his sort of boldness both unfamiliar and frightening. "You're both gay?"

"I know. Such a cliché, right?" Gideon had a musical laugh, the sort that made people want to laugh right along with him. "And it was almost twenty years ago when we married, twenty-five when we started dating. Marrying my best friend was easy. Coming out was harder. But she did it, so I did too, and I was happier for it. How about you?"

"Me?" Apparently, somewhere in his whirlwind of

sharing, he was asking for my coming-out story, but I needed a second to collect myself. "I...uh..."

"I'm sorry." Shuffling his feet, he shifted his gaze downward. "I'm being presumptuous. I saw your little logo and simply assumed..."

It would have been easy to just nod or maybe say that we did a lot of business with the LGBTQ+ community, but something about the way he'd deflated made me more talkative. "You didn't assume wrong. But you're also right. Twenty years ago, things were different. My parents died. I had to get custody of Brandon."

"I'm so sorry." The overwhelming sympathy in Gideon's eyes was a huge reason why I seldom shared even this much. Glancing over at Jim lying in her plaid bed, I focused on the rise and fall of her furry chest so I could get the rest of the story out quickly.

"Even if I'd been out, a single gay guy in his twenties was gonna be a harder sell to the social workers. So I kept my head down. Then when Brandon left for college, I could finally breathe." I shrugged like the whole thing had been simple, like those early years hadn't fazed me at all. Sharing the near past was far easier. "I had a lot of same-sex couples as clients by the time Brandon graduated. He and my couple of close buddies had long since known, so I told myself that putting the little rainbow up to try to get even more LGBTQ+ business was simply good advertising, nothing to get all worked up over like coming out to the social workers would have been."

And if my hands had shaken when I'd ordered my new logo, well, I sure as hell wasn't telling Gideon that.

"That's still a long time to hold your breath." Gideon nodded like someone who'd know, and I supposed maybe he would.

"Yeah," I agreed, but in a tone that didn't invite follow-up questions. "Tell me about the other deals you've arranged."

"Okay." Gideon's tone was overly bright like he knew I needed a topic change and was having to work to restrain his always overflowing curiosity. "Now, the living room will require more imagination."

"Try me." He wasn't the only one who could fake a hearty voice. Tapping into Gideon's enthusiasm was way more interesting than talking about me. And he was rather cute when he got excited, all big gestures and fast-talking.

"Now, Cheryl had a living room set with a large couch for sale most of the fall. No takers despite a more than reasonable price. It's still in their garage taking up space, and none of her boys want it."

"What's the catch?"

He laughed like I'd said something rather smart. "You got me. It's ugly as sin and twice as heavy."

"Sounds like a score." I was more okay taking the unloved couch than I was with Gideon strongarming his ex into a dining set upgrade. "But hey, a couch is a couch, right?"

"We're going for more than function here." He gave me a withering look. "Cheryl's sons and prospective buyers lack my vision. I found a cranberry-colored slipcover for a song. It'll look divine with these walls, and the size means it'll make a striking statement. Add some seasonal throw pillows, and voila!"

"Voila!" I echoed him, and he beamed at me with all the gratitude of Jim when I accidentally added too much kibble to her bowl.

"Exactly. And Cheryl really wants that garage space back before the snow arrives, so again, you're doing her the favor."

"Sold. But I'm paying her asking price, and I'll buy the slipcover myself."

"I've got the links ready for you." He handed me yet another sheet of paper, this one helpfully labeled, "Paul's To-Do List, Part One."

"The part one business is scaring me." I was only half-joking.

"Stages, remember?" He patted my arm, and unlike the other night, I didn't dodge his touch. He had a warm, wide palm, and the heat from his touch lingered far after he was back to shuffling papers. "If I give you the whole list at once, you'll get overwhelmed. And there's no fun in that."

"Yeah." I had to swallow hard. I couldn't remember anyone caring about my stress level before. Whether I was overwhelmed or not had been largely irrelevant the last twenty-odd years. Someone rationing out my to-do list was a novelty, one I probably shouldn't get used to. "And how do you know all these people getting rid of stuff?"

"Well, for starters, I'm on the neighborhood app. Aren't you?"

"No." I'd heard about it, of course. People complaining about porch pirates and the late-running teens and ill-behaved dogs. I was still old-fashioned enough to be on the email list for the neighborhood association, and even then, it was a crapshoot whether I actually opened the newsletter.

"Well, people get rid of stuff constantly. I'm just good at keeping track."

"So I see." I shook my head because he really was something else, eagle eyes and constantly whirring genius brain.

"Now, show me to the bedroom!" he demanded.

"Pardon?" My mind homed in on *bedroom*, heading

straight for places that would probably shock my design guru here. Fussy might not be my usual taste, but my body sure did like the idea of showing him the finer points of my mattress.

"The guest room?" Gideon prodded, cheeks pink. "I have all sorts of ideas for there too, but I need to see the space."

"Ah. Yes. Right this way."

Chapter Eight
GIDEON

Free: Giant reindeer head, gently worn. Must pick up! ~Penny Jordan posted to the What's Up Neighbor app

Perhaps "show me to the bedroom" wasn't my best line. Making Paul sputter and turn light purple was a pretty nifty feat though. He didn't fluster easily, so that was an A-plus job of inserting my foot into my mouth. *Again.* However, I'd been here at least thirty minutes now, and Paul hadn't kicked me or my big ideas to the curb.

That was something, as was him seeming more amused than irritated at my bossiness. I was rather impressed myself at how well my ideas were coming together.

"For additional seasonal decor, I'll take you to my favorite bargain-hunting secret," I said as Paul led me upstairs, trying to distract myself from how his jeans pulled against his ass. "I've got lights covered, but you'll want some odds and ends to round out the Christmas decorations."

"I can't let you pay for the lights." Mr. No Charity gave me a withering look over his shoulder.

"I bought too many on clearance last year at the day-after-Christmas sales. I wake up at five each year to get the best chance of nabbing good lights."

"That's just bizarre enough to be the truth." Paul blinked and paused at the top of the stairs, a cute landing area with built-in bookshelves and a bench seat.

"It is," I assured him, patting his arm again. I really needed to stop touching the guy. He wasn't one of my friends, who were far more used to my casual touches and freely given hugs. "My attic is full of boxes of unused lights in search of a good home. And I already added the ones from my surplus inventory to the schematic for your outdoor decor."

"I'm not surprised." Paul's voice was dry, but he also wasn't shutting down my plan. "What is it with you and lights anyway? Why be so invested in the whole neighborhood glowing like a landing strip?"

His incredulous expression said he expected to hear about my geeky love of timers and circuits, but I gave him honesty instead.

"Growing up, my parents fought constantly. Then they divorced. The one constant was Christmas at Holiday House in this very neighborhood. I looked forward to my grandparents' big celebration all year, and my grandfather would take me walking to see the neighborhood lights. Away from all the bickering, it really did feel like a magical wonderland. I want to be that feeling for others who might need the lights this time of year."

"I...uh...*wow*." He gulped audibly. The oversharing was too much, undoubtedly, but he'd asked. "Holiday House? That's your place now?"

Now it was my turn to frown. "I wish. The Morrisons

beat me to buying my grandparents' old house. After my divorce, I decided to move back to my favorite neighborhood, even if I couldn't get the house I truly wanted."

"I'm sorry." Paul sounded like he really meant it, eyes softer than I'd seen them.

"Don't be." My back muscles going tight, I made a dismissive gesture. I'd shared my story for accuracy, not sympathy. "My place at least had a big head start on renovation. I'm no DIY champ like you. The Holiday House needs a ton of work, not that the Morrisons agree."

Seeing the sorry state the house had fallen into was a constant burr in my side. I could live with a happy family filling the place, but an ill-tempered Scrooge who lacked any sort of appreciation for its distinctive features soured my stomach every time I jogged by.

"Yep. It needs work. Paint, windows, landscaping, and that's only the exterior." Paul ticked off the items on his long, blunt fingers. Their purposeful movements were enough to make a few sparks zip up my spine. I wanted to see what else they could do. *Danger. Back to your story, Romeo.*

"I used to dream about how I'd renovate when I grew up and had money, but my dad convinced Grandma to sell in my teens, and I put aside those drawings."

Paul nodded solemnly, more of that unexpected and not entirely welcome empathy. "I used to draw too. Had the crazy idea I might be an architect."

"That's not absurd." The glimpse at his childhood self made my chest hurt.

"Yeah, it is. My family didn't have college funds to start with, then Brandon came along, a huge surprise for my parents. Plans changed." His tone was matter-of-fact, but when he met my gaze, an entire weather system of emotions filled his eyes.

And lord how I understood plans changing. My childhood was littered with broken promises, canceled weekend visits, postponed vacations, and forgotten plans. Even my current life was largely a reaction to the way my divorce had upended all the plans I'd had with Lori. Sometimes hoping *hurt* and rolling with the punches was the only way to avoid hitting the floor.

"Yeah," I said softly, not breaking away from his gaze, air thickening and energy gathering. I flexed my fingers, the urge to reach out overwhelming, but then he abruptly strode away to the first door off the hallway.

"Anyway, this is the guest room." His tone was curt, putting an end to our emotional show and tell. The room was small, but the dormer windows, refinished hardwoods, and built-in dresser gave it character. The walls were a light blue, a pretty shade that would be fun to coordinate with.

"Run out of cream paint?" I joked.

"Brandon always did like blue." If there was a certain yearning to Paul's voice, I knew better than to offer my understanding.

"Well, then, we'll go for blue-and-white bedding." I kept my tone bright even as my chest clenched again. "And yes, the saw and sawhorses are going to have to leave."

"Yeah. I can buy a bed. I keep debating upgrading my own to a king, but it's only Jim and me. Seems ridiculous to get new simply because my bones are getting creaky and memory foam sounds good."

"Well, here's your chance." I tried to convey practicality and not reveal how my brain was now besieged by images of him in a too-small bed, big muscular frame spread out. And certain parts of me were only too ready to volunteer to help him test a new mattress. "Move the smaller one in here, and treat yourself to something appropriate for your advanced years."

"Hey." He laughed, and damn, I liked being able to make him chuckle. He didn't do it often, but he had a warm, rich laugh that could fill a space, instantly changing the mood.

"I'm just saying." I gave him an arch look. "My orthopedic mattress is one of my favorite investments. And it's only me as well, but I've totally got a king now."

"How is it you don't have a boyfriend?" Paul frowned, then shook his head. "Never mind. That was rude."

"I don't mind," I assured him. "And hey, I'm flattered you think I should have one. But I have terrible luck with dating. I've seen a few people since Lori and I split, but nothing stuck."

Calling it luck was kinder than admitting my bossy ways tended to chase potential partners off. I ran a hand over the built-in dresser, picturing a few accent pieces for the room.

"How about you? Now that you've got your breathing room, I would think you'd have a line of prospects."

"Ha." Paul snorted. "I'm cranky, set in my ways, and lack the necessary skills for modern dating. Missing most of my twenties and thirties means I never got good at that sort of thing. Bar scene sucks, and I'm a slow typist on my phone. The apps baffle me."

"I'm not big on bars myself, but trust me, you could pull any number of guys willing to help you make up for lost time." It spoke to my stellar restraint that I neither volunteered myself nor pointed out that being slightly less prickly might improve his chances.

"Thanks, but the scene seems to skew toward young dudes." He shuddered. "And I don't care how old the mirror says I am now, I'm not looking to play Daddy games."

I laughed because he was *such* hot silver-fox Daddy, but

I got what he meant. "I feel you. Most of the guys our age around here are either into that dynamic—more power to them—or already coupled up."

"Yup. Trust me, I know. My client list is full of happy husbands. Like you said, more power to them, but I'm just not cut out for the domestic."

Far be it from me to argue with his resolute tone, but all evidence pointed to the contrary. Hell, forget shirtless pics. All he'd need to do is share snaps of his gleaming hardwoods and DIY prowess, and he'd have an inbox full of dudes ready to play house. But I didn't want to cross the line into flirting.

Okay, that was a lie. I was *dying* to cross that line, but I wanted to help him more, and every instinct I had said he'd shut me down cold if I made a pass.

"Speaking of domestic, you want to show me your existing decorations? We won't want to duplicate anything you already own, and setting out your familiar pieces will be welcoming for Brandon."

"Doubt he cares. He's always got his head in the clouds, worrying about some equation or model." Paul's tone was fond as he headed back into the hallway, where he pulled down an attic ladder from the ceiling. "I'll grab the box."

He really did mean box, singular. At my house, I had a line of plastic storage totes, each neatly labeled. Green for lights and wiring supplies. Red for outdoor decorations. Blue for indoor. I added to the collection every year, to the point where it took me a decent amount of time to carry everything down each year. But Paul was scarcely gone thirty seconds, returning with a single large box that had once held computer equipment.

"I remember that model." I pointed at the label. "Talk about a blast from the past."

"Yeah, that was Brandon's first computer. Had to save a good few months, but he sure was excited that Christmas." Paul set the box down and crouched in front of it. "There's not much in here."

"It's okay." My heart was hammering as I crouched next to him, struggling to keep my voice even as he revealed the tidy collection of treasures inside the box. In my head, I could hear my grandmother's voice as she unwrapped a particular ornament, telling me where it had come from and why. I'd blithely demanded Paul share, but now I wasn't sure I was worthy of this glimpse into his heart.

Part of me wanted to tell him he could pack it back up again, but then he unwrapped a heavy platter, holding it tenderly. It had a Norman Rockwell holiday scene in the center and a scratch on one edge.

"There was a fire," he said softly. "Not much was salvageable. Few things of our mom's favorites, like the stockings and this cookie plate. There's only the one."

"It's beautiful." I was shocked I had any voice at all. It went without saying that I was sorry, so terribly sorry, about his parents, but something about the moment felt eggshell fragile, as if the wrong words could shatter the immense trust he was placing in me here. "Your mom had good taste."

"Yeah, she did, didn't she?" His smile was faraway and heartbreakingly boyish. Setting the plate carefully aside, he revealed a small box full of craft stick and pipe cleaner ornaments, glitter raining onto his fingers. "These are a couple of things Brandon made as a kid. I didn't have the heart to throw them out."

"Of course not."

When he set the small box of ornaments aside, I carefully replaced the lid. Next, he pulled out a tiny tabletop artificial tree and a wooden advent calendar.

"Man, Brandon always loved that countdown calendar. Think we got that on clearance. You'd approve."

"I do." My voice came out all thick and muffled, sinuses clogged and eyes burning. I picked up the calendar to admire it more closely. "I definitely approve. We'll use all of it."

"All of it?" Paul frowned. "That tiny tree isn't gonna cut it for the proposal."

"No, but it can occupy a place of honor on a side table." I had the perfect end table hanging out in my own attic. "Trust me. Brandon will remember it."

"And laugh at me keeping it." He snorted like being sentimental was a character flaw, like he was vaguely embarrassed he'd dared keep these little treasures safe.

"I doubt that." My voice came out all emphatic. I'd do battle for his right to be as sentimental as he wanted. Hell, I'd trade almost all of my loaded down storage totes if it meant keeping his precious memories safe.

"Gideon," he warned, packing stuff back up. There were a few other items in there, and I truly did plan to use them all. "Don't make more of this than it is. It's just a box."

"It's not *just* anything," I argued right back. I remained dangerously close to tears. I lacked the words for what his sharing this had meant to me. "Trust me, I know. My dad kept almost nothing of my grandparents. The couple of keepsakes I have, they mean the world to me. It's okay to keep special things around, no matter how humble the items."

"If you say so." He gave a tired sigh as he finished closing the box. "Probably should just plan on buying all new."

"Absolutely not." I reached for my bossiest of tones. Paul couldn't let himself admit how much these items meant and would undoubtedly shrug me off if I gave him the hug I so desperately wanted to, so I went for logic instead. "If nothing else, your sentimental future sister-in-law is going to love hearing Brandon's stories about being a kid. Let her have that."

"All right. I'll carry this downstairs then." His expression was stony as he hefted the box up, his granite jaw and resolute nose were bulwarks standing guard over the heart he usually hid so well. But now I'd seen it, and I wasn't ever forgetting.

Understanding him far better now, shame swept through me. In my zealousness, I'd forgotten how truly painful the holidays could be for some. We all had our coping methods, and if he wanted to hibernate the holidays away, who was I to try to fracture what little peace he'd managed to find through boxing everything up tight?

"Let me help." I had no clue how to apologize for any hurts I'd stirred up with all my efforts to get him to participate over the years, but I was going to give this decorating project my absolute all, give Paul and his brother the chance at some new memories.

"I've got it." He gave me a sharp nod. And maybe he had everything under control, all his emotions locked down, but I sure as hell couldn't say the same.

Chapter Nine
PAUL

Big thank you to whoever left a tin of British cookies on the porch! First gift of the season! The kids loved them! ~Molly Reed posted to the What's Up Neighbor app

Gideon was back to erecting statues in my honor. I could tell. He'd heaped compliments on my box of old decorations like I'd revealed a whole collection of mint condition rookie cards, and he'd sat on my living room floor with his stack of papers, adding my items to his plan. Finally, he'd headed back to his place, but not before thanking me yet again for trusting him to help.

Thanking me. He'd drawn diagrams of my various rooms, made lighting schematics for my exterior, and drafted a schedule for what decorating was happening when, and he was thanking *me* for the privilege of adding a hell of a lot more work to his month. And now, here he was, giant cheery smile on his face, crack of dawn on Sunday, two cups of coffee in his hands as he made his way to my truck.

"Thanks for humoring me," he said brightly. More thanks from him. I might not survive this outing. I gave a curt nod.

"No problem."

"But we really will have the best selection if we get there early." He held out both coffees. "Left has cream, right is black. I can drink either."

How on earth Gideon managed to make being flexible about his coffee preferences sound so sensual, I had no clue. Maybe my body wanted to remind me how I often spent the early hours on a Sunday, using the lack of an urgent wakeup for a little solo time. Not today, and now my sex drive was all haywire. And I had a full day of Gideon to get through.

"Black coffee is fine." I grabbed the closest cup. "And you're sure this is worth the trek to South Philly? We've got the various big-box options and downtown Evergreen and other stuff closer."

"Trust me. You've never seen anything like this holiday outlet." He stamped his feet, whether from the nippy air or excitement, I wasn't entirely sure. "We'll be able to cross a ton off your list. They even have sheets and seasonal linens!"

"Awesome." I tried to sound suitably enthusiastic. After all, Gideon had made the ridiculously detailed list. He could have sent me on my own to the store, let me pick up the items needed. But apparently, he thought I needed company. "Thanks for coming along."

"Oh, it's no problem." He followed my lead and got into the truck. I'd had it warming even before he'd emerged from his house with the coffee. "And it's not that I don't trust your selections, but—"

"You don't trust my taste. It's okay." I took a sip of the coffee, which was extra-strong and bracing. Probably a

French press or something similarly fussy. I got by fine with my ten-dollar old relic, but I couldn't deny Gideon made good brew.

"No, it's not okay." Gideon sagged back against the seat dramatically. "I'm a terrible control freak. This is supposed to be your project. But when I get into something, I tend to micromanage every little detail."

"Manage away." I was dangerously close to telling him his bossiness was cute. I took another sip of coffee. "I'm good with letting you lead."

"Really?" He brightened considerably.

"I have to have that same level of concentration on the job. I appreciate the attention to detail." Gideon's obsessive planning put my own organizational efforts to shame, but there was only so much praise I could dole out. I pointed the truck out of the neighborhood, which, despite the early hour, had more than one household out working on exterior decorations. "But it's been a long time since I've done Christmas, and I'm way out of my element here. You're the holiday expert, Mr. Holiday."

"I am." He preened, and my decision to get underway was a good one because the temptation to touch him was particularly strong.

"Letting you be the one with the opinions, it's relaxing," I admitted. Felt like I'd made enough tough calls and big decisions for two lifetimes. And I'd keep right on doing it. But if Gideon wanted to save me worrying about bedding patterns and garland length, more power to him.

"Well, in that case, I am full of opinions with a side of perfectionism. Leave it to me." He did the closest thing to chair dancing I'd seen in years. His excitement made me want to give him more things to be decisive and bossy about. *Whoa, easy there.* Before I could get ahead of myself, I took the on-ramp to head toward Gideon's preferred destination, a holiday outlet near the airport where people were already lined up and waiting when we arrived.

"See?" Gideon gestured at the crowd. "Early pays. With any luck, they'll still have flocking."

"Excuse me?" My brain was apparently still stuck on sex.

"Fake snow, Paul. You must need a good flocking." He grinned wickedly, and yes, yes I did. "For your mantel. It'll show off the stockings perfectly, and we'll get one for Elaine."

"If you say. You're the boss." I followed him out of the truck, our coffees long since finished and the morning possibly even colder than when we'd left.

"Don't worry, I'll remember the budget," he promised as we stamped across the lot. "I have estimates by each item already, and the spreadsheet app on my phone will alert me if I start to go over."

Nothing about Gideon should have surprised me at this point, but I still blinked. "You have an app for that?"

"I've got an app for everything," he said, full of cocky swagger as we joined the line. "Including my lights. I can put one on your phone or add your setup to mine?"

"Whichever you prefer." This not-deciding thing was awesome.

"Mine it is." He grinned as he pulled out his phone, thumbing it open to a color-coded spreadsheet. "Told you. Control freak."

"Don't apologize." I glanced at the list on his phone, where items were grouped by type. "Add candy canes to the list. Brandon was always nuts for them. I'd let him have a whole box to hang around the place, but they never lasted."

"Three boxes. Check." He added the request, then marched in place, shivering. I had the strangest urge to pull him against me, warm him up. The line was full of happy couples and excited families, more than one duo in matching coats and a number holding hands. If I grabbed Gideon's hand, at least I could keep his fingers from freezing. But, of course, I didn't.

"You want to get back in the truck?" I asked instead. "I can turn the heater on."

"Thanks, but no. I don't want to lose our spot in line." He was all bluster and pink cheeks.

"Suit yourself, but I'm getting you something hot if they have a drink stand in there."

"They do." He sounded all pleased. It was just a drink. I'd do it for any freezing buddy.

Lies. Well, okay, I wouldn't be here at a Christmas Mart with any other buddy. But if I couldn't—wouldn't—warm Gideon up the fun way, a beverage was no big deal.

Finally, the place opened, and I grabbed Gideon a hot chocolate from a snack stand decked out in red and white while he fetched a cart. Or rather, *two* carts.

"Really?" I gestured with the hot chocolate as I handed it over.

"I might see something I can't live without." He gave a sheepish smile.

My chest fluttered, but I ignored it, following Gideon into the maze of displays and aisles.

"Nothing with sound," I said when he stopped by a grouping of musical lawn ornaments. "It'll freak Jim out."

"Gosh, Paul, I don't know. Seems like you might have opinions after all." He laughed merrily.

"Only about practical stuff."

"Right. Leave the color schemes to me." Not sounding at all put-out, he headed to a display of winter-themed sheets and bedding. "Blue snowflakes for the guest room. And for you—"

"What do you mean for me? I'm not the guest."

"You're about to have a king size for the first time," he reminded me. "And these are super cheap, especially for flannel. Now, moose or snowpeople?"

He held up two packages. And damn if I didn't picture him in that king bed. And not all spread out naked either, but in pajama pants reviewing his stack of plans. I was losing my damn mind.

"Moose," I said before I realized they were wearing scarves and stocking caps. *Whoops.* Too late. I wasn't supposed to have opinions. The moose sheets landed in the cart along with a fuzzy brown king-size blanket. For the guest room, he went for a matching snowflake comforter set. Gideon would totally be the type to envy the duos in coordinating coats and Christmas sweatshirts we kept passing.

And why I suddenly felt murderous toward some faceless dude who might be game for matching pajamas probably had to do with my blood sugar or something. I couldn't give Gideon that, but I could at least be decent company. To that end, I laughed as two blue accent pillows hit the cart quickly, followed by ones with fake needlepoint designs for the couch.

"I'm gonna have to learn to live with pillows, aren't I?"

"Yup," he said smugly, heading away from the bedding aisle and toward a grouping of ornaments.

"Don't complain when Jim shreds them," I warned.

"Is Jim that bad?" Gideon sounded legit nervous, and I regretted the tease.

"No. Not at all. She's remarkably laid-back." I assured him. "Her breed is known for being really sweet. You're afraid of big dogs?"

"Oh, it's kind of silly." He made a dismissive gesture,

narrowly missing a stack of red globes. "My stepdad had a mean mutt. It never liked me."

He shuddered, and I wanted a whole bunch of words with that stepfather.

"Bad owner," I said without thinking. *No bad dogs.* I heard my dad's voice, clear as day for the first time in years. I picked up a package of glass ornaments. Another long-held memory sparked, and I turned the box over in my hands.

"No kidding." Gideon plucked the box from my hands, added it to my cart. "Both of my stepparents are pieces of work. There's a reason I'd rather spend Christmas alone than with either of my parents and their new families."

Alone. That word hit me square in the chest. I'd never thought of Gideon as lonely. This many years into living right next door, and I'd never realized Mr. Holiday was alone on Christmas.

Like you. Yeah, but I didn't count. This mattered to Gideon. "You shouldn't be alone."

"Oh, I usually end up at some friend's for dinner at some point," he said breezily. "Don't worry about me."

But damn it all, I did, a heavy feeling I couldn't shake even as he moved on to the next display.

"Where do you stand on roof decorations?" He stopped in front of a line of cutout reindeer designed to be strapped to a roof. An oversized sleigh and a jolly Santa were also available. Gideon sighed like we were admiring some French painting. "The slope of my roof is all wrong for something fun like this, but yours…"

"Is it in the budget?" I asked, testing the heft on one of the boxes.

"Really?" His whole face lit up. "Because, yes, we're well under budget thanks to all the bargains I've scored."

"Humble, aren't you?" Shaking my head, I laughed

before sliding the box onto the shelf on the bottom of my cart.

"Hey, I know when I've done a good job." He beamed and crouched to pat the box of reindeer. Scared of dogs. Soft spot for plywood creatures. He truly was something else. "These will go perfectly with the simple lighting scheme I've laid out for you. They can be the one touch of whimsy."

I was pretty sure that role was reserved for Gideon. Humming softly, he moved on, but I lingered a moment, appreciating the way his bouncy steps showed off his backside. Plain khaki pants, but round, firm, bitable ass. Damn it. He was here to do me a favor, not rev up my body to new levels of awareness. But it was getting harder and harder, literally, to remember that.

Chapter Ten

GIDEON

※

Be careful out there! Snow is forecast for later, and it could get icy! Don't freeze your fannies off! ~ Cheryl Bridges posted to the What's Up Neighbor app

PAUL FROST WAS A SECRET SOFTIE, AND I NOW HAD AMPLE evidence. His box of treasures was the first clue, but watching him shop was another. Even though he wanted to defer to me, I had a wonderful time letting his clues guide my selections. He gravitated toward classic themes and items with an old-fashioned feel. His eyes would linger on an ornament featuring a retro sled or vintage truck hauling a tree, then he'd sigh and move on.

And I'd quickly add the item to his cart while he scolded me about budget even as his lips curved into the barest of smiles. We made an excellent team, and by the time we reached the checkout lanes, I was floating on a shopping high that lasted all the way back to our driveway.

"I'm glad we took my truck." He deftly backed the truck in, lining up the full truck bed with his back porch like he was leveling up for a video game. "I'm surprised there's anything left in the store."

"Ha. If we unload fast, we can still get some lights up before the weather turns." It had been cold all day with gray, ominous skies but no snow yet. Hopping out, I went right to check on the load. Paul had secured everything down with a tarp, but I was still relieved we'd made it back without anything blowing away. I grabbed two bags and started stacking items by his back door.

"You still want to string lights today?" He groaned, but he didn't sound completely opposed to the idea as he set his armload next to mine. Inside, Jim let out a series of excited woofs. "Do you have an extra battery pack or something? How do you keep going and going?"

"Go let Jim out," I ordered as I loaded up another armful of purchases. "I'm going to go pick us up some hoagies. You'll be less hangry with food."

"I'm not hangry." He gave me an absolutely withering look, but I wasn't fooled.

"No, you're perma-grumpy." Not thinking, I patted his cheek. Oops. Forgot about my resolution to stop touching him. And the way his whiskers prickled my palm made my whole body hum. His expression shifted from irritated to something far more potent. And dangerous. I stepped back in a hurry, all breathless. "I'll be back with food, my lighting schematics, and timers to get started."

"Only you could make that sound exciting." His tone was resigned, but his eyes twinkled. I was glad I could amuse him if nothing else.

"I try." And I took advantage of him being distracted by wrestling the box of reindeer to get him to tell me a sandwich order. After a lightning-fast trip to the sandwich joint on the other side of the park, I returned as promised, balancing the bag of hoagies on one of my big plastic tubs of lights and equipment.

"Thanks." Paul led me to his kitchen table, dog fast at his heels. "Ignore her. She smells food. Jim, go lie down."

"She's okay." I still gave her a wide berth as I took a chair. "But thanks."

"God knows I've got enough dog beds. She can sniff your food from over there." He waved Jim toward the padded mat in the corner. Paul caring about my comfort level and nerves made my chest all warm and light.

"How did you end up with a girl dog named Jim?" I asked as I unwrapped my turkey and avocado on wheat.

"Girls can't be named Jim?" He raised an eyebrow.

"Point taken." I should have ordered a meatball hoagie like Paul because his sandwich smelled far better than mine. "I meant more like, how did you convince Jim to put up with your stellar temperament?"

"Maybe she doesn't think of me as cranky." His mood was definitely improved by the food, not that I was going to point that out. "And we found her at a worksite. She was still a young dog, under a year, and in a sorry state, huddled under a wheelbarrow. Crew member I was with, Jim Rivers, convinced me to take her home for the night while we tried to locate an owner. I called the dog Jim in his honor to get his goat. It was supposed to be temporary."

"So your one-night stand became a long-term relationship?" I laughed. "If only it were that easy the rest of the time."

"Yeah, but dogs are easy. It's people that are the problem." Paul caught a stray drop of marinara with his tongue.

"Says the dog person," I retorted, enjoying watching him eat far too much. It had to be a sign of how hard up I was that his big appetite joined the growing number of things that turned me on about him.

"Animals do tend to like me." Paul adopted an arch tone as he started in on his chips. "We had a couple of terriers when I was growing up. Sucked that I couldn't have a dog for Brandon while we were in an apartment. And he, of course, was all over the notion of me keeping Jim around soon as he heard about her. Made the mistake of sending him a cell picture. I promised she wouldn't go to a shelter while we tried to find her a permanent home."

"How'd that work out for you?" Yup. He was one hundred percent a soft touch, and uncovering the good person at the core of his gruff exterior was my new favorite hobby.

"Three years now." He tossed the dog a look so fond I was almost tempted to go lie on the mat myself. "Had some offers for her, but nothing was a good enough fit. So she stayed."

"I have a feeling nothing short of royalty with a private dog walker might have passed your test."

"That's what the real Jim said too." Laughing, Paul finished the rest of his lunch and cleared away our trash. "All right. Show me this schematic of yours. How many extension cords are we talking about?"

"A couple," I hedged as I handed over the lighting diagram. "But most of what we need is in this box. Plus the reindeer."

"Can't forget the reindeer." He gave a crooked smile, and it was only for an instant, but his expression went as indulgent as it had been for the dog. My pulse skittered. That. I wanted more of that. And then the smile was gone, and he was all business again, handing me back the plans. "Here, let's slide the reindeer and supplies out the guest room window."

"Smart." Carrying the storage tote, I followed him upstairs. He brought along the big box that held the reindeer cutouts. Using a pocketknife, he neatly unpacked all eight. Add another turn-on to my list because men who could expertly wield box cutters apparently did it for me. "Nice tool."

"Thanks." He smirked. "I had my dad's old multipurpose knife for years. Rusty thing finally gave up the ghost, and Brandon got me this fancy one a few years back."

"Nice brother."

"Yep. Genius and nice. He got all the good genetics." Chuckling, Paul placed the reindeer and their stands right outside the window. "Now we can get the ladder, but I'm leaving the window open just in case."

"Sure you're not the genius brother?" I asked as we trooped out to his garage.

"Ha. I've got the English grades that say otherwise, but it's only common sense to have an escape route." He opened the garage door to reveal an impressive array of power tools and renovation supplies. My zest for organization approved of the neat rows and orderly bins, although I could see where a better labeling system might improve things. "In fact, I'm gonna grab two ladders. We can't both be stranded."

"Oh, the gossip mill would love that. Trapped on a roof together. They'd have us engaged by dinner."

Pausing mid-reach for his ladder, he made a strangled noise, and I rolled my eyes at his obvious panic.

"Breathe, Paul." I clapped him on the shoulder before grabbing the second ladder. "No one's proposing quite yet."

"Like anyone other than Jim would put up with me." He laughed, and so did I, even if I didn't agree. He was a catch. He might not know it yet, but hell if I was going to tell him before I finished rescuing his holiday.

"You need gloves." He thrust a pair of thick work gloves at me. Yup. He was *such* a catch. And him being oblivious somehow made him all the hotter.

"Thanks. I have some in my coat pocket, but these are better. I did wear my nonskid shoes for the roof."

Paul cast a disapproving eye on my loafers. "Those aren't work boots."

"Nope, but I'll be fine," I assured him as we made our way around the house to the front roof.

"All right. Put me to work," he demanded, surveying the ladders and the rest of our supplies that weren't already on the roof. I did love how he seemed totally fine with my bossiness. In my experience, big, tough guys like him didn't tolerate my take-charge attitude very well, but Paul was the perfect assistant, placing plastic hangers without argument, stringing lights, and meeting my every requirement, sometimes even before I asked.

"Going to need—"

"The black extension cord. On it."

"This should be—"

"Farther to the left. You're right. I'll move it." He was a marvel, and I wanted to do lights with him every year. I'd enjoyed decorating my place on my own, but working with another person was a whole different level of joy.

"Do we turn everything on now?" he asked as we finished securing the last strand. The air tasted like snow, but we'd had only a few rogue flakes find us up here on the roof so far.

"You're eager. I like that." I waggled my eyebrows at him, gratified at the flush that spread across his cheeks. I kept conveniently forgetting I wasn't supposed to be flirting. He made it so darn easy though. And fun. "No lights yet. We need the reindeer for the full effect."

"You're the boss." Returning to the window where we'd stashed them, he hefted the reindeer into place. "Hell. These things didn't seem so heavy in the store."

"Here. Let me help." I reached out, but he waved me away.

"I've got it." It was the first time in several hours he'd been short with me. Wait. We had been at this all afternoon. The light was starting to fade. I probably needed to feed him again.

"Let's get these bolted down, then I'm going to fetch some cookies for while we admire the finished product."

"I don't need cookies."

"Yes, you do." Starting to get irritated, I turned to find the staple gun, but I misjudged my balance. Or maybe it was starting to ice up, and I hadn't realized. Whatever the cause, I was sliding. My knees hit the roof, then the rest of me. My coat bunched up around my middle and my fingers scrambled for purchase. My pants caught on something rough, but it wasn't enough to stop my slo-mo descent.

"Gideon." With a mighty roar, Paul grabbed me right before I reached the edge, hauling me back up and onto the roof. We landed in a heap together on the flat space by the dormer. "Fuck. Fuck. Are you okay?"

"Never better." I smiled at him. I was probably in shock, but his arms were still around me, and I wasn't sprawled out on his front lawn, so life was pretty damn good if you asked me.

"Liar. We're getting you inside." He hustled me in through the window, pulling at my askew coat. "Let me see how bad you got scraped. Fuck. Your knee is bleeding. I told you those shoes weren't up to the job. You could have broken your fool neck."

His face was ghostly pale, eyes stricken as he removed my coat and examined my various injuries, tone growing ever more alarmed. Maybe I wasn't the only one in shock.

"But I didn't," I assured him, pushing at his shoulder. "Paul. I'm okay. I didn't fall. You saved me."

"Almost didn't." He'd removed his gloves, and his fingers were warm against my scraped-up side. "I'm going to need to patch you up."

It had been thirty-five odd years since anyone had shown this level of concern over my welfare, and that it was him, my grumpiest of neighbors, had my eyes stinging.

"Thank you." I tilted his face up so he'd stop searching me for new wounds. But that brought his face level with mine, his bristly chin in my hands, hazel eyes cloudy with pain like he was the hurt one, mouth parting like he was going to deliver more scolding.

And I did the only thing that made sense and slid my mouth over his.

Chapter Eleven
PAUL

Needed: Snowblower battery pack. The snow is finally sticking, and the rechargeable battery for our snowblower won't charge. Anyone have a spare? Don't want to be without a blower in the morning! ~Ricky Adams posted to the What's Up Neighbor app

Gideon kissed me. Or maybe I kissed Gideon. I was a little fuzzy on the order of events, what with Gideon almost breaking a leg. Or worse. I didn't want to think about worse. What I wanted, apparently, was to kiss Gideon. My heart felt ready to pound out of my chest, the way his scent and warmth revved my engine. I was an eight-cylinder diesel cutting through a frozen January morning. And I hadn't realized how chilled to the bone I was before I had Gideon in my arms. He was as messy as I'd seen him, clothing all twisted, skin scraped and bruised, hair a rumpled wreck.

And he had never been hotter. *Alive.* Vital. In one piece. But he kissed like a dying, desperate man.

I couldn't get enough.

My grip tightened on his torso. He was smaller than me, but solid. Compact energy, a spark plug, and lord did he light me up. He purred, arching into my touch while cradling my face as though I were the one at risk of bolting. His fingers dug into my jaw, holding me there.

Bossy man. Even his kisses were brash, taking charge with his soft lips and demanding tongue. His brand of bossiness was so damn appealing, at least to me, and I relaxed into his touch, let his soft mouth show me what he wanted, *needed* from me.

And he did, his bossy demands meaning less guesswork for me. More going along for the ride as Gideon kissed and kissed me until I was trembling like I was the one who had nearly fallen to my doom. I clung to him, bodies pressed so closely together that I could feel each inhale and gasp as if they were my own. And still, I needed more.

He backed me up against the wall, and I ate up every bit of contact. He sucked on my tongue, and I almost came in my pants. The surge of pleasure was so strong that my hips shot forward, rubbing against him. I swept a hand up his side, trying to gather him even nearer.

"Ah." He made a pained noise that worked like a bucket of ice water dumped over us both. Damn it. He was injured. How had I forgotten that? I broke away from the kiss, dropping my hands from his scraped side.

"Sorry. Sorry." I straightened his clothes like that could make up for this lapse in judgment.

"I'm fine." Gideon batted my hands away. "Don't freak out."

"I'm not freaking out," I lied, shaky voice giving me away and making Gideon laugh.

"Yes, you are." He patted my cheek. "And we still have

reindeer to secure, cookies to eat, and lights to admire. You having a meltdown isn't going to help."

My ears buzzed with how fast his brain could switch directions. "You're thinking about the reindeer? Now?"

My own mind was still locked on that kiss, the taste of him still fresh on my tongue, lips extra sensitive, and I sure as hell hadn't been thinking of a to-do list during. I supposed I should be glad he was being mature and not dwelling on the kiss, but his composure irritated the fuck out of me.

"We can't leave them half-done."

I was more than half-done myself. "So I'm supposed to pretend I didn't just maul you?"

"I kissed you." Gideon's tone was all patient and reasonable and utterly maddening. "You didn't do anything I didn't actively demand."

"This is true." Hell, even the reminder about his bossy ways had me most of the way hard again.

"And I'm definitely not forgetting that kiss." He winked at me, but all I could do was groan.

"Me either."

"You don't need to sound so sad about that. Let me find some peroxide and maybe a bandage, and I'll be all for a repeat." He twisted around, trying to see his own side.

"Fuck. I was supposed to be patching you up. Come this way." I steered him into the hall bathroom and had him sit while I dug for the first aid kit.

"Nice tiles." Gideon ran a hand down the backsplash, a complicated arrangement of hexagons that had taken far more hours than I'd allocated. And damn, if I didn't want to trade places with the tile, let him run those hands all over *me*.

"Hold still." Trying to focus, I knelt in front of

Gideon's knee, which was probably the worst of his various scrapes and bruises. Luckily, his pants had torn in such a way that I could doctor his cut without him removing them. Gideon in his underwear might be more than my weak willpower could stand.

"You don't have to do it for me."

"Yes, I do." Even with me being as cautious as I could, I still winced right along with him as I cleaned the cut. "Sorry."

"Quit apologizing. You're the gentlest medic I've ever had. It's not your fault that it stings. And it's not your fault that I kissed you."

"Thought we weren't talking about that," I grumbled.

"No, we're not flipping out over it," he corrected as I positioned a bandage over the wound. "Oh, and by the way, I'm tested. In case you were worried about that."

"I…thank you." Said something about where my head was at that it hadn't even occurred to me to worry about getting Gideon's blood on my hands. "Me too."

I moved to cleaning his side, each long scrape making my stomach clench all over again. Such a close fucking call.

"Excellent. So, we're two single, consenting guys who happened to kiss. And we could schedule that repeat. Or we could move on. But what we are not going to do is make some huge deal over it, abandon all our plans."

"You don't quit with the bossy, do you?" I had to laugh because that was the most rational response to an *oops* kiss I'd ever heard. And how very Gideon that he was more worried about me not wanting to decorate than about the kiss itself.

"Nope. And you like it."

"You did work awfully hard on those plans. Color

coding and all." I sidestepped his observation, even if he was right on the money about me liking him taking over. And maybe he had a point. Maybe this didn't have to be some huge deal. After securing a gauze pad over the worst of the scrapes, I patted his shirt back into place. "There. All fixed up."

"Thank you." His grin was so tender that I braced for another kiss, which didn't come. Instead, he gave me a hand up as he cheerily announced, "Now we can finish the reindeer."

"You really think I'm going to let you back on the roof?" I stared him down.

"Let?" There were undoubtedly European princes with less indignant tones.

"I don't want you falling," I admitted because clearly trying to order him around wasn't going to work. "Once was enough."

"It's sweet that you care so much." His expression softened again, another moment when I thought he might reach for me, but instead, he headed back to the guest room. "Honestly, I want to get back out there so I don't let myself develop a fear about it."

"I can respect that," I grudgingly agreed. I didn't like it, but I did understand where he was coming from. And it was another totally Gideon thing to press ahead even when someone else might have shied away from repeat danger.

"But I'm going to be extra careful." Touching my arm, he met my gaze. I had no clue what he saw there, but then he nodded like we were having some unspoken conversation. "Maybe I can kneel near the window and hand you pieces."

In the end, we did exactly that, and I lined up all eight reindeer surprisingly fast, bolting them in place. As we finished the last of the outdoor decorations, the wind shifted, gray sky darkening further, twilight and incoming weather combining to bring night on in a hurry. But, of course, snow flurries didn't deter Gideon from dragging me out to my front lawn while he fiddled with the lighting app on his phone.

"Now for the big moment," he announced dramatically. I was pretty sure nothing was going to compete with that earlier kiss as far as big moments, but I nodded. He was so damn cute concentrating hard on his app.

"Let's light it up." I clapped him on the back, hand lingering as he finished telling the lights to turn on. I pulled him tighter against me, arm around his shoulder, something for me to hold on to as the house transformed. His nearness felt less like a turn-on and more like a necessity as if I physically needed him to keep myself upright and grounded. And he fit so naturally against my side as if we were two metal fastenings clicking into place, made to stand like this. "Wow."

I had to swallow. I'd seen holiday lights every season, but they hadn't been *mine* in so very long that I'd forgotten about the magic, the fluttery feeling as something so familiar became something so precious and beautiful. The house looked...hopeful. I'd put hours and hours into this place, but in all that work, I'd never had an ounce of sentiment, never tried to assign it a personality.

But now here it was, stretching skyward, each white bulb a tiny lighthouse waiting to chase away the darkness and welcome someone home. *Home.* A word I tried never to dwell on. And this fucking hurt, the reminder of what I'd been missing.

"Damn." I tried for a whistle, but it came out all broken.

"Are you all right?" Leaning more into my chest, he

peered up at me. "I'm sorry. I didn't mean to drag you into something painful."

"It's okay." It really wasn't, but he'd gone to a ton of trouble here. And it did look good. "Brandon's going to love this. I used to bring him here. Back in the early days, when we didn't have a lot, I'd drive around various neighborhoods, especially Christmas Eve. More than once, I drove until he fell asleep, but he was always awake for this one."

"Oh. I love knowing that." Gideon made a delighted noise before stretching to kiss my cheek like he was rewarding me for sharing the story. "And that's why you got the house, isn't it?"

"I was planning to flip it like I said. Got it right as Brandon was about to graduate from college. Figured we'd take the summer, rehab it together." Even now, I couldn't help my heavy sigh, the way my voice shifted. "But then he got this huge research opportunity and a full-ride to get his doctorate out in California."

"I'm sorry." Gideon wrapped both arms around me. I wasn't a hugger. I didn't need hugs like some seemed to. But hell if I didn't cling to Gideon right then, standing on my lawn, full view of the neighbors.

"Don't be sad," I ordered him when he made a sniffly noise. God knew I'd lectured myself enough over the past few years. "I'm proud of Brandon. Him sticking around here wasn't meant to be."

"It's okay to want things, Paul. Everyone needs a dream." Releasing me from the hug, he took my hand.

"Yeah," I said gruffly. I wanted to know his dreams. The things he wanted. My own dreams might hurt to touch, but his, I wanted to know. And he was wrong. Wanting things was damn dangerous. I knew better. And still, as we stood there, holding hands, I *wanted*.

"It's snowing for real now!" Gideon cheered as big fat flakes rained from the sky. His tongue darted out to catch one, and never had I been so tempted. His enthusiasm was maybe the best thing about him, and I hoped he never changed one bossy trait. The world needed more Gideon. And maybe I did too.

Chapter Twelve
GIDEON

Who needs an exercise bike? Finally got a taker for my couch, so I'm about to have enough room to park in my garage if I can get rid of this darn bike too! Free to a good home! ~ Cheryl Bridges posted to the What's Up Neighbor app

It was only a matter of time before I ended up kissing Paul senseless again. Watching him out my kitchen window, I tingled with the memory of Sunday. He was so hot, even doing something as mundane as opening his garage, and I wasn't sure how much longer I could hold out.

Left to my own devices, I'd been known to eat pie for dinner and skip the entree at a restaurant known for dessert. Not to mention, my shopping habits alone said I was crap at resisting temptation. And Paul was both sweet and tempting. Had he not reacted so stricken, I would have kissed him a second time right there, injuries be damned. Or later, when we stood on the lawn, his arm around me, the moment so perfect.

Too perfect. I hadn't wanted to ruin it with another kiss and possible meltdown. The only melting I wanted to do around Paul was the fun kind. As it was, the way he'd tiptoed around me all week said he was feeling awkward. But I was determined to find a way to rescue his holiday *and* have guilt-free kissing. He deserved it. I deserved it.

But here it was Saturday, and I lacked a plan to achieve the kissing part of the goal, which irked me. All my other plans were coming together beautifully, so why not that too? I waited for him to back the truck into the driveway before I left my house via the side door, saving him the trouble of texting or coming to knock.

"Ready to play furniture movers?" Smiling broadly, I slid into the truck, setting my bag on the floor. No matter how strange the kissing had made things between us, this was going to be a fun day, picking up both the dining set from my ex and the couch from Cheryl's garage.

"Yep. Is this going to be weird?" he asked before putting the truck in gear.

"It was only one kiss, Paul." I bristled because things were already weird, and his bringing it up only served to remind me how desperate I was for more.

"Um. Yeah." A ruddy flush swept up Paul's neck as he looked sheepishly down at his hands on the steering wheel. "I meant seeing your ex."

"Oops. That. Sorry." Calling myself ten kinds of idiot, I tried for a super casual tone, like that could make up for me being the one fixated on that kiss. "No, not weird. I see Lori all the time, and her wife, Simone, is someone who has been part of our social circle since college."

"Well, at least you avoided the whole who-keeps-the-friends breakup question." Paul sounded like he too was having to work for a light tone. Perversely, I preferred him grumpy and real to this too-hearty version.

"Yeah. I worked hard to make sure no one felt awkward." I added a smile because I'd been successful in that effort. But then Paul stopped for a light, and the sympathy in his eyes said he knew I'd been the one feeling awkward even as I'd rallied the troops around Lori and Simone.

"You're good at that." His expression stayed solemn, and I wasn't sure I liked being this seen, so I forced a laugh.

"I try." I let the conversation drift off, focusing instead on giving him directions to Lori's house, which was two townships over but not that far in light Saturday traffic. Their friendly split-level was all decked out for the season, complete with a lopsided snowman in the front yard. I didn't even have to knock before the door flew open to reveal my favorite pair of kindergarteners.

"Uncle Gideon!" Piper, the bigger and louder twin, threw both arms around me. "Did you bring us anything?"

"Of course." I held up my bag. "Cookies, but ask your moms first, and this Santa puzzle fell into my cart last weekend."

"You're funny." Joey gave me a toothy grin as he dug in the bag.

"Who's that?" Piper demanded, pointing at Paul.

"This is Paul." I followed the kids into the living room, where a toy explosion joyfully mingled with Christmas decorations. "We're here to move your table."

"The new one has a bench. We can slide back and forth," Piper reported as Simone made her way down the hall.

"Hi, Gideon." Simone greeted me with a hug before pointing at the two giant cookies Joey was holding up. "I see you brought their weekly ration of sugar."

"Lori can scold me later."

"What did you do this time?" Lori swept in, long purple sweater flapping behind her.

"Was utterly horrible and brought your kids cookies." I pretended to be contrite as we hugged.

"I guess I can let it slide. This time." Rolling her eyes, she patted Joey's dark head. "They're all hyped already, though, because we told them about Christmas."

"What about Christmas?" I asked.

Simone's face went from its usual friendly openness to wide-eyed horror. "Lori, tell me you told Gideon."

"Oh my God." Lori slapped her forehead. "We had teacher conferences and a bout of strep, and then Simone had a work crisis, and I thought I told you. We're going to Simone's folks. They have a new condo in Florida. Christmas and Disney both. The kids are over the moon."

"I bet." My chest went tight, but I kept my voice easy.

"We're so sorry." Simone's eyes were misty, which only served to make my spine that much stiffer.

"No worries at all. The grandparents will be thrilled to see the kids."

"We'll miss you though." Lori rubbed my arm. Damn it. I never had been able to completely hide from her.

"And we'll miss your potato-peeling skills," Simone added with a laugh, but her face was still concerned, as was Lori's.

"Eh. My fingers could probably use the break. I hope you have a wonderful time." I made the mistake of glancing over my shoulder at Paul. His soft eyes were even worse than Lori's and Simone's sympathy. Pity was the absolutely most pointless emotion, and I'd happily endure fifty trashcan placement lectures from Paul than have him look at me like that. "And I'm being rude. Lori, Simone, this is Paul. My neighbor. Show us to the table, and we'll be out of your hair shortly."

"Right this way." Lori led us to the dining room, which was crammed with both the new and old tables. Someone had stacked the chairs on top of the old one, and the four of us made easy small talk as we carried first the chairs then the table to the truck. Lori being Lori, coffee and whole wheat muffins were offered, but Paul was all business and predictably declined. Simone went to check on the kids as Lori and I watched Paul secure the load. Predictably, he'd waved off both our attempts to help.

"He's quite the silver-fox hottie," Lori whispered from our vantage point on the front porch. "Silent type, but nice."

"Lori," I warned.

"What?" She laughed, two-plus decades of friendship earning her more right to tease than most. "I can't tell you to set some fox traps?"

I shrugged. "Maybe I don't have the right kind of bait."

"Nonsense. He keeps looking all murderous when I touch you." Making her point, she threw an arm around my shoulders. Fascinatingly, Paul glanced up from his work with the bungee cords and frowned.

"Interesting." I smiled as he looked away fast.

"All set," he called as he hopped down from the truck bed and walked over to the porch.

"Thank you both. So much." Lori gave us both hugs, and Paul's resulting blush was damn cute.

"No problem." Paul shuffled his feet, kicking some rock salt loose off the sidewalk.

"Drive safely. And seriously, Gideon, are you going to be okay for Christmas dinner?"

"Of course." I waved away her concern. "Don't worry one second about me. You know me. I've got plenty of options."

"Yep, that's you. Stack of invites." She laughed fondly before hugging me a final time. "Take care."

My gaze met Paul's as I released Lori, a restless feeling gathering in my gut. I'd been wrong. This was weird. But it wasn't the ex-factor or even the memory of the kiss. It was Paul and how damn much he seemed to see, even stuff I'd worked years to put a pretty spin on. All my uncomfortable energy wanted to *do* something. Run. Hide. Kiss him stupid. Maybe especially that last one.

Chapter Thirteen
PAUL

Wreaths for sale! One of the grandkids is selling wreaths to raise money for the school band. Every door could use a nice wreath!
~Cheryl Bridges posted to the What's Up Neighbor app

Gideon was in a mood after leaving his ex's house. Which was funny as I had thought he only had settings for chipper, perky, and sappy. Him all grumbly was alarming, like gum in a set of gears. Gideon was supposed to be the happy one. And I hadn't realized how much I depended on that fact until he wasn't. I put up with his one-word answers and fake smiles while we brought the table into my place. But when he stayed quiet before we could go to Cheryl's for the couch, I took a quick turn out of the neighborhood.

"Where are we going?" Even in porcupine mode, Gideon was still cute, looking down at his ever-present plan folder, which even included a schedule for today.

"Coffee break." For him, I even added a smile.

"You turned it down at Lori's." His eyes narrowed. He

was in jeans so stiff they had to be new, a sweatshirt for the campus LGBTQIA group, and those same shoes that were only marginally suitable for the weather. No active snow, but there was still plenty on the ground. "Granted, her muffins require extra coffee to wash down, but we could have had some there."

"So we could have." Honestly, my reluctance to linger had had a lot to do with Gideon's tense body language while we were there. And the muffins had looked like doorstops. But now, I had a better reason to slow the day down. "This new German bakery place recently opened between here and the downtown Evergreen shops. Best whoopie pies I've ever had and excellent coffee."

Myself, I seldom sprang for coffee out. Jim Rivers and some of the crew had insisted I try this place, though, and now I was glad because it gave me a good excuse to distract Gideon from his funk.

"I don't need cheering up." He slumped in the passenger seat, lower lip coming out.

"Nope." I knew better than to disagree. I started looking for a parking space. Typical December crowd, all the little stores filled with gift-hunters and weekend leisurely lunch goers. "You're hangry like you're always accusing me. This is self-defense. If the couch is as heavy as you say, I need you properly sugared and caffeinated.

"Well, okay." He still had suspicious eyes. "But really, I'm all right."

"Yep. And you'll be better with food." Two coffees and two whoopie pies later, we were both full of the oversize fluffy sandwich cookies with their trademark creamy filling —his pumpkin, mine chocolate—and he was decidedly happier.

"Maybe you were right," he allowed as we walked back to the truck.

"Maybe you should listen to me more often." Somehow it was easier to joke with him when he was coming back from being cranky. Weird, but I almost liked him better like this. Real. Less of a cardboard cutout of the perfect neighbor. And I was a little proud that my coffee idea had worked.

"Yeah. I was perhaps a teeny bit down." He shrugged before shoving his hands in his pockets. "I love Lori and her house. And Simone and the kids. It's only that sometimes…"

"It's too much," I supplied. "I feel that way at the human Jim's place. Happy house, full of people. I'm always welcome, but I'm the boss, not family."

"That's it exactly." He sighed as we climbed into the truck. "I'm always a little outside the core."

"I know how that goes. Kids seem to love you though."

"Yeah. They're great." His voice was back to wistful. Damn it. I shouldn't have brought up the kids. "I'll have to make their presents small enough to go on the plane. And something for Lori and Simone too. Still strange, thinking of them as moms now."

"You and Lori…" I trailed off because that was undoubtedly another minefield of a topic. Better to get to Cheryl's with him at least a little restored, so I shook my head and gave him a quick pat instead.

"No, no kids." Gideon guessed my question anyway. "We talked about it, especially early on, but fertility was a factor and trying was hard. Hell, regular sex was hard, let alone on a schedule. So the issue faded, too difficult for us to discuss. But then she and Simone decided to try, using Simone's eggs and Lori's brother's sperm. I offered, of course…" There was a world of hurt in that "of course." My hand was still on his thigh, so I squeezed, wishing like hell I could make it better.

"I'm sorry," I said quietly as we turned back into our neighborhood, all the cheerful decorations countering the seriousness of the conversation.

"It's fi—"

"No, it's not," I said sternly. I knew plenty about running from topics better shoved in a drawer and left alone, but something about Gideon's brand of pretending wanted to break my heart.

"Okay. No, it's not." Frowning, he waved a hand in front of his face. "But it is what it is, and the kids are adorable. And they love me, like you said."

We both got quiet as I backed into Cheryl's driveway.

"Jim's kids are all into the handheld devices," I offered awkwardly, not sure how to end on anything other than a downer. "He told me what game to buy. Tiny cartridges. That might travel well."

"That's a great idea." He beamed at me like I'd handed him another cookie.

"No problem," I said gruffly.

"And thanks for the treat. I needed that." He touched my coat sleeve, and I turned toward him, mouth already parting. My stomach quivered, whole body revved, and—

"Hi, neighbors!" Cheryl bustled out of her house, and I stifled a groan. Without her interruption, I totally would have been kissing Gideon right then.

"Gotta have strength for this monster couch," I joked as we exited the truck, trying to pretend like I hadn't been centimeters from planting one on him again.

"Wait till you see." Gideon had a hug for Cheryl, who seemed utterly delighted to see us. She had a red Christmas sweater on, and she'd sold Gideon on a wreath for some fundraiser even before she had the garage open. Raising the door, she revealed a packed garage. Boxes.

Furniture. Ancient exercise bike. And a massive, incredibly ugly blue couch.

"Wow. This is the perfect nap couch." I whistled as I approached the beast. Gideon's forehead furrowed, clearly confused. "Sorry. That's what my dad called a similar one we had that he refused to part with. Loved that big old, lumpy workhorse."

Running a hand along the back of the couch, I had to closely study the worn fabric rather than let those memories take over.

"So you'll take it?" Cheryl asked eagerly.

"Yep. I've got your cash here." I dug out my wallet, but Cheryl batted at my hand.

"Put that away. Your money's no good here, Paul Frost."

"I can't take it for free." I'd told Gideon. No charity. But Cheryl was shaking her head with a determined glint to her eyes.

"You're saving it from the dump. If you feel guilty, come help me plant a few blooms come spring. Not one of my sons has your green thumb. I hear glowing things about your company."

"Thanks. And will do. You'll have the best yard on the block if I have any say in the matter," I promised.

"You're too kind." She blushed and tugged on her sweater. "I'm going to go wrap up a cookie platter for each of you while you load up the couch and the chairs. And anything else you spy here is fair game as well."

"Excellent." Gideon wandered away from the couch, same expression he had in the Christmas store when he sniffed a bargain. "Paul could use this lamp and side table."

He carted them both to the truck before I could object,

and Cheryl was chuckling as she made her way back to the house.

"You're a good guy," he said as I sized up the couch, trying to decide how best to approach it.

"Not really." I lifted one corner, testing. "If I do good work for Cheryl, that's word of mouth for my crew. Smart business. That's all."

He wagged a finger at me. "Uh-huh. I'm on to you."

He could be on me any time he wanted, but of course, I didn't say that. "Let's scoot it as close to the truck as we can. The less lifting, the better."

"Aye, aye, boss." Gideon followed my directions as we wrestled the couch into the truck. Me being in charge was a nice novelty, but I was too busy hefting a zillion pounds of couch to enjoy Gideon taking orders.

"Damn. This truly is an elephant," I grunted as I shoved.

"Warned you. Mind your back." Gideon was couched low, voice as strained as mine.

"I'm fine. More worried about your knees," I shot back. I wasn't *that* old, even if I would likely feel this for the next few days.

"Oh, my knees still work." Gideon batted his eyes at me, eyelashes almost long enough to brush his glasses lenses. Why had I never noticed exactly how expressive his eyes were before now?

"Behave." I meant me as much as him. I needed to focus on the job at hand. With one last shove, the couch was finally in position. "Here comes Cheryl."

"Cookies for the road," she announced, holding out two wrapped paper plates. "Feel free to swap with each other."

She tittered like she'd accidentally made a dirty joke, which made my skin heat. Last thing I needed was neighborhood matchmakers. Gideon was tempting enough without people pushing us together.

I needed to put this stupid fascination with him aside, but hell if I didn't like working with him, watching his sturdy body flex and bend back at my place as we unloaded. Back in bossy mode, he directed me this way and that as he positioned the furniture. Jim watched us from her bed, letting the foolish humans do all the work. Finally, after endless rearranging, Gideon made a satisfied noise that went straight to my dick.

"It's a start." He stepped back from straightening one of the chairs.

"It's more than a start." I flopped onto the couch, suddenly aware of exactly how exhausted I was. And turned on, a day in Gideon's company doing wonders to make my internal furnace hum like it was July. "It's like a real house now."

"Yep. How did you survive this long without a couch?" Gideon sat next to me, voice still perky, but he had a weary set to his shoulders and eyes. Fading light from outside wiggled in past the cracks in the front blinds.

"Eh." I stretched an arm along the high back of the sofa. "I've got a futon in the basement where I've got my weights and my desk where I handle business after hours. Got a TV down there. Don't really need much else."

"Don't tell me such things." Gideon leaned back like my arm was there especially for him. And maybe it was. "Now I'm picturing you working out."

"Is it a good picture?" I couldn't resist asking.

"It's a very good picture." Turning toward me, he licked his lips.

"Great," I whispered, not doing a damn thing to move away. The room seemed to crackle with new energy. "You lift? You could come over…"

Eyes still locked on my mouth, he raised his eyebrows. "For the chance to see you all sweaty? I'll risk pulling a hamstring."

"I'd spot you." I lowered my arm to his shoulder, and Gideon wiggled into my embrace like he'd been waiting for exactly this moment all day. God knew I had.

"Excellent." He did a breathy exhale, head tilting back. With an invitation so clear and a whole day—okay *years*—of anticipation, no way could I keep fighting how much I wanted him. Leaning in, I closed the last few centimeters between us, mouths colliding.

And apparently, Mr. Bossy was occasionally good with someone else leading, even without a giant couch to lift, because he let me explore his mouth at my own pace. The other kiss had been frantic, all raw power and no chance to slow down. Here, I went slowly, so slowly, remembering how very much I liked kissing and how seldom I got to indulge.

His lips were sweet, little hints of the cookie from Cheryl's platter he'd swiped earlier. And warm. Everything about him was so warm. Warm hand on my side. Warm tongue meeting mine. Warm little gasps. I'd put my body into the deep freeze for so long, and Gideon kept melting away every layer of ice I'd built up. He made it so damn easy to figure out what he liked—friction, movement, little bit of teeth, the sort of active kissing that had me harder than the fireplace mantel in no time flat.

"That's nice." He gave me a dreamy smile when I finally let him up for air.

"Nice?" I faked outrage. "That's the best you can say?"

He stretched like a cat against me. "Hey, you want to earn stupendous, be my guest."

Using his momentum, I tumbled us backward onto the

couch. We ended up with him sprawled on top of me, both of us stretched out, legs tangled.

"That sounds like a challenge." I grinned up at him before tugging him right back down for another kiss. This one was hotter, less sweet, more spice. He was back to being bossy, and I welcomed it with a low groan. Holding my face in his hands, he claimed my mouth until he wasn't the only breathless one.

He broke away to offer me a wicked smile. "See? Couch was an excellent idea. We both fit."

"You gonna admire my couch, or you gonna kiss me again?" I demanded. Hell, I'd bronze this thing if it got me more of Gideon.

He pretended to have to think, then laughed. "Kiss."

Making out with him was such a joyous thing, all that optimism and humor he walked around with coming out in kisses that felt like basking in the spring sun.

"Fuck," I groaned against his mouth as he moved his hands to my shoulders. The slight shift in position brought our denim-covered cocks into perfect alignment. I swept my palm down his sides, and he shivered. Hell. His scrapes. "Sorry."

"Don't you dare stop. I'm all healed. Promise." He arched into my hand like a touch-starved pet. And lord, I wanted to give him everything he needed. "But I'm going to die if you don't kiss me again."

"Can't have that." I pulled him back down, mouth as hungry as the rest of me. His lips were delicious, but so were his jaw, his neck, and his ears. Drunk on him, I explored every inch he let me. Still bossy, he had no issue directing my mouth to the exact spot on his neck that made him gasp or stretching, so I had no choice but to capture his ear. He was a fucking wonder, and I wanted to do this until New Year.

"Paul." Shuddering, he surged against me, grinding down, and all of a sudden, lasting another five minutes wasn't going to happen, let alone the rest of the month. He was hard and solid, the perfect counterpoint to each of my own thrusts. Our hands became greedier as our movements gained momentum, me grabbing his ass and him wedging a hand under my shirt to clutch at my side. His fingers dug into my ribs, and I groaned.

"Fuck. You're going to get me off."

"Do it." He was all wide-eyed wonder and husky demands, and hell if I could deny him a damn thing.

"You too." Hand on his ass, I urged him faster, our kisses turning clumsy and that much hotter for it.

"Oh, I'm there. I'm there." Crying out, he bucked hard against me, pushing me deep into the couch cushions, and that desperation was enough to pull me along with him over the edge.

"Fuck. Gideon." I came in big, gasping waves, head falling back, eyes closing, lost to everything except how good this felt for long moments.

"Damn." Voice drowsy, he rested his head on my chest, and I stroked his back, touch way gentler now.

"All that genius vocabulary and that's the best you can offer?" I laughed and kissed the top of his head.

"It was nice," he mumbled, still-trembling body countering his faint praise.

"If that's you angling for a repeat, you might need to wait." I laughed because as much as I'd come in my pants like a horny teen, I wasn't twenty anymore, and even with Gideon as incentive, I needed a minute before I did something about that *nice*.

"I can be patient." He managed a fake humble tone before breaking off into musical laughter. "Did we scare the dog?"

I glanced over at the now-empty dog bed. "Apparently, she decided we needed privacy."

"We did." Gideon snickered. "You were right as well. Perfect nap couch. Damn. I needed that."

"Yeah. Me too." Fuck. It was scary how much I had, how quickly we'd gone from furniture moving to making out, and how damn badly I wanted to do it all again. And shouldn't for a whole host of reasons that had me scrubbing at my hair.

Making a clucking noise, Gideon calmly removed my hand and returned it to his back. "You're thinking about freaking out. Don't."

"Because you have decorating to do?" I wasn't entirely joking. Much as he'd been into the making out, he was entirely too invested in the decorating plans, and I didn't doubt that he'd throw me over for a perfectly placed garland or sparkly ornament.

"Exactly." He nodded sharply, chin digging into my chest. And it would be easy, so easy to simply let him have his way. But I shouldn't. Because it wasn't going to be December forever, and we still had to live next door to each other come January.

"Gideon…"

"That is a 'we need to talk' voice. And we don't." His tone was so stern I almost expected him to whip out a ruler. "We had stupendous orgasms together. I'd like to do it again."

"Well, at least I earned a stupendous there." I laughed because I couldn't argue with the wanting to do it again. I wanted that too. So much that my brain was already buzzing with possibilities, things I'd like to try, ways I might coax out more laughter, more praise.

"You can earn more. Later."

"Later." I wasn't sure exactly what I was promising.

Maybe he was right, and this was as simple as some kissing we both wanted to do. Whatever the case, he was absolutely right that examining it too closely would be a bad idea. *Later.* Later I would figure everything out, but not before I soaked up some more of Gideon's holiday magic.

Chapter Fourteen
GIDEON

Looking for a tree? My oldest has his first real part-time job at Murphy's tree lot on the other side of the park. Stop by! He'll load you up! ~Molly Reed posted to the What's Up Neighbor app

"The time has come," I announced as Paul opened his front door. His kitchen light had been on as I came home from work, but I hadn't wanted to be presumptuous. Even if we did have an appointment.

"Oh?" Paul's heated look as he ushered me into the dim foyer said he most certainly had not checked the schedule.

"To get you a tree." I held up said schedule, helpful smile firmly in place. Him thinking I was there on a sexy mission was nice though. The last few days, we'd alternated awkward chitchat and flirty innuendo, but as of yet, we hadn't repeated the couch tango. Maybe this would be my lucky night. But first, I had a mission. "The tree lots are packed on weekends. Wednesday night is a good time to get a nice one, rest it on the porch, then decorate it when we're ready."

"Hold up. A real tree?" Paul frowned, deep furrow across his forehead. Like me, he'd probably recently arrived home because he still had on thick work socks, faded jeans, and a T-shirt advertising his business.

"Yes. Of course. You want the best backdrop for Brandon's proposal. And I still need a tree for my place." I'd been looking forward to this for days now. I'd probably still end up decorating mine on my own, but the coziness of joint tree shopping was too appealing to pass up. "We can each—"

"Gideon." Paul's expression was way too serious as he cut me off. "I can't do a real tree, sorry. The fire hazard…" He took a shuddery breath. "I thought you knew."

"I should have," I said miserably, bitterly disappointed in myself. With someone else, I might have tried logic, explaining how regular watering cut way down on the risk, but this was Paul, and he was deathly pale. *There was a fire…* An apology, not an argument, was what was called for. "The fire hazard. You're right. I'm sorry. So sorry."

"It's all right." More of Paul's Philly accent came out when he was upset, the "all right" rough. "Just one of those weird quirks. It wasn't even a tree fire, just faulty wiring, but I can't do candles at all either. No open flames. Fire pits and grills make me antsy too. But it's not your fault."

The way he said it, all quiet and resigned, hit me square in the gut. This was a guy who knew self-blame a little too well, and I hated that for him.

"Hey, I thought we agreed the other day that it's okay to say when something sucks." I shifted from foot to foot, mind racing to find a way to save this evening. Having upset him made my stomach roil.

"Yeah. It does suck. But I don't mean to push my phobias on you." His mouth twisted.

"You're not. It's not even that weird of a quirk. Everyone has their fears. I'm scared of the dark," I blurted, hating the self-deprecating way Paul kept talking. I rarely shared that information, but if it made him feel better, I could humble myself a little.

"You? King of the lights?" Paul laughed, but his eyes were kind.

"Maybe that's part of why I love light displays so much. But I'm forty-two, and I still sleep with the hall light on because my inner six-year-old still isn't over being alone in the dark and hearing my parents argue. So I get it. Some fears you can't outgrow."

"Yeah." Reaching behind him, he none too-subtly flipped on the light for the dark living room behind him. "Think there's room in the plan for an artificial tree?"

"Absolutely." I'd already arrived at a good solution on the fly. "And not a big-box store either. There's that historic hardware store in downtown Evergreen. They always have a display. Top-quality ones. We'll go tonight."

I rubbed my hands together, liking this new idea more and more.

"We can still get a real one for you," he offered. "I don't want to ruin your plans."

"Don't be silly." I waved his concern away as Jim wandered in from the back of the house. "It's just me this year anyway. I should get a nice tabletop one as a backup for years when a real one is harder to come by anyway."

Usually, I could count on Lori and the kids coming by, at least once, and other friends as well, but this year was looking decidedly lean. All the more reason to appreciate the distraction of Paul and this project.

"So, you were thinking of going right now?" he asked,

stooping to pet Jim's furry head. The dog really did seem to have a sweet disposition, and my own quirk about big dogs was something I wanted to get over, and not simply because I wanted more repeat invitations to Paul's house.

"Um, yeah. The—"

"Schedule." Paul nodded and headed toward the kitchen, Jim and me both following. "Got it. Let me feed Jim real quick."

"I'm the one with the neuroses," I admitted as Paul fetched a dog dish. "Neither of my parents know how to plan. Visitations were always getting changed at the last minute. I never knew which house I'd be at on any given weekend. And after my grandfather died, my dad talked my grandmother out of her previous plans, got her to move to Florida with him on a lark. I *need* my plans."

"I understand, Gideon." Pausing his work, he squeezed my shoulders. "I don't color code, but if I don't check the smoke detector batteries on the third of every month, I get antsy."

"We're a good pair." I laughed. It felt nice, not needing to hide and finding something of a like soul. My shoulders felt lighter than they had in years, laughter that much freer.

"We are." Looking up from feeding Jim, he met my gaze, but I couldn't tell whether he was matching my humor or maybe something more serious. Still trying to make sense of his expression, I hung back while he grabbed his coat from a hook near the kitchen door. "I'll leave the lights on for when we're back."

My face heated. He was so good to me. "You don't have to do that."

"It's two lights." He shrugged. "And I'm not twenty-five with way more month than pay. I can leave a light on."

"Thanks." I held out a hand, and he took it, fingers interwined the whole way to his truck, which was better suited to hauling a big box with a tree than my car. His grip was warm and solid, and I liked how naturally our hands fit together. I'd intended the gesture to be playful, but there was nothing humorous about the way my stomach fluttered from the contact.

The historic downtown Evergreen, right on the mainline train from the Philadelphia city center, did December *right,* everything from the train depot to the little shops decked out in white lights and each streetlamp featuring a jaunty red bow.

"I always forget how pretty downtown is all lit up." I slowed our pace so I could admire everything as we walked from the lot where we'd finally found parking toward the collection of shops that rimmed the town square.

"It really is." Like me, Paul had his hands in his pockets. No repeat of earlier when his hand in mine had felt so right. But even without holding hands, our stroll still felt romantic with the decorations all around us. In the center of the square, a seasonal Santa's village display was closing up shop for the night while a caroling group strolled around, singing familiar tunes. Local groups raising money for various charities alternated nights to carol, adding to the throwback feel of the area. "Brandon used to say it was something out of a movie, the trees and carolers and display windows."

"I bet his girlfriend will love it too. It's hard not to love. I always feel like a kid coming down here."

"I know." He gave me an indulgent smile, not unlike the one he gave Jim before we left. My chest swelled. Paul made me want so much more than simply another round of sex. Every time he looked at me like that, like I was *special,* I ached with wants I thought I'd packed away a long time ago.

The hardware store played up its early 1900s roots with

a Victorian-themed window display and gleaming wood fixtures festooned with greenery.

"We need the biggest, fluffiest artificial tree you have," I told the young clerk near the door.

"You're in luck. We have just one box left of the deluxe model." She led us over to a grouping of decorated trees near the front of the store. The largest tree was taller than Paul, wide with dense branches and impressively authentic fir tree coloring.

"Oh, that's gorgeous." I could already envision it in the corner at Paul's house.

"It's sure massive." Paul whistled before circling the floor model. "Will it fit?"

I snorted. "Trust me. I measured. This is prime proposal backdrop."

"Oh, congrats!" The clerk grinned wide enough to strain her freckles.

"Not us," I said hurriedly. "His brother. But we need perfection."

Oblivious to the clerk trying to marry us off, Paul had knelt down to admire the train set rimming the display model's tree skirt. His eyes had a distant cast to them, and his half-smile made my heartbeat faster. I knelt next to him.

"Paul," I whispered urgently. "Get the train."

"Why?" He frowned, but his gaze was still on the train chugging around the tracks. "A train probably won't show up in the proposal photos."

"Get Brandon to put the ring box on one of the coal cars." Tapping my temple, I tried to come up with more ideas before he could talk himself out of it. "Or load the cattle car with candy canes for him."

Paul wouldn't buy the train for himself, but he would

for Brandon. I'd happily use that excuse because Paul *needed* this train.

"All right," he allowed at last, standing back up.

"Good choice," the clerk enthused. "Only one box left of that too. I'll grab the tree and train both for you."

"See?" Straightening my coat as I also stood, I grinned at Paul. "This was meant to be."

"I see." Tone solemn, he was studying my face intently. The air seemed to quicken, all my nerve endings vibrating. Something was happening. What, I wasn't sure, but *something*. "Do you want dinner after this?"

"Out?" Was Paul asking me on a date? Yes. The answer was yes.

"If you want. I was thinking more of cooking for you."

"Even better." I wasn't simply being polite. I ate far more takeout than I should. Someone cooking for me was a treat I wasn't about to turn down.

"I have some meat in the fridge. Wait. Do you eat meat?"

"Yes, Paul, I eat meat." I snickered like a twelve-year-old. "That sounds great."

"Good. You can help set up the tree while I cook." His tone was very matter-of-fact, but my heart still beat faster. Visualizing the scene alone was enough to give me goose bumps.

"It's a…" I trailed off because I didn't want to risk spooking him by calling it a date if it was more about him being hungry.

"Plan," he supplied with a rare full smile.

"Yes. Exactly." His understanding was a gift, a rare one. I had many friends and acquaintances, but few got me on the level Paul seemed to. And not only did he understand, but he seemed to embrace my bossy nature and obsession with details. And like the best gifts, I couldn't wait to unwrap Paul under that tree. Soon.

Chapter Fifteen
PAUL

Needed: some tenors! Our group is short two tenors for our turn caroling in the square! All are welcome. Please message me if you can sing! ~Randolph Clark posted to the What's up Neighbor app

"I CAN HELP NOW. THE PORK CHOPS AND POTATOES ARE finishing in the oven," I announced as I returned to my living room to check on Gideon and the tree. Jim had been supervising my cooking, but she followed along behind me. "Put me to work."

"Well, the hard part is done." Holding a string of lights, Gideon gestured at the tree, which truly was huge. It filled out the corner nicely though. Gideon would probably call it a focal point or some such. "It came with lights already wired on, but I'm adding a few additional strands."

"I see." I helped him finish draping the lights along the fluffy branches. "Nice assembly job on the tree."

"Thank you. It was mainly just branch fluffing." His eyes twinkled when he said *fluffing*, and the back of my neck heated. "The tree parts snap together. I didn't even need to go back home for my drill."

"I have plenty of tools here."

"Yes, but do you have my favorite drill?" Gideon's smile widened, and the only thing preventing me from tumbling him backward onto the couch was the prospect of burnt dinner.

"Somehow, I'm not surprised you have a favorite tool." I shook my head.

"I do." Gideon's expression turned hot. Possessive. I'd walked right into that one, and hell, charred meat might be a risk I'd have to take, especially when he added, "Now, you can have the top."

"Uh..."

"Of the tree, Paul. Of the tree." He handed me my box from the attic before dragging more containers of ornaments over to the twinkling tree. "For your treasures. They should be up higher."

"Ah. Yeah." My tongue felt too big for my mouth. I tried to follow orders and hang a few pieces, but my brain kept wanting to leap back to sex. Sex was far easier than the memories the old ornaments sparked, that was for sure. Which Gideon seemed to sense because he laughed knowingly.

"If you're asking, I wasn't kidding the other day. My knees aren't *that* creaky yet. And you can *top* whatever you'd like."

I made a strangled noise. Outside of a few brief forays into the wild world of hookup apps, I hadn't many occasions to quite so frankly discuss my bedroom likes. "Wouldn't have figured you..."

Fuck. I needed to stop right there before I said the wrong thing. Or the right one.

"Ha." Gideon stopped sorting a box of jewel-toned

glass ornaments to pat my cheek. "You're cute if you think I can't be bossy and bottom at the same time."

I swallowed so loud even the dog looked up. "Good to know."

I liked topping, and in my limited experience, it was what people tended to ask for from me, but the one part I struggled with was trying to read the other person's mind, figure out what they needed and when. With Gideon, there would be no such guesswork. He told. He directed. He managed. And lord, I wanted that. I licked my lips. He did the same.

"How long does the dinner need?" he asked huskily.

"Not nearly long enough," I groaned and stepped away before I could kiss him until we both forgot all about the food.

"What?" He waggled his eyebrows at me. "I was only asking for decorating reasons."

"Uh-huh." The dog wandered over to us, pushing her head against my leg. Good. Welcome distraction. "Hey, you." I petted her soft ears. "What do you want?"

"Um. Will she eat the low-hanging ornaments?" Gideon cast a critical eye on the glass bauble he was holding. For all that he'd been over several times now, Gideon was still wary around Jim, giving her an almost comically wide berth.

"I seriously doubt it." I moved from petting the dog to rubbing Gideon's shoulder. "For all I joke, she has a pretty mild manner. I'll still likely shut her out of here while I'm at work, to be safe."

"Good." Gideon's spine was still stiffer than the pole at the center of the tree.

"How about you give her a treat?" Thinking fast, I dashed back to the kitchen for the zippered package of dog snacks. "She'll be your buddy for life for these duck and sweet potato things I found."

"Oh. Okay." Gideon took a deep breath and plucked a treat from the bag. I was so proud of him for trying that I very nearly praised him, not the dog. Instead, I held my breath, watching, hoping this wasn't a terrible idea.

"Here. You want?" He held it out, and Jim swept it up with her tongue, utterly delighted to not have to sit or otherwise do work to earn the reward. And when Gideon gave her a second, she nudged him with her head, giving him a big doggy grin. "She likes them!"

"Told you." My heart thumped, a weird mix of adrenaline and joy at watching Gideon pet Jim for the first time. Damn it. Now I had to kiss him. No choice. Needed—

Beep. Beep. The timer dinged in the kitchen. "That's the dinner."

"See? Now the humans will eat." Gideon talked to the dog as they both followed me into the kitchen. "Let's break in your new table."

Vivid images of how we'd christened the couch danced through my head, and I coughed.

"Dinner first." His laugh was downright wicked.

"Good idea." Working together, we fixed plates and carried them into the dining room, where the oval table that had looked so big when it was only me in the house felt friendly and cozy with him across from me.

"I didn't know you cooked." Gideon admired the dinner, which really wasn't all that. Thick-cut pork chops. Easy mustard sauce. Oven potatoes with some rosemary. Roast carrots and onions tossed in next to the potatoes. But he seemed impressed, which was nice. "This is really good. We won't discuss how much I live on delivery and takeout."

"Yeah, well, eating out adds up fast with a growing kid

like Brandon. And frozen is fine in a pinch, but I taught myself the basics if only to save us from scurvy. Had to get some vegetables into the kid."

"You're a good big brother." His expression softened, more of that willingness to hand me a medal for simply doing what had been needed.

"Eh. More like I knew Mom would haunt me if I didn't get some green stuff into him. She was a pretty good cook, making do with what we had. You would have liked her rolled sugar cookies. She did dozens every Christmas."

"I'm sure I would have. Do you have a recipe?" Gideon leaned forward, all eager, pork chop promptly forgotten.

"Recipe? Not one of her own. She had this red cookbook, one of those old plaid three-ring binders everyone had back in the day. All her desserts came from there."

"I know the one. My grandmother had the same book in her kitchen, dog-eared and well-loved. I've got my own I found at a flea market for the nostalgia factor. You want to make some cookies for Brandon and Elaine? I'll help." Predictably, he already had his phone out, likely to schedule cookie-making time.

"They might burn," I hedged. Two decades had passed, and I could still remember the smell of our little kitchen in the days leading up to Christmas. Hadn't occurred to me to try to duplicate it. "I'm good at meat. Not fiddly stuff."

"If the first batch is crap, we simply try again." Gideon shrugged with the confidence of someone who'd never worried about the price of butter. "Or we order some, but we should try baking our own first."

"All right." It was easier to go along with the Gideon express. I could afford some wasted flour these days. "I don't have the shapes though."

"Cookie cutters? I have you covered. I've got a collection." He made another note on his phone before setting it aside.

"Somehow, I'm not surprised." I shook my head. He was somehow too much and exactly right at the same time, and the rest of dinner was similarly easy as he finally turned his attention back to the food.

"Dinner was good," he said as we finished and carried our plates to the kitchen. "You should make something like this for your guests."

Oh crap. I was going to need to feed Brandon and Elaine too. And he'd probably developed more refined tastes out in California than the endless bowls of cereal he'd lived on as a teen.

"Don't suppose you do menu planning as another side gig?"

"I can help you brainstorm, absolutely." Gideon nodded as he helped me load the dishwasher. "Left to my own devices, I tend to revert to easy options, but I like cooking for others. Entertaining."

"That sounds fancy."

"You're cute when you get suspicious." He waited for me to toss in the dishwasher soap pellet before shutting the door. "Let's go assemble your train, then I can help you start thinking about a menu and shopping list."

"The train can wait." Merely watching his bustle around my kitchen in his starched white shirt and plaid bow tie had the need to kiss him bubbling up again. And without the risk of ruining dinner, I was done resisting.

"No, it can't." He tugged me back to the dining room, totally missing my I-want-to-eat-you-alive vibes. "Come on."

"You're worse than a kid," I complained. I was still kissing him, but I could give him this first. He was already carrying over the big box that held the Christmas train set.

"Guilty. But I'm fun. Or so I'm told." He set the box in front of me as we both knelt by the tree.

"You're fun," I agreed.

"Really?" His eyebrows shot up like he'd expected an argument.

I shrugged. "Guess you're growing on me."

"Good." He puffed up like Jim after she earned extra treats. "Open the box."

I pulled off the lid and slid out the pieces, and Gideon immediately set to examining the various train parts.

"Ooh! The ring box could go right there." He pointed to one of the cars, which did have an opening that might hold a small box. "And look! They even have a tiny engineer."

"Nice." I took the engine from him, studying the little details that gave it an old-fashioned feel. "Had a grandfather who worked freight trains. His father too. I had a set when I was little. Used to think it would be fun, driving a train."

"I'm very much enjoying the image of you with an engineer's hat." Gideon gave a happy sigh. "My grandfather's family ran a haberdashery, fine men's furnishings, down near the city center."

"And now we know where you get your sense of style." Laughing, I pointed to his jaunty bow tie.

"Oh, my grandfather was a much snappier dresser than me. I've got the cuff link collection to prove it. He never left the house without a hat and always had a linen handkerchief on him."

"That's nice that you kept his collection."

"I had to beg my dad to let me have it when they were selling everything off." Gideon made a sour face, and any jealousy I had about him getting to keep more pieces of his past faded. The more I understood his little collections and traditions, the more I appreciated him, the way he'd fought to keep certain things going.

It didn't take along before the train was assembled, track going around the base of the tree. It did look nice there, train waiting patiently on the tracks.

Gideon, however, was not so patient, thrusting the controller at me. "There. Last piece. Turn it on."

"Demanding." I shook my head simply to make him whine. "Ask nice."

"Please." He leaned over for a lightning-fast kiss on my cheek. He could have gone for my mouth, heated things up in a hurry, but the sweetness of the cheek kiss melted even more of those frozen places inside me.

"Yeah." My voice came out all rough as I flipped the switch for the train. It chugged around the track, little engine working hard, real train sounds filling the room. For an instant, I was seven or eight again, long before Brandon, when it was just me and an old train chugging around my room. The years had long since swept away most of those memories, but now they were back, that same quiver of excitement at the train rounding the bend. "Well, would you look at that?"

"Wow. It's so pretty." Exhaling, Gideon dropped his head to my shoulder. "Exactly how I pictured it."

"You've got a good imagination." I didn't. I hadn't pictured this. Hadn't pictured him. Hadn't realized how much I needed this until I was here, arm around him, train sounds filling my once-empty room, soft lights bouncing off the walls.

"I do." He sent a longing glance toward my couch, head digging in more against my collarbone. "But even the best imagination can benefit from proper…inspiration."

The brush of his hair against my neck was enough to make me shiver. "Quit looking at my couch, Gideon."

"Oh. Sorry. Um, maybe I should go…" He tried to pull away, but I wouldn't let him.

"I didn't mean *leave*. I meant I have a bedroom."

His grin was more dazzling than any of the ornaments on the tree. "You do."

Chapter Sixteen
GIDEON

It's going to be a cold one tonight! Remember to take steps so your pipes don't freeze! ~ Cheryl Bridges posted to the What's Up Neighbor app.

"Is your cat fed?" Paul asked, all serious as he turned off the train before we both stood up. Fireworks went off inside me. Apparently, I wasn't only being invited to see the bedroom but to sleep over. *Score*. I would have been happy with a couch make-out session in front of the tree, but now I was ecstatic.

"Yes. Fed. Litter. Water. He's fiercely independent, despite all my efforts to the contrary." I beamed at Paul, not even trying to cover my delight. "He'll be fine until morning."

"Good." And then he was on me, backing me toward the stairs even as he kissed me fiercely. I liked Paul all compliant and taking orders, but I fucking loved him on the verge of losing control. Desperate. Hungry.

Like me. I kissed him back, yanking at his shirt. Ever

helpful, he pulled it off, tucking it under one arm before tugging me up three steps. Then another kiss. And another. His hands were rough, and his mouth was urgent as he pulled me tight against him. He was deliciously hard, and the temptation to blow him right here on his polished staircase was high. But I did like both our necks in one piece.

"Let's not do it on the stairs," I said, breathless and dazed as I broke the kiss.

"Yeah. Don't want to fall." His voice was gruff before he grabbed me for another kiss. Then a mad dash to his room, our sock-covered feet sliding on his hardwoods, making me feel young and even more reckless.

Giggling like this was my first time, I collapsed against him the second the door shut. He'd flipped the light on, a soft glow warming up the sparsely furnished room. Double bed that really did need that upgrade and soon, gray bedding, single bedside table and wooden chair in the corner. His bare chest was warm against me, and I had to step back so I could get a better look.

"Fuck. You're hot." Fuzzier than I would have guessed with a few gray strands here and there. Dark nipples. Sculpted muscles. Clearly not loving the scrutiny, Paul turned to come around me, revealing a tattoo. That was unexpected, especially for Mr. Frugal, but there was a Victorian-looking angel on his upper left shoulder blade. *His mom.* My breath caught. "Your tat is beautiful."

"Thanks." His tight smile said he wasn't taking questions. Instead, he wrapped his arms around me, undoing my tie. "Your turn."

"Afraid I'm not as much to look at." I gasped as he made fast work of my buttons, peeling off my shirt.

"Your dress shirts drive me crazy," he growled against the back of my neck. "You're plenty hot under them too."

He nipped at my shoulder before taking my shirt and tie to join his clothes on a nearby wooden chair.

I had to laugh. "I'm charmed that even urgent lust can't get you to put clothes on the floor."

"Urgent lust, huh?" Returning to stand in front of me next to the bed, he kissed me slow and sweet, the brush of our bare chests almost too much but not nearly enough either.

"Hurry up and get your pants on the chair," I ordered, breaking away to undo his belt.

"Lucky you're so cute when bossy." He obeyed, shedding his jeans before eyeing my pants meaningfully. "You too."

But I needed a second to appreciate his powerful thighs and flat abs and that cock. My mouth watered. Cut with a broad head and the sort of width I loved. Not porn-star huge, but more than enough for me. Perfect.

"Pants." He helped out by unbuckling my belt.

"Sorry. I needed to write an ode to your cock."

"Oh? Come up with a good one?" He pushed my pants down, waiting for me to step out free before they too joined the pile on the chair.

"There once was a fellow—" I didn't get farther than that before he was kissing me again, finding my mouth with his, tongue delving deep enough to make me moan.

"What do you want?" he asked against my ear. I liked how he asked instead of assuming that my bottoming confession earlier meant I was up for that tonight. I did like fucking, but right then, I was dying to taste him.

"I want to show you how good I am on my knees until you scream." I started to sink down, but he pushed me to sit on the bed.

"Doubt I can come standing up. Your knees are safe with me." He sprawled on his back. "Have at me."

That was nice, the way he didn't argue with me or go all tough guy insisting on getting me off first. No, he took my words at face value. If I wanted something, he was going to give it to me, and that was heady stuff. My head buzzed and my hand trembled as I ran it down his torso.

He shuddered like he too was hovering on the edge. And damn, he was gorgeous, each firm muscle sexy as fuck, especially when countered by the softness of his fuzz.

"I need to get way more committed to weights if this is the result." Moving so I knelt next to him, I stroked his stomach. "I jog, but I've always thought that washboard abs were a trick of Hollywood lighting."

"Ha. This is called nothing to do in the evenings." He stretched, a clear bid to get my hand lower, but I didn't take the bait, instead switching to touching his biceps.

"I could give you something to do."

"So you could." He regarded me carefully through half-lidded eyes. I'd meant my comment as a flip retort, but something more serious sizzled between us, something best not mentioned. Chuckling, Paul rocked his hips. "How about you give me a preview of your evening suggestions before I lose my damn mind?"

That I could do. I kissed his shoulders, loving his impatient wiggling as I moved lower, blessing his arms and chest with little licks and nips. I kissed his abs right above his straining cock, then moved to his thighs.

"No fair." He let out a pained groan as I nuzzled all along the crease at the top of his leg. "You missed a spot."

"So I did." I imitated his deeper tone, and we both laughed right before I captured the head of his cock with my mouth. I swirled my tongue all around the tip before slowly going lower.

"Fuck. Fuck," Paul cursed and clutched at the bedding. "This is where I warn you it's been forever…"

I winked at him as I jacked his shaft slowly. "Glad I can jog your memory about what you like, old man."

"Hey!" He half-laughed, half-groaned, then full-out moaned when I took him deep in my mouth. Some skills got better with age, and I was only too happy to show off everything I knew and some tricks I made up on the spot. He gasped when I used my tongue on the underside, so I did that even more, going deep and teasing at the same time until he was thrashing against the bed again. "Jesus. Slow down. I wanna remember this."

"I'll give you the long version later," I promised, way too gone on how good he felt in my mouth to be able to make this last. The power of coaxing all those sexy sounds from him had my own cock hard and leaking against my stomach as I stretched out next to him. My cock could wait, though, because every sense was locked on him and his responses. His salty taste. His scent soap and spice and so good I wanted to drown in it. His abs under my head and firm thighs tensing against my palm. "I want to get you there."

"You are. Fuck. You are." He rocked his hips up to meet my mouth, a deeper thrust than I was expecting, and I had to quickly pull back to avoid coughing. He stroked my hair with gentle fingers. "Fuck. Didn't mean to choke you. Sorry."

"No sorry. Do it again," I ordered, more ready for his movements now, craving them even, moving my hand to the base of his shaft so I could control the depth of his thrusts. "Love making you lose control."

I sucked hard until he got the idea that I truly wanted this. He started to rock again, a shallow motion that quickly escalated to him fucking my mouth. I tried to keep giving him the tongue action he'd been loving, but I had to let go of that idea and simply hang on for the ride. It was sloppy and fast and loud and so fucking hot that I almost got there before he did.

But then he groaned low, body bowing upward as his hand tightened on my shoulder. "Fuck. There. There."

The taste of his come, the way he filled my mouth, made my cock pulse over and over. I had to seriously clamp down against my own orgasm and focus on swallowing.

"Fuck." Paul hauled me up next to him. "You're incredible."

"Thanks." Nestling into his side, I reveled in how harsh his breathing still was, the way his rugged features were softened, the way he kept looking at me with such wonder. He made me feel like I'd won a gold medal in sex, and that thrill was almost better than coming myself. Almost. My cock twitched against my belly, and I finally gave into the urge to reach for it.

"Wait." Paul stopped me with a hand over mine. "I wanna play too. Come up here."

Gesturing at his chest, he licked his lips, intent clear. Him so eager to please made my cock pulse even harder. And weirdly, his desire made my chest ache as well, turned this from something hot I'd done for him to something shared, something more than I'd expected but sure as hell wasn't about to turn down.

"This good?" I scooted around until I was straddling his chest.

"Yeah. Too lazy to move, but I wanna taste you too." Reaching behind him, he stuck a pillow under his head. He urged me closer with his powerful hands on my hips.

"I'm close," I warned, not sure how much more I could endure.

"Even better." Eyes flashing darkly, he gave a mischievous grin. I held my cock loosely with one hand while he licked all around the head. My ass and hips burned from resisting the urge to fuck his mouth. He tried to suck me deeper, and I did a controlled thrust, keeping it shallow. His grip on my ass tightened. "Come on. You can give me more than that."

"You want more?" My voice sounded like the train earlier—fast chugs and breathy whistles.

"Fuck. Yes." He urged me forward until I had no choice but to brace my hands on the wall in front of me. And his eagerness was even better than his warm and welcoming mouth, each desperate sound and greedy suck getting me there in record time. Control shattering, I thrust hard and fast, and he took it all. I reached one hand down, touching his hair, and somehow that one point of contact catapulted me into free fall.

"Oh. Damn. Coming." I came in hard shudders, and he swallowed it all, sucking hard until the stimulation was too much, and I had to collapse next to him, narrowly avoiding kneeing him with my limp-noodle legs. "Okay. I'm dead now. Wow."

My legs weren't the only things wrung out. My insides felt all loose, like all the screws that usually held me together were loosened, undone by him and that unexpected connection. All the solo orgasms couldn't hold a candle to how good it felt, sharing that with Paul, knowing he wanted it as much as me.

"Fuck. I almost came a second time, feeling you go." Wrapping an arm around me, he held me close.

"Yeah?" I loved knowing that, loved having turned him on that much. I shifted to reach for his cock, but he captured my hand instead, holding it in his.

"I'm good." He laughed, sounding as drunk and loose as I felt. "So good."

"Me too." Even my sigh was giddy. I was sleepy but still

wired, flying high on every damn amazing minute of the whole evening.

After adjusting his pillow, he stretched, pulling the too-narrow cover over us both. "Hell, I really do need to go bed shopping."

"Yes, you do." I was one hundred percent in favor of him planning for a repeat. "A king will make sleepovers more fun. But I don't want you miserable all night. Should I go?"

"Fuck no." He held me closer, and I settled my head on his broad chest. "I'd be more miserable if you left."

"Good." I rewarded the admission with a kiss right over his heart. I couldn't help my smile either. Paul wanting me to stay was like having leftovers of an amazing dessert, knowing more would be coming later. "You can have the pillow. I'm happy right here."

Warm hand still on my back, he kissed the top of my head. I was happy. So happy I wasn't sure I could survive it. And he could have the pillow, steal the covers, and talk in his sleep, and I still wouldn't rather be anywhere else. Bring on the mattress shopping because I was sure as hell planning on making this a regular thing.

Chapter Seventeen
PAUL

Free dishes! Ugliest set of stoneware ever to grace a table. Heavy as you-know-what. Service for sixteen. Free to a good home (or not so good! No judgment here! Just come take it!) ~Penny Jordan posted to the What's Up Neighbor app

"Explain to me why I can't accomplish this online?" I asked Gideon as I put my boots on. I needed more than my boots to be willing to brave a shopping center on a Saturday in mid-December.

"Because you need to test the various mattress options." Gideon looked up from his crouch on the floor near Jim. Still concerned that she might bother the tree or the train, he'd brought her a bribe, a plush stuffed Grinch dog toy. I'd probably be hearing the thing's squeaker in my sleep, but bless Gideon for trying to make friends.

"Oh?" I put some extra heat behind my gaze, not that I had to work that hard around Gideon lately. Apparently, my body liked the whole regular sex thing because I thought about Gideon constantly. "They're going to let me throw you down right there on the showroom floor?"

"Not that kind of test." Gideon had been in a funk ever since his arrival that morning. I should have come up with an excuse to get him to sleep over Friday. Then I could have guaranteed a better mood for both of us, but I hadn't been able to come up with a plausible enough excuse for three nights in a row. Thursday, I'd gotten him to add menu planning to the schedule and kept him so busy afterward that he'd forgotten to leave. But right then, he was frowning like a guy who hadn't gotten laid in six months. "Not everyone has the same definition of firm—"

"You're telling me." I was going to get him to smile even if it took an emergency stop for whoopie pies to do it.

"Behave." He rolled his eyes when usually he was the one snickering at juvenile jokes.

"You're in a cranky mood." Finished with my boots, I grabbed my coat from the hook, but I'd enjoy this whole undertaking a lot more if Gideon would either return to normal or tell me what was wrong so I could fix it. "I thought I was supposed to be the foul-tempered one."

"You're not so bad." Standing back up, he managed a half-smile. "And sorry. I'm simply frustrated because my coat rack collapsed on me, and despite my best efforts, it appears broken for good. It's an older cherry one I picked up at an auction. Furniture breaking is a stupid thing to let bother me—"

"Show me," I demanded, having to work to not grin. Smiling would be bad, but I was relieved that his funk had nothing to do with the sex we'd been having, Christmas plans, or anything I'd done. "Broken wood? I'm your man."

"Of course you are." He laughed, which was an excellent start, but shook his head. "We're supposed to go mattress shopping."

"The schedule can wait fifteen minutes," I snapped without thinking, only to watch his face fall. Damn it. I'd forgotten how important plans were to Gideon. Reaching for his arm, I softened my voice. "We'll go. Promise. Let me take a look before you send your favorite coat rack to the dump."

Gideon nodded and waited for me to lock up. He was weirdly quiet on the short walk across the driveway, eyes all shifty and steps slower than usual. He seemed reluctant to step aside at his kitchen door before finally ushering me in. "Apologies for the clutter."

"I'm sure it's fine." I'd never actually been inside Gideon's house, so I took time to look around as he led me to the front hall. I knew his place had been remodeled some before he'd bought it, so the kitchen was updated like mine, but the similarities ended there.

Each space was a different color, a coordinated muted palette, and each area had been staged like something out of a magazine. Maybe one of those ones dedicated to collectors because there was a lot of stuff, true, but it all worked. Vintage plates rimming the wall above the cabinets. Mural landscape wallpaper above the chair rail in the dining room, which featured two packed china cabinets. Catalogs littered the dining table, but no other mess. The living room was decked out for the holiday, the tabletop tree he'd bought downtown with me on display in the front window. Little buildings for one of those holiday village type things lining full bookcases.

"This isn't clutter." I touched his shoulder as we entered the foyer because he seemed all twitchy. "Addiction to fake snow, maybe, but it's pretty."

"It's a lot more stuff than your place."

"So you're more ready for entertaining than me." I shrugged. It was more than I'd ever own on my own, but I could appreciate the care that had gone into his rooms. Everything was very welcoming like he was ready for a gathering at a moment's notice. "It's fine. I like the decorating. It's very you."

"Oh, good." Gideon exhaled hard before giving me a tentative smile. "I've been wanting to have you over, but I didn't want to scare you off with how much I own."

"I'm not scared off." I gave him a fast kiss. Well, I intended fast. The actual kiss turned slow and sultry and had me glancing at the stairs behind us as we broke apart. "Show me the broken thing before we forget all about mattress shopping."

"Right here." He indicated a wooden coat rack, which was laying on the floor, blue drill next to it, one of the arms askew.

"Hmm." I knelt to examine the problem. The arm had pulled away from the central pole, and it was a bigger issue than simply tightening some loose screws but still highly doable. This time I didn't hold back the grin as I looked up at him. "I can fix this. Screws are stripped, but I've got some that will work better. Main thing is to shore up the loose screw holes and repair the crack before it spreads."

Gideon snorted. "I do hate a loose hole. And spreading crack."

"Glad to see you amused." I was. I liked him back to normal and with me being the reason why. He was rescuing my whole damn month. Least I could do was fix some furniture.

"You really think it's worth saving?" Kneeling next to me, he ran a hand down the polished wood. "They don't make them this sturdy anymore. It reminded me of a piece my grandparents had."

"Yeah." My voice turned husky because that was exactly what Brandon had said when he'd first seen my house. *Think it's worth saving?* Clearly, I had, even if I'd grumbled a lot during the doing. And with Gideon, *so* much was worth saving, every item linked to a memory, something that mattered. "You'll want to turn this arm to the back, maybe use it more for hats and light stuff, but there's a lot of use left in this piece. Good bones."

"Thank you." His gaze was soft, and he was damn lucky there wasn't a bed nearby and that I appreciated his need to follow his schedule.

"Let's cart it to my garage. I've got the right tools and glue and clamps there."

"Kinky." His voice was teasing, but his eyes were still hot enough to melt the crusty snow covering the lawn out front. Bitterly cold day, and I wanted nothing more than to get warm with Gideon.

"Wood clamps. And if you keep looking at me like that, I'm not going to require a mattress."

"You need a mattress." Rolling his eyes at me, he straightened back up and dusted off his pants. I filed away my need to push him against the nearest flat surface for later, and we were on our way to the big shopping center in a nearby township in short order.

I wasn't entirely clear on why Gideon needed to tag along for me to pick out a bed. Strictly speaking, this wasn't part of the holiday plans where I needed his input or assistance, like with the decorating or furniture moving.

"I hope I'm not stealing you away from any other parts of your to-do list," I said carefully as I drove. I didn't want to sound unappreciative, but I also hated the idea that I was monopolizing his time.

"You're not." His voice came out surprisingly somber, then he forced a laugh, but even his lighter tone had a blue edge. "I always think I'll be busier in December than I am. I pre-plan so much ahead that I wind up at loose ends."

"That sucks." I didn't know what else to say because it did suck. I might not share Gideon's love of the season, but I did know lonely. I coped by refinishing floors to ballroom-worthy levels while maybe he coped by taking on decorating projects and social obligations. My insides turned sour. My own solo life was practically an old friend at this point, broken-in boots I was reluctant to replace, but his loneliness cut me to the bone

"Maybe next year I'll take up baking like Cheryl. Anything to keep busy." He sounded so resigned that I gave his leg a squeeze while we were stopped at a light. "I even volunteered to take an extra shift collecting donations from cars driving through to see the lights tonight."

"You're going to freeze your ass off." We weren't expecting more snow yet, but a cold front hung over the region, bringing low temperatures and a biting wind.

"Yes, but we got an excellent writeup on an entertainment blog that focuses on local attractions. We should get good traffic tonight. Someone needs to be there to do the donations, so I put myself on the schedule."

Ah. The schedule. Stubborn man. I groaned. "I'll make you a thermos of tea. It'll be too late for coffee, and I don't have any decaf. Do you have long underwear?"

"You're going to help me?" His eyes were wide. Outside, the line of cars crawled along toward the retail center, shoppers undeterred by the cold weather. Finding parking was going to be a chore.

"Well, yeah. I was going to put your evening to better use, but if volunteering is what you need to do, you're not getting hypothermia on my watch. I've got insulated coveralls from work you can borrow too."

Shifting in his seat, Gideon released a dreamy sigh.

"Paul Frost, this may be the nicest thing someone has done for me."

My neck heated from his praise, and I was glad for the distraction of the jam-packed parking lot. I forced a laugh. "Would I ruin it if I said I had a vested interest in certain parts of you not freezing?"

"You offering to warm me up after?" Sadness gone from his voice, he coupled his playful tone with dancing his fingers along my thigh.

"Absolutely." I tried to remember where I'd put my spare blanket. I could make the bedroom a little warmer as well. "I can't leave Jim, but I do have a hot shower I installed myself in the master."

"Oh, baby, talk DIY to me." He laughed as I circled the lot in a fruitless hunt for a space.

"If that does it for you, I did the tile in there too. Needed a whole new sub-floor. Weeks of work."

"I'll come to you after I finish my shift. We can move the old bed into the guest room in the morning." Clearly pleased to have a schedule, Gideon pulled out his phone, adding notes. "After, I need to figure out what to get my secret Santa person for our annual work luncheon next week."

"What do they like?" I asked as I finally spied an open space.

"Helene is a huge Eagles fan. The football team, not the band, alas. Her cube is a monument to bobblehead football figurines."

I zipped into the parking spot before grinning at him. "Luckily, I'm a football guy."

"Why am I not surprised?"

"And one of my best landscaping clients works in PR for the team." My shoulders lifted. I fucking loved being able to help Gideon. Furniture repair. Football advice. I wanted to do whatever it took to get more of his musical laughter. "Would a signed poster work? I got one of those for human Jim's teen son. Or maybe some discount tickets?"

"Oh my God, you're a lifesaver. Yes. A poster would be perfect." Leaning over, he gave me a swift kiss. "Now, let's find you a bed."

"I like you happier." I followed him out of the truck.

"I like me happier too." His face was back to soft and sentimental, and when he grabbed my hand, I let him. We held hands on the trek to the mattress store, but he dropped mine in his excitement as we entered the store.

"Look! Big year-end clearance." He pointed to a sign.

"Find me a bargain suitable for my ancient back," I ordered as he launched himself onto the nearest bed, spreading out like a snow angel.

"Will do. And not this one. Too firm."

"No such thing." I offered him a hand up and settled in to enjoy watching Gideon have the thrill of the hunt.

Naturally, Gideon got the life story of the clerk who arrived to help us, passing out holiday dinner tips in between testing other mattresses and trying to wrangle deals. We made our way from the cheap box spring models to higher beds with fluffy tops and price tags discreetly hidden. Even I got into the spirit of trying, and lying next to Gideon on a plush mattress with the helpful salesperson hovering nearby was definitely one of the more surreal experiences of my life.

"Your sides each adjust individually. A ton of spouses love that feature." The clerk showed off matching controllers. He was young and earnest, and like the rest of the world, entirely too eager to marry Gideon and me off.

"Ah…" Sitting up, I made a strangled sound. Spouses? We were barely…*huh?* I couldn't finish that thought. We weren't a couple, but this sure as hell felt like something other than hooking up.

"He's not that picky," Gideon covered smoothly for me before turning to me and lowering his voice. "Get what you want. This one is super comfortable, but that other one was the better deal."

"Actually, I can get you twenty percent off this one," the clerk offered as Gideon pet the quilted pillow top.

"Sold."

Gideon flushed an adorable shade of pink. "You don't need…"

"My back liked this one most," I lied. Actually, I'd been fine with every bed we'd tried, but following Gideon's lead to make snow angels while trying beds had been too fun to cut it off at the first mattress.

"Excellent." Gideon rubbed his hands together. "Let me see if I can get you an even better deal like some free pillows."

"Ask for two." I laughed, not sure shopping had ever been this fun. "Do your thing."

As he hustled over to the clerk, I was already counting down to when I'd get to warm him up later. I didn't even mind the delay. Somehow, I knew this wouldn't be the last time I waited up for Gideon. He deserved someone watching out for him, someone to leave a light on, and if he'd let it be me, well, I liked that. It also terrified me. But not enough to dampen how much I wanted to be *someone* for him.

Chapter Eighteen
GIDEON

REMINDER: Can people with deliveries PLEASE ask the truck drivers to respect the driveways of others? We noticed some neighbors were blocked in for over twenty minutes today. ~ Ernest Morrison posted to the What's Up Neighbor app

"Did it arrive?" I asked breathlessly as Paul opened the side door. I'd come over as quickly as I could, but a networking emergency had kept me at work longer than I would have liked. Then a fast trip to the store and quick attention to an indifferent Butterscotch before I hurried across the drive.

"Hello to you too, Gideon." Laughing, Paul ushered me into the kitchen, which smelled divinely like garlic and butter. "How was your day?"

"Oops. Sorry." I set my brown paper bag on a corner of the counter before kicking off my shoes to set them next to his boots. "When you texted to ask if I was coming over, I didn't mean to presume…"

"Presume away. Please." He smiled, but the lines

around his eyes and mouth were deeper than usual, even his beard looking a little weary. "You eager to see my new bed is the highlight of my day. Damn. It was a long one."

"What went wrong?" Crossing over to where he stood by the stove, I then rubbed his meaty shoulders.

"This cold snap isn't helping any for one thing."

"Even with your insulated coveralls?" I teased. He'd insisted I borrow a pair Saturday night, and not only had they kept me toasty warm, but I wasn't sure I'd ever had a more romantic gesture. Oh, maybe some wouldn't see the romance in Paul filling his big thermos with tea and plying me with extra-thick gloves, but I'd felt so cared for I'd practically floated into his place hours later, where I'd proceeded to show him my extreme gratitude with my mouth. Best Saturday night in a long time.

And now it was a new week, still nasty weather, but Paul hadn't gotten tired of me yet, so there was that. He stretched into my touch, groaning loud enough to startle Jim, who was having her dinner in the corner.

"I had on more layers than a head of cabbage and my feet are still half-frozen." Paul rolled his shoulders in a none-too-subtle bid for more. "And supplies for one project are delayed, so I had to be on the phone way more than I like and had to rush to make it back here to deal with the mattress delivery crew."

"Oh, poor baby. You had to deal with *people*." I craned my neck so my lips were near his ear. "My turn to warm you up properly tonight."

"I'll take that." He pivoted toward me, turning my chaste kiss on his temple into something feral and potent when he found my mouth with his. But right when I was ready to yank him toward the stairs, he released me. "However, I'm testing a recipe for dinner. Like you said last week, I don't want to serve anything I haven't made at least once before."

I was amazed Paul remembered a damn thing from our menu planning session because even with a stack of notes on my phone, all I remembered from that evening were the toe-curling kisses and five-star-worthy orgasms.

"Mmm." I made a pleased noise as I looped my arms around his neck. "You invited me over to see your new bed *and* you're going to feed me? Oh my."

"I plan to make you work it off after," he said huskily, giving me another quick hard kiss before turning his attention back to the stove.

"Of course. I can stage the guest room—"

"You know what I meant." He waved the spatula at me.

"Oh. That." I played dumb for the sheer purpose of earning one of his patented scowls. Once he was all mock grumpy, I hugged him from behind. "I'd be in favor of late dinner. Just saying."

"It's a spinach Parmesan stuffed chicken breast and mashed potatoes." He gestured at the bubbling pot on the stove before removing a large cast-iron skillet from the oven. "This recipe was way too fiddly. But it's almost ready. We better taste-test it while it's fresh."

"I bet Brandon loves whatever you cook. Elaine too," I praised as he plated the food. "The place is looking amazing."

"Thanks to you." Voice distracted, he arranged the chicken on the potatoes.

"No, thanks to *you*. I'm not the one who did all the rehab work. I'm more like…the garnish." I swiped a cherry tomato from the salad on my plate.

"Yeah, well, apparently I like garnish." He gave me a fast kiss on the head before carrying the pair of plates to the dining room. My head tingled from the kiss, a good feeling that radiated down my spine. I'd been so worried about him seeing my place. But every time I was certain Paul was about to head for the hills, he surprised me most pleasantly. He might like my flourishes and finishing touches, but I liked *him*, a scary-yet-wonderful thought that carried me through dinner.

He told me about the supplier delays, and I told him about the network malfunction, and it was so cozy, I was practically vibrating with happiness by the time we were on to clean up.

"Now dessert." I grabbed the brown bag I'd brought in with me off the counter.

"I was wondering what was in the bag." He shut the dishwasher and dried his hands.

"A big slice of checkerboard cake to share." I held up the cake and then removed the other two items, watching closely for his reaction.

"Condoms?" he asked as a big grin spread across his face.

"And lube. I came prepared to break in your bed."

We'd had a lot of fun thus far with hands and mouths, but the new bed seemed as good an occasion as any to mix things up. Since we were both coming off dry spells, I hadn't wanted to leave him having supplies up to chance. The cake was simply a happy bonus.

"I see." Paul's gaze was so hot it was a wonder my vision didn't steam up. "Tell me the dessert can wait."

"The cake can definitely wait. But I'm bringing it with us." I grabbed two forks from his silverware drawer. "I have a feeling I'm not going to want to move after."

"I'm planning to make sure of it." He winked at me before we both headed up the stairs.

Stopping in his open doorway, I let out a delighted gasp at how the room was transformed. "Ooh, it's so big."

"Flattery gets you everywhere, but I haven't even undressed yet." Paul bent to kiss the back of my neck. Plucking the cake out of my hands, he set it on the nightstand along with the supplies.

"Hush. Let me properly admire your bed." I walked around it slowly, petting the fuzzy blanket and moose sheets before I added my glasses to the collection on the nightstand. They had a tendency to go missing with Paul around, and I didn't want to have to hunt them later. "You even put the new bedding on."

"Figured I might as well." That he blushed over having prepared the bed was the cutest thing ever and made my chest as soft and warm as the new blanket.

"I like it," I pronounced as he peeled back the covers.

"I like you." Standing next to me, he kissed me tenderly and so carefully that I had to work to avoid swooning like a Victorian virgin. My chest felt more light and fizzy than a bottle of New Year's Eve bubbly. This wasn't my first time, but Paul had a way of making everything seem brand-new again.

"Clothes off," he ordered as he released me, already peeling off his own shirt.

"Thought I was the bossy one." I laughed as I added my own garments to the growing pile on his chair.

"You are." As soon as both of us were naked, he tumbled me onto the bed. "Tell me what you like best."

"You." I liked him. I liked him asking. I liked the way he listened even more. I liked his new bed and the soft flannel sheets. But I utterly loved Paul Frost flat on his back, loved how willingly he let me reverse our positions until I was straddling his waist and holding his face so I could kiss him again. "This. I like this."

"Me too." He made a show of lying there all obediently while we kissed, bare chests rubbing together, my cock dragging against those amazing abs of his. But as always, I was impatient to get to the good stuff, and I was the first to reach for the lube. Paul laughed, but he didn't try to take it from me. "Do I get to play, or am I supposed to lie here and look pretty and let you do all the work?"

"Look pretty." I winked at him as I slicked up my fingers. Rising higher on my knees, I worked myself open. And apparently, even without being able to see what my hand was up to, Paul liked my show. His cock twitched against his belly as he groaned low.

"Fuck." He ran his hands up my thighs. "You're killing me, Gideon."

"I suppose you could play for a second." I handed him the lube.

"Yes, your highness." Chuckling, he explored my rim with slick fingers that felt way better than my own. I never had much patience for a ton of prep, but his fingers were long and blunt, and one had me gasping while two lit me up, pressure so good.

"More." I rocked down to meet his fingers

"Fuck. You feel amazing."

"You too," I panted, what little patience I had evaporating with each thrust of his fingers, deep but not deep enough. "Going to feel even better on your dick."

I grabbed the box of condoms, loving how he groaned and strained toward me. "Fuck yes."

As soon as he withdrew his fingers, I opened a condom and rolled it on his cock. Even with this, he didn't try to take over, letting me lube him up and position us both to my liking. I wanted this badly, and my solo play included a couple of favorite toys, but my body still tensed, his cockhead feeling tree-topper huge against my rim.

"Talk about having been awhile..." Groaning, I tried to remind my body how this worked.

"It's your show." Paul folded his hands behind his head, the picture of serene control. So much power in his chiseled body, and he was handing it all over to me. "Do whatever you want."

His supplication encouraged me to try again, holding his shaft in one hand while I lowered down. Teasing myself with the tip, like he was a toy, had us both moaning.

"Sadist." His chuckle was tight, but his hips stayed riveted to the bed even as he complained. "Probably gonna end me for real. Enjoy the cake and take care of Jim for me."

"Ha." Laughing worked even better than teasing for getting my body to relax. I slid farther down, seeking the right angle where the burn turned sweet and hot. Lower. Enough to remove my hand. I canted my hips, still searching, then a sharp explosion of pleasure had all our laughter turning to moans. "*There.* Okay. That's better."

"Fuck yeah, it is." Paul's gaze was hot and needy as I found a rhythm that had us both panting. "More."

Taking him at his word, I found the angle and pace that pleased me best, but his moans matched mine. The way he watched my every movement made me feel sexy and alive and so fucking powerful, but I needed more than his intense stare.

"Touch me," I demanded. Instantly, he freed his hands from behind his head, running them all over my torso, ass, and thighs. Everywhere but where I wanted him most. "Evil tease."

"This?" Smile twisting mischievously, he traced my cock with a single featherlight finger.

"Do it right." I stilled my motions until he started

stroking me the way I wanted, long, slow pulls that countered the pressure and fullness in my ass.

"Bossy." He said it like an endearment as I started riding him again, faster now, keeping his cockhead pressing on my prostate, the stretch having gone from too much to exactly perfect.

"You love it."

"Fuck. I do." His gaze locked with mine, my cheeky tease transforming to something tender, almost fragile. My breath caught at the sheer amount of wonder in his tone. "I really do."

"Good." I had to close my eyes, only so much emotion I could take, especially coupled with pleasure this intense. His grip tightened on my cock as I rocked more urgently against him. The firmness of his body under mine and the solidness of every last inch of him was freeing like he could take everything I wanted to give him and then some.

Letting go, I rode him hard and fast, trusting him to not break and drinking down his every moan and curse. "Fuck. Gideon. Get there. Use my cock."

I was supposed to be the one making the demands, but I was way too far gone to point that out. I sped up, him moving with me now, pushing up against me, deeper, harder. "Going to…"

"Do it. Please." His broken "please" did it, that hint of begging and desperation, the way he was coming apart under me, and that even more than his hand on my cock, tipped me over. The orgasm rocketed through me as I painted his abs and chest with my come. Seeing him so messy and marked was enough to tease one last spurt out.

"Yes. You too. Now." My voice was more needy than bossy, climax leaving me breathless and desperate for him to go too. And he must have been waiting for that signal because his body bucked, fucking hard into me. I'd thought

I was done, but watching him come apart was enough to have my ass clenching again, powerful aftershocks that pulled him right over the edge until he was coming too.

"Fuck." He groaned over and over like his orgasm was even more endless than mine had been.

"Oh. My. Fucking. God." I collapsed onto his chest in a messy heap.

"You can be in charge whenever you'd like. Damn." He grinned boyishly at me before rolling slightly to fetch a small towel from the nightstand.

"You really mean that?" I asked as he cleaned us both up. Old worries about being too much, scaring people away, fluttered around like moths in my otherwise well-pleasured brain.

"Hey, when I let you lead, good things happen." He kissed my forehead, and the anxious moths fled. "You bossy is a win for me."

"Me too." I sighed happily and settled more comfortably against his shoulder, the spot that was rapidly feeling like mine and mine alone. "And that totally earned us some cake."

"We'll get crumbs in the new bed," he warned.

"Grouch." I kissed his bristly neck. "I'll do the sheets for you."

"Deal." He tipped my head up so he could find my mouth with his, and the moment was sweeter than any dessert could ever be. It was cuddly and domestic, and I wanted it to be December forever.

Chapter Nineteen
PAUL

Remember your vitamins! Nasty cold going around to match this nasty weather! But Gideon reports that we're up to record donations thanks to the lights fundraiser. Way to go us! ~Cheryl Bridges posted to the What's Up Neighbor app

"Your dog is wearing a coat." Gideon eyed me suspiciously as Jim and I walked up to the small popup canopy tent over a table near the edge of the park where signs funneled cars out at the end of the neighborhood lights spectacle. He sat alone in one of two folding chairs.

"So she is. It's her Christmas present from human Jim and the kids." Jim's ridiculous outfit was styled to look like a tracksuit, complete with hood and fleece-lined legs. She had enough fur to make any sort of clothing unnecessary, even in these brutal temperatures, but I'd wanted to see Gideon smile. "She wanted to show it off, but also, it's about to snow."

"I know." Gideon sighed and wrapped his arms around himself. He'd borrowed a set of my coveralls earlier and had his own coat on top, but they were no match for a wicked wind and rapidly dropping thermometer. "But Cheryl has a cold, and I promised."

"So you said." He'd been in a rush when he'd stopped by earlier, taking a rain check on our casual plans for dinner and scrambling for warm gear. I'd managed to make it through a solitary meal and a workout before worry over him won out, and now, here I was. I held out my thermos. "I brought tea. And a stadium blanket."

I tucked the thick blanket around him before taking the other chair. He was missing his glasses, probably because they kept fogging in this blasted cold.

"You're staying?" His eyes narrowed further even as he untucked enough blanket to share with me.

"Eh. Nothing better to do. Jim can catch snowflakes." Uninterested in that suggestion, Jim flopped at our feet. I'd taken her on enough of a walk on the way over that she wasn't restless and was probably wondering why I wasn't in my warm basement office like usual. I was wondering that too. "I can dream up new ways to break in my bed better here."

"But now we'll both be cold," he complained, but there was a pleased undercurrent to his tone. Car traffic was woefully sparse, not nearly the usual steady stream the neighborhood saw this close to Christmas.

"Yup. We will." Winking at him, I took his glove-covered hand under the blanket. "We can squeeze into my shower together after."

"This is true. I'll duck home to check on Butterscotch and grab a change of clothes." He pulled out his phone to use the voice recorder feature to add a reminder to his calendar because, of course, he did. Note done, he glanced my way again. "Why'd you really come?"

Damn him and his way-too-smart brain. "I can't be

worried you're gonna turn into a human ice pop?"

"That's sweet." He patted my knee. Near us, a car slowed for the driver to push a few cash bills through the slot in the drop box for money donations. "But you have more nervous energy than a poodle. Even your dog is concerned,"

"Ha. She's fine." Jim's head was currently resting on my boot, swishing tail catching Gideon's calves. Not seeming reassured in the least, he continued to stare me down until finally, I cracked. "Okay. I'm worried I'm going to forget some important piece of the plan."

"Ah. We're down to days away from the arrival and your nerves are hitting." He gave me a fond smile, but there was something else there. At some point, we probably needed to chat about this thing between us, the regular dinners and sleepovers and decorating projects that were more convenient excuses at this point. But things were going so well, and I had a lot of history to say I sucked at having important conversations. Better to not jinx things, but I did need Gideon to know how appreciated he was.

"You've done so much to help me. You've saved my whole darn month." I patted him again, and his smile deepened. "But I'm not like you with the spreadsheets. It's a lot to keep track of. Plane times. Food. Presents, of which I'm still lacking an engagement one."

"Breathe," he ordered, pulling out his phone again and removing one glove long enough to type around. "Here."

My own phone dinged in my pocket. "What's that?"

"Now you have a copy of the planning schedule. I've updated it with a food shopping list and the menu you settled on and the arrival times you mentioned."

"Thanks." I exhaled hard as I leaned forward. "You kept track of all that? Wow. I thought you'd be done with the spreadsheet after the last strand of garland."

A strange look flitted across his face. "Of course, I took notes. I like to plan."

"You're good at it." Another car pulled up, this one with a toy for the box on the table. Gideon fetched the donation, then returned to squeeze my biceps.

"This is going to be fine, Paul." He gazed deeply into my eyes, the steady calm I really needed right then. These nerves weren't like me at all. "He's probably going to be so happy to see you that he won't notice if you miss a step on the plan."

"Yeah."

"He doesn't know, does he?" Gideon asked softly.

"Know what?" I wasn't playing dumb. Sometimes Gideon's brain made these big leaps I couldn't quite follow.

"How hard it was on you. Him moving away." His voice was as warm as his grip on my arm. Grounding.

"It wasn't," I protested weakly.

"Paul. It's just us here. You don't need to pretend."

"All right. It sucked." I studied my thick gloves before gazing off into the frigid night. A few more snowflakes filtered down. "And no, he doesn't need to know. He went off on his grand doctoral adventure. It's all I ever wanted for him. Him to reach for the stars, maybe catch one."

"You're a—"

I held up a hand to cut him off. "Good brother. I know. I just did what needed doing. What else was I supposed to do? I couldn't leave him."

"No, you couldn't." Gideon grabbed my hand, held it tightly. "You did the right thing, but that doesn't make it any less hard or sucky for you."

"Yeah." I wasn't sure I'd ever admitted this aloud before and my voice was scratchy. "It was hard."

"You did good. I bet he doesn't have a clue how difficult it was." Gideon's tone was more admiring than pity.

Understanding. Which shouldn't have been a surprise. If I'd learned nothing else over the last month or so, it was that Gideon was the master of putting on a cheerful face even when highly stressed.

"And that's a good thing. I kept food on the table. Found a safe school for him, although that meant a tinier apartment. It was bad enough he lost his folks. Didn't need a daily struggle too."

"*Paul.*" Gideon tilted my face toward his. "You lost your parents too."

Oh. I hadn't let myself dwell on that, not ever, and lord, his words sliced deep. My chest ached like the air inside my lungs was turning as icy as the rest of me. "I wasn't a kid."

"Barely. And you held it all together for Brandon for so many years. That's something to be proud of. You raised him well. But that doesn't mean it didn't suck for you."

"I miss them." Some of that ice around my soul cracked off.

"I know." Gideon didn't say he was sorry, but he put an arm around me, and somehow, I was a little less chilled, a little less alone. I neither wanted nor needed his pity, but his understanding and his strength were unexpected gifts. I slumped against him.

"I tried never to show any sadness around him. Couldn't let him see me down. Never talked money either. If he needed something for school, I made it happen." The admissions were coming faster now as Gideon and his quiet comfort chipped away at years of staying quiet.

"You're good at getting things done." He squeezed me closer. The traffic had thinned out to nothing, just him and me out here holding down the dark. "There wasn't insurance?"

"Nope. My folks always rented, and they were too broke for renter's insurance. Life insurance had lapsed.

Brandon got survivor's benefits, but that went to his education much as I could manage it."

"And now he's what? An actual rocket scientist?" Gideon's expression was soft and proud. I was proud of Brandon too, so much that the pride was what had often kept me going. "You did good."

Wait. Gideon's pride was for *me*. I had to swallow hard, force a rusty laugh.

"He says he's not a rocket scientist. Physicist. He's better at explaining his specialty than me." An uncomfortable thought strode through my head, made me groan. "Oh fuck. What if we have nothing to talk about anymore? I don't speak fancy science well."

"You have football. Let's move your TV upstairs." Gideon was nothing if not quick with the practical solution. "You can put on a game of some kind if it gets awkward."

"Won't that fuck with your decorating scheme?"

"I'll work it in." Out came his phone again, but he had a small smile as he made the note.

"Thanks. You're a good friend." I kissed his cheek, and he made a surprised, happy noise. "What?"

"You called me friend. Not neighbor."

Geez. If he thought that was a step up, we really did need to have that talk. We'd passed neighbors weeks ago.

"Well, yeah, Gideon, I—"

Honk. A waiting car at the donation box cut me off.

"Just a sec. Let me take their donation."

I nodded. He was so much more than a neighbor or even friend. Friend was someone you watched a game or had an after-work beer with. Gideon was...*special*. He'd laugh if I called him that though, wave away the praise. I needed better words, the *right* ones, words that he'd take seriously. He deserved that.

Chapter Twenty
GIDEON

Need a last-minute gift? Crocheted hats! Twenty each, but make me an offer! Might take payment in fudge! ~Molly Reed posted to the What's Up Neighbor app

One more touch. I'd been thinking of last little details for Paul for days now, and I could hear my grandmother, who had taught art history part-time at the same college where I now worked, laughing about how an artist's work was never done. There was always one more thing to fix, something to add, elements to tweak. And honestly, I was happy for it. Each small adjustment meant another trip to Paul's place, another excuse to hang out.

He could undoubtedly be entrusted to run a load of sheets and make the guest bed himself, but why should he have to when doing it together was so much more fun? Even cleaning the guest bath this morning had shown the power of teamwork. He scrubbed, and I hung three small art prints, fluffed towels, and took care of other last-minute presentation things.

"Fancy soap." Paul touched the small basket I'd set next to the sink. Nestled inside were three wrapped soaps shaped like a snowman, a tree, and a wreath. "I never would have thought of that. And it matches the towels."

"You noticed." I'd discovered the holiday-themed hand towels among my own unused seasonal decor, some impulse purchase that hadn't yet found a purpose. The soap had been a lucky find at the Christmas market with Paul. That seemed so long ago. We hadn't even kissed then, and now I craved his taste more than any other seasonal treat. This had been the fastest, best December of my life, and I wasn't at all ready for Christmas to be two days away. I swapped the position of the snowman and tree soaps and straightened the washcloth. "I guess this is done."

I hoped I didn't sound too reluctant. In a couple of hours, Paul would head to the airport, and I would return home, job well done. And if I peeked out the window when he came back with his guests, well, that was my own business.

"Brandon's going to be impressed." Paul clapped me on the shoulder. "I'm pretty sure I'm still using the same basic brand of soap I did the whole time he was with me."

"I like your usual brand just fine," I reassured him, soaking up these last minutes of his nearness.

"Elaine's folks probably have imported soap from some remote mountain village." He held me closer.

"Don't stress." I tipped my head back against his shoulder. "She loves Brandon. She'll love you too, and if she doesn't, she's the wrong kind of genius."

"Thanks. You're kind." He kissed my ear. "What do you say to a shower in the master bath? We both got all sweaty with this last-minute cleaning round, and thanks to you, we're actually ahead of schedule."

"We are." Spinning, I looped my arms around his neck. "But that sounds like a recipe for getting dirty, not clean."

"We can multitask." He kissed me, and I watched us in the mirror, wanting to memorize how damn hot we looked, even rumpled and dusty from the morning of cleaning. Well, I was the rumpled mess with smudged glasses while the hot part was mainly Paul, all muscles and silver scruff that somehow got even more attractive sweaty. And in that moment, he was all mine. *Guess I found some fox bait.* I couldn't help the little giggle that bubbled up.

"My kissing is funny?" Grinning, Paul pulled back. "I clearly need to try harder."

"You're plenty hard." I bumped meaningfully against him. "I was merely amused at how good we looked in the mirror."

"We could look even better." Paul swept his gaze over the mirror, sexy speculation rising in his eyes.

"Not here." Chuckling but also serious, I squirmed away. "We just cleaned."

"The master bath has a mirror too." He tugged me out of the hall bathroom, and we were halfway to his room when his phone buzzed. "Fuck."

"Better check before I distract you further." My back prickled. Somehow, I knew it was Brandon even before Paul pulled out his phone and cursed.

"Crap."

"What?" I asked as he clicked around on the screen.

"Their connecting flight got canceled because of weather in the Midwest. They couldn't get a different one out until tomorrow."

"That sucks." My shoulders slumped right along with Paul's. Damn weather. Paul didn't need any more disappointments in his life.

"Yeah, it does. Brandon's trying to find other options, but it's looking like tomorrow afternoon at the soonest."

"That still puts them here in time for his big Christmas plans." I deliberately brightened my tone.

"Which is good, except he was supposed to sneak out to pick up the ring tomorrow morning in the city center while Elaine had a manicure date with a friend from undergrad."

"She's totally expecting the ring if she's getting pretty nails. I don't think Brandon has to worry about the yes."

"Yeah, but now he might not have the ring." Paul glanced down at his phone as it chimed again. "He's asking if I can do it today. That way the ring is here at the house at least."

"That's a good idea."

"Hope I can beat rush hour." Groaning, he leaned against the doorframe to the master bedroom. "And good luck finding parking near Franklin Square this time of year, but God knows I hate being on the train's timetable even more."

Optimism returning, I touched his arm. "That's close to where my grandfather's shop was. I love that area."

"Don't suppose you'd want a trip downtown?" Paul seized my hint, exactly like I'd hoped. "I bet you speak fancy jeweler better than me too."

"Flattery gets you everywhere." I laughed like I actually needed convincing for this field trip. Technically, I could volunteer to do the errand without Paul, but company, especially his, was always preferable.

"Good." He pulled me close enough to kiss my head.

"We can take my car for a change. Way easier to park." My mind leaped ahead to the practical details, but my insides stayed strangely buoyant. I didn't want to wish bad weather on Brandon and Elaine, but if it delayed my return to my empty house and got me more time with Paul, I was at least going to enjoy the change in plans. "If we hurry, we can still shower, then I can grab some more suitable clothes at my place."

"Do jewelers have dress codes?" Paul harrumphed a sigh. "You're totally gonna make me wear something with buttons, aren't you?"

"Poor Paul. Such torture." I patted his fuzzy jaw. "Do you even own a dress shirt?"

"I'll have you know I do."

"This I want to see." I doubted Paul's usual jeans and black T-shirt would get us kicked out of the jewelry store, but I wasn't turning down a chance to dress him up. "Oh, if you don't have to rush back, we could deal with rush hour by getting an early dinner down near the square, wait out the traffic rush. I know some places."

"Yeah, food sounds good. Jim should be okay alone for a couple of hours."

"It's a plan." I couldn't keep the happiness from my voice as I turned to steer us both toward the master bath. "Now, shower first."

"Gideon?" Paul paused inside the bedroom, expression going more solemn.

"Yes?" My heart rate sped up.

"Thank you. A lot." He licked his lips. "I'm not good with words—"

"It's my pleasure." I interrupted him because I didn't want to ruin what was looking to be an unexpectedly good afternoon with a "thanks for everything" speech. Instead, I winked at him. "And I've got better uses for your mouth."

And it was my pleasure. One more rescue mission for Paul, one more chance to play hero for him. I should probably be thanking him, not the other way around.

Chapter Twenty-One
PAUL

Needed: Extra chairs! The in-laws are unexpectedly joining us for Christmas dinner. All six of them. Who has extra folding chairs we could borrow? Please! ~Penny Jordan posted to the What's Up Neighbor app

For once, bumper-to-bumper traffic didn't irritate me. The shower not-so-quickie with Gideon had been worth the hassle of increasingly worse traffic in Gideon's little roller skate of a car. He was a decent driver, even if all his radio presets were playing Christmas tunes, and better him than me for zipping around lumbering trucks. Also, unlike me, he knew downtown parking tricks from his years working in the city center in the banking industry, doing corporate IT work.

"Do you miss working down here?" I asked as he locked up the car in the garage several blocks from our destination.

"Nah. I mean, Franklin Square sure is pretty this time of year with the light display and holiday festivities, but the college is way more flexible. They put up with me. We're like a big family."

It totally fit that Gideon would value a close-knit working group, but I couldn't let him talk himself down like that. I made a scoffing noise. "Put up with you? They're lucky to have you and your color-coded plans."

"Aw. You're sweet." He grabbed my gloved hand, and I let him. Another chilly day, but at least the snow was predicted to hold off until after Brandon and Elaine were here. "And Helene loved her signed football poster. It was a huge hit, so thank you."

"Anytime. Wish I was as good at my own present hunting." I followed Gideon across the street. He cut through the square, which was packed with people waiting in line for attractions like seasonal mini-golf and a carousel.

"Are you still deciding on an engagement present?" Gideon asked.

"Burned cookies don't count?" I laughed. We'd attempted Christmas cookies twice now. The first burnt batch was entirely my fault for distracting Gideon while they were in the oven. The second batch had been missing some key ingredient like baking powder. Like finding the right present, maybe the cookies simply weren't meant to be.

"Hey, I'm not giving up yet." Ever the optimist, Gideon gave me a sunny smile. "We can try another batch in the morning before they come if you want."

"Sounds good." Far better than me pacing and worrying about plane schedules. "And everything I think of seems cheesy. I got them a gift card to a restaurant, but gift certificates always feel like the easy way out. What would you want?"

"What would I want?" Stopping near a giant snowman, Gideon frowned.

"If you were newly engaged, and it was Christmas, and you were visiting a strange city?"

"Something sentimental," Gideon said thoughtfully as we resumed walking, heading out of the square and onto one of the surrounding city streets. "A welcome to the family sort of present. Lori's folks gave us a set of heirloom wine glasses. I gave them back when we split, naturally."

"Hmm." I squeezed his hand. I wasn't sure whether he missed the in-laws or the glasses more, but his faraway tone made me want to hunt down some crystal. "I don't have much like that. Nothing fancy. I was thinking maybe earrings for Elaine."

"Earrings?" He stopped by the sign for the business we were hunting, which had a large display window of holiday jewelry. "I'm sure they have something here, but not sure you need to go jewelry price tag big on a gift."

"Not buy. I've been debating giving her a pair of Mom's earrings. They're pearls, not diamonds—"

"Yes. Do that." Gideon's eyes went misty. It figured that he'd like this idea. "I bet you could find a nice case here, something where she could keep those and her other wedding jewelry."

"That's a good idea. Should have known you'd think about presentation."

"Details matter." Nodding sharply, he smiled. "It's sentimental and perfect. If she doesn't love it, snatch the earrings back."

"Deal." I followed him into the jeweler. A very upscale place with muted jazz on the speakers, plush carpeting, and sparkling display cases. The decor made me glad I'd let Gideon talk me into a nicer shirt. He, of course, fit right in with his crisp white shirt, gray pants, and jaunty plaid bow tie.

The sole clerk was busy with a young couple when we

came in, so I let Gideon show me various jewelry box options in a display near the door.

"Too sappy?" I asked as my gaze landed on a silver case etched with a quote about love from a famous poet. I wasn't much on poetry, but the line about carrying the heart of another was pretty.

"Quit second-guessing your instincts." Gideon touched my arm. "It's perfect if you ask me. You want her to take good care of Brandon's heart. It's a good message."

"I trust you more than my instincts. I'll get it."

"Sorry about the wait, gentlemen." Finally free, the clerk strode over. His black suit was as stiff as his hair. "Do I sniff a spring wedding, perhaps? I have a lovely selection of men's rings, including some unusual offerings."

"Uh." Why perfect strangers seemed so ready to marry Gideon and me off, I wasn't sure, but I really needed to work on a response that wasn't an awkward noise.

"Not for us." Smooth as ever, Gideon covered for me. "We're here to do a pickup. Should be under Frost."

"Of course." The clerk strode over to a discreetly placed tablet, typing with a manicured finger. "Do you have ID?"

"Yeah." I dug out my wallet and handed my license over.

"You're not Brandon?" The man frowned.

"No, I'm his brother. Didn't he call?" I tried to keep the frustration from my tone, but I hadn't come this far to fall five yards short of the goal. "He said he'd clear it for me to do the pickup."

"I understand, sir. Let me go check our phone messages." The clerk retreated to the rear of the store while I tried and failed to reach Brandon.

"Damn it. He's not answering."

"Probably means they succeeded in finding a hotel

room." Gideon's eyes twinkled as he patted my shoulder. "This will work out. They're simply being cautious, which is a good thing."

"No message that I could find." Still frowning, the clerk returned, no ring box in hand.

Fuck. No holding back my annoyance now. "I need—"

"Paul, show him the text messages with Brandon." Keeping his hand on my shoulder, Gideon countered my rising irritation with his calm voice, reminding me that getting cranky wasn't likely to get results.

"Oh, right. Sorry." I pulled out my phone and clicked over to the messages with Brandon before holding out the phone. "Here."

"Hmm." The clerk studied the screen, and sweat gathered in my lower back. But right as I was about to give up hope, my phone rang. Brandon.

A quick conversation followed, and suddenly, the clerk was back to overly polite.

"Sorry about that, Mr. Frost. I'll be right back with the ring."

"See? It worked out." Gideon smiled patiently at me as the clerk bustled off to the back again. "And now you totally deserve a cannoli with your dinner."

"A cannoli, huh?" Crisis averted, I could joke again. And after his deft talent for defusing the situation, he was the one who needed a reward, and I fully intended to deliver.

"If you're good." His eyes sparkled.

"I'm very good," I promised, fully intending to light him up brighter than the square as soon as I could.

Chapter Twenty-Two
PAUL

Can we get a bigger sign with the park hours on it? These teenagers have not been respecting the sundown rule. They need to find a new place to canoodle. ~Ernest Morrison posted to the What's Up Neighbor app

WAS IT POSSIBLE TO BE OUT ON A DATE AND NOT KNOW IT? The whole ride back to Evergreen, I stewed on that question. Gideon and I'd had an amazing dinner at this small Italian place he knew that didn't have the same crowds as most of the more popular spots in the pre-Christmas Eve crush. My lack of dating experience gave me few experiences to compare our dinner with, but we'd held hands walking back through the square to reach the restaurant, sat way closer than friends might, and I'd let him steal bites of my meatballs. We certainly *felt* like a couple, which was good because it meant that maybe we didn't need some big talk. Accidental dating? Was that even a thing? Maybe we could make it one.

We talked so long at dinner that it was well after dark

before we returned home to our twinkling neighborhood. Franklin Square had been more spectacular with acres of lights, but I preferred the homey familiarity here.

"You win," I said as Gideon parked near his garage. "That dinner was worth the stress of getting the ring."

"It was good, wasn't it?" He smiled at me, but he seemed a little tired, shoulders sagging and eyes drooping.

"Even the cannoli." I winked, fully intending to hustle him up to bed in short order. All the driving had to be exhausting. Thanks to Gideon's timers, the lights on both our houses were glowing brightly and his small tree sparkled in the front window like it was waiting to welcome a party. Or maybe just Gideon. I probably wasn't ever getting as lighting-happy as Gideon, but I was starting to understand why he liked coming home to his decorations. "Your tree looks nice."

"It does." He still sounded weary, exiting the car slowly and standing in the driveway to admire the lights. "Guess I should sleep in my own bed for once."

Darn. I had kept him over most of the previous week. Jim had likely seen more of him than his cat, and that wasn't fair of me. Trying for a neutral tone, I nodded. "All right."

If he was already exhausted, I wasn't going to add my disappointment to his burden, but when he turned to go inside with little more than a nod in my direction, I stopped him with a hand on his coat sleeve.

"No good-night kiss? Did I do something?"

"Oh. Sorry. No, I'm not mad at you." He grinned as he pulled me close, but his expression still looked a little tight. I wanted to follow up on his mood, but then his mouth was sliding across mine, and I was lucky to remember my own name. We were in full view of the neighborhood, standing there between our houses, yet we kissed like we were locked in my bedroom.

He started soft like he truly was intending a fast goodnight, but then his mouth parted on a gasp, and next thing I knew, our tongues were playing tag, and I was harder than the icicles dripping from the nearby tree. I held him closer against me, and he clung to my shoulders, and still, we kissed.

"Damn." Breathing hard, Gideon pulled back only far enough to rest his lips against my cheek. "Why do you have to be so good at this?"

"Give me ten minutes to let Jim out and stow the ring in my safe, and then I can come over," I suggested, giving up all attempts to play this cool. I needed him too damn badly.

"You want to come over?" His eyebrows flew up higher than his foggy glasses, but he didn't sound uninterested in the prospect.

"Well, yeah." Skin heating, I ran a hand along the back of his head, letting his silky hair filter through my fingers. Neither of us had grabbed our gloves on our way out of the car, and it was too cold for these outdoor shenanigans, but hell if I could resist one more quick kiss. "If you need to be home tonight, I get it. Your cat probably misses you. But maybe we could make out in front of your tree before I have to get back to Jim?"

"I'd like that," he said quietly, eyes pleased and mouth soft and kissable and so tempting.

"Ten minutes," I promised.

And at nine minutes and change, I arrived back at Gideon's side door. I'd left Jim with a rare treat of a long-lasting chew as an apology for hurrying her up outside, and the ring was locked in the basement safe.

"Hey." Gideon had removed his tie and shoes, which

only made me want to unbutton him further. "You really want to see my tree? I could come to your place."

"I really want to see *you*." I kicked off my own boots, set them next to the door. "The tree is a bonus."

"Well, the tree's ornaments are probably more worthy of admiration." Expression strangely guarded, Gideon led me through the kitchen and dining room into the living room.

"Trust me, I plan to appreciate your ornament plenty," I teased, wanting to find that light and easy place we'd been in earlier. All the lamps tucked into corners and little decorating touches here and there made his place warm and inviting. Every time I visited, I noticed something different, but right then, all my attention was for Gideon.

He stopped near the tree, drawing the curtains closed, and as soon as he finished, I swooped in for a kiss that took up right where we left off in the driveway. I used all the things I knew he liked, my lips and teeth and tongue, until he shuddered in my arms.

"Couch. Now." Spinning him slightly, I pushed Gideon onto the sofa. But instead of sitting next to him, I knelt in front of him, nudging his knees apart.

"What are you about?" he asked in a husky voice. He trailed a finger along my jaw, ruffling my beard.

"Maybe you're not the only one who has big ideas." Winking at him, I ran my hands up his thighs, spreading his legs farther.

"Oh?" Wiggling around, he got more comfortable, ass sliding toward me and back pushing into the overstuffed cushions. "Your turn to be bossy?"

"Uh-huh." I nuzzled against his lap. His dick was already hard and straining inside his dress pants, and the combination of hard cock and slick fabric made my blood thrum. "You stay there, enjoy the lights, and let me play."

This wasn't the first time I'd sucked him, but he usually preferred blowing me first then giving me a quick taste. Which was hot as fuck, and I loved that and sixty-nine both, but tonight, I wanted to focus on him. Holding his gaze, I slowly unbuckled his belt and unzipped his fly. I rubbed my face against his black briefs, which were a step up from my own basic cotton boxer briefs. The soft, slippery fabric dragged against my lips, and a desperate noise escaped my throat.

"I'm enjoying the view, that's for sure." Keeping his eyes locked on mine, he bumped his hips forward as I withdrew his cock. The heft of his shaft in my hand made me even harder. He fit my fist so perfectly, letting me jack the shaft while teasing the head with my thumb. Holding him loosely, I ran my tongue along my fingers, loving his low moan. "Fuck. Might need to count reindeer if you're going to do that."

"Count away." The last of my laughter died as I swallowed him down. My cock ached from the weight of him on my tongue, the hint of salty precome near his tip, and the soft moans escaping his parted lips. I sucked harder, trying to find a rhythm that would drive him wild without ending this too fast.

"So good." Eyes shutting, he tipped his head back. His hands kept drifting to my shoulder and the back of my head. But every time he flexed his fingers, he quickly drew his hands away.

"You can touch." Releasing his cock for a moment, I grabbed his hands, put them on my head. "I'm not going to break, and it turns out I like you driving. Show me what I do to you."

"*Yes.*" Gideon's voice was a mix of enthusiasm and need, and this time when I went back to sucking, his hands stayed put. It only took a few long, slow strokes of my tongue before he started pushing up to meet my mouth. I moaned around his cock, encouraging him. He tightened his grip, not painful, but enough that he could direct my rhythm and push me to where he wanted.

Fuck. Now I was the one who needed something to count. I held on to his thighs to avoid the temptation to jack off against his couch. I was close to the edge simply from his taste and smell, and the pressure of his demanding hands added to that. Not having to guess what he might like was fucking incredible, letting go and letting him use my mouth however he wanted. Each time I took him so deep that my lips brushed the fabric of his pants, my cock pulsed as we both moaned.

"Paul." The desperate edge to his voice was one more thing pushing me closer. His cock grew stiffer in my mouth, thrusts more purposeful. "Paul."

Him chanting my name was the sexiest fucking thing ever. I retreated enough to suck in a breath. "That's it. Take my mouth, baby."

Seemed like he'd been waiting for that final bit of permission, despite me allowing him to set the pace, because his moans came faster now. His whole body vibrated under my hands as I took him as deep as I could, let him go as fast as he wanted.

"Now. Oh. Now. Coming." He held me fast as he came, filling my mouth. My own cock had never been harder, and I trembled. Swallowing, I milked him with my tongue until he finally released me and pushed at my shoulder. "Wow."

"Wow is right." My voice was rough. Dazed. I legit had to check in with my body, verify I hadn't come because it had been that near a thing.

"Get up here." Gideon grabbed my arm and hauled

me up next to him. I wound up half-sprawled, one leg up, one leg down, shoulders against his chest.

"Yes, Bossy." I slumped against him almost-but-not-quite spent, but he was busy kissing my temple and undoing my fly. Just the brush of his fingers had me groaning. "Fuck. Your hand feels good."

"Yeah? Did sucking me get you close?" Gideon's tone was as demanding as his grip. With his free hand, he held me tightly, palm spread wide on my chest, right over my heart.

"Always." I wasn't ever going to get tired of blowing him, couldn't imagine a time when I didn't crave his taste.

He inhaled sharply as if he was the one about to shoot. "I like that."

I liked Gideon. More than liked. And I needed to tell him that, but then he sped up his hand, thumb sweeping across my cockhead, and every word I knew fled, replaced by a low shout as I came, hard enough the first spurt hit my beard and some likely got him too.

"Fuck." I didn't understand how pleasure could be so much more intense with him, like he found an extra gear on my internal transmission, some sort of overdrive button that belonged to him and him alone. "Jesus."

"Oh, you were worked up, weren't you?" He sounded very pleased with himself indeed, and I had to laugh even if it came out more like a squawk. Chuckling along with me, he stroked my chest. "More wow?"

"All the wow." Sighing happily, I adjusted my position so my head was more comfortably against his chest, both legs outstretched. My nice shirt was a wreck, but I was in no hurry to clean up. "Don't boot me out too fast. Not sure I can walk after that."

"Nah." He kissed the top of my head. "Stay cozy for a bit. Enjoy the lights."

"I am." I gazed up at him, admiring the way his cheeks were still pink and flushed, hair a little sweaty, eyes glassy. I couldn't get enough of how he looked at me either, the tenderness and wonder there. Like he couldn't quite believe I was here, which was funny because I wasn't sure I was ever leaving.

Chapter Twenty-Three
GIDEON

Reminder! Car traffic to see the lights will likely be dense tonight! Make sure any Christmas Eve guests are aware and give yourself extra time if you're heading out to services. ~Cheryl Bridges posted to the What's Up Neighbor app

PAUL'S KITCHEN SMELLED LIKE CHRISTMAS—sugar, butter, and flour combining for that magical scent that no candle or room spray company could ever hope to duplicate.

"This time they'll work," I assured him as he slid a tray into the preheated oven.

"Only for you would I get up early for baking cookies." He laughed like he hadn't been the one texting me after his walk with Jim, wanting to know what time I was coming over and if he should make extra coffee. I'd been there, French press and cookie-cutter collection in hand, five minutes later.

"Hey, this way you can have one for second breakfast."

I finished rolling another round of dough and moved so he could help place the cutters.

"Is that a thing?" Paul frowned, and I laughed because I'd forgotten that not everyone had spent two decades running with a decidedly nerdy crowd.

"Well, it is for hobbits. Clearly, your pop culture education is lacking."

"You'll have to fix that," Paul said, almost absently like, of course, we would have time to watch a famously long trilogy. But he hadn't said anything concrete about a future beyond Christmas. Neither had I. This was too good to jinx. But it had certainly felt like a date last night. And he'd seemed genuinely disappointed I hadn't slept over. Not to mention how he'd steamed up my living room with that epic blowjob.

"Sure thing." Maybe in a few days, after Brandon had returned home, I'd text Paul offering a movie marathon and a chance to tell me how things went. And I'd try not to hold my breath waiting for a reply. Damn. I liked him far, far too much.

"Huh." Chortling, Paul pointed at the tray of unbaked cookies. "Upside down that snowman looks like..."

"No phallic cookie jokes." I pretended to scold him even as I snickered because he was right. "He'll look fine after we frost the cookies."

"There's decorating too?" He groaned, but his eyes were still twinkling.

"*Paul.*" I continued the chiding tone to see if I could get another laugh. He laughed more these days, and I was more than a little addicted to his deep, rich chuckle. Rare enough that I felt like a rock star when I earned one, but powerful enough to change a room's energy with a single note. "There is always decorating."

"This is true." He patted my shoulder with a floury

hand. We were a mess, owing to being inexperienced bakers but also our inability to stop touching and kissing each other. "Speaking of decorating, you wouldn't want to help me wrap that jewelry box for Elaine, would you?"

"I would be honored." I kept getting all choked up when I thought about him giving his mom's earrings to Elaine. She damn well better appreciate the gift. "I can do it before I head out if you have paper. If not, I'll duck home, grab something appropriate from my wrapping cupboard."

"You have a wrapping cupboard?" He shook his head as he set another misshapen snowman on the sheet.

"Of course." I gave him an arch look before retrieving more dough from the fridge.

"You're something else." His tender smile did things to my insides. I loved how he could tease me without a trace of mocking, turning my quirks into warm, shared jokes. But then his smile slid away, replaced with a frown. "You have to head home? Is your cat doing okay?"

"Butterscotch?" I had no clue why Paul was suddenly concerned about my cat. "He's as foul-tempered as ever, but he did let me brush him the other day, so there's that."

"I love that you, with all your endless sunshine, have a cranky cat."

"Apparently, I attract grumpy things." I kissed his bristly cheek before plunking the dough onto his kitchen island, which we'd covered with parchment paper to make a rolling station.

"That you do." Turning toward me, he turned my quick cheek peck into a long, sultry kiss that lasted until the oven timer dinged.

"Cookies!" Head still spinning, I tossed the potholders at him in time for him to rescue the sheet from the oven.

The cheerful shapes were browned but not burnt. "Just in time. Now they need to cool."

We were using a rack more suited to roasting chicken pieces as a cooling rack, and one cookie cracked as I transferred it over with a wide spatula.

"Oops. Guess this one can be our sample."

Laughing, I fed Paul a piece of still-warm cookie. His face transformed from lightly mischievous to something far softer. He chewed slowly and licked his lips before speaking in a hushed voice. "Oh. It's like I remember."

"I'm so glad." I exhaled hard to relieve some of the rising pressure in my chest. Nope. Still too full. His shining eyes met mine, and in that moment, the whole month was worth it. Every garland, each spreadsheet entry, and the growing risk to my heart, all of it was worth being the cause of Paul's awestruck expression. Christmas magic, indeed.

We both opened our mouths to speak right as the doorbell sounded. Paul's phone clattered on the counter, his doorbell app flashing with a door camera picture. His eyes snapped wide open.

"It's them."

"Oh my." Heck. They were way early. Paul had been scheduled to go to the airport that afternoon. But the last thing Paul needed from me was a disappointed tone that our time together was cut short. I set the spatula aside. "I'll just sneak out the side door."

"Why would you do that?" He frowned, voice shifting from excited to confused.

"Hello?" A male voice sounded from the foyer. "Paul?"

"Stay," Paul said sternly, and I wasn't sure whether he meant me or the dog, who was trailing behind him, clearly no intention of obeying. As for me, I paused partway to my shoes. I could see the foyer through the wide opening on the other side of the island, which gave a clear view of the dining room and then the living room beyond that.

"Brandon!" Paul called out as the front door opened to admit Brandon and Elaine and several bags and rolling suitcases. They looked much like their photos, a little more wrinkled from travel and Brandon had different glasses, but still a cute, younger couple. Elaine had the sort of adorable elfin face that looked good even without makeup and her hair was in a scrunchie. Although her tired eyes said she was probably running on little sleep.

"Sorry." Brandon greeted Paul with a huge backslapping hug. "When you didn't answer, I tried the knob, and it opened."

"It's okay." Paul glanced down at Jim, who was dancing back and forth, doggy excitement at an all-time high. "Down, girl."

"She's fine." Brandon bent to pet Jim's dark furry head and floppy ears. "What a good puppy."

"You have company." Elaine's eyes went wide as she caught sight of me, and then all three of them were turning toward the kitchen. *Oh fuck.* I was in my socks, dusty with flour, smudged glasses, and undoubtedly sporting beard burn from the earlier kissing.

"Oops." Brandon's cheeks went pink. "I thought we'd save you the airport trip and surprise you when we scored an earlier flight. Elaine loves trains, so I figured we'd catch it instead."

"That's fine." Paul didn't seem nearly as uncomfortable as I would have expected, smiling even. "I wanted you to meet Gideon anyway."

Say what now? Paul wanted what? I blinked. Then blinked again.

Brandon's jaw dropped as if he were preparing for a tonsil exam. "You have a boyfriend?"

Chapter Twenty-Four
PAUL

Christmas Eve Miracle Needed! My trusty food processor bowl cracked! Anyone have a spare one I could borrow until my replacement bowl gets here in two days? ~ Molly Reed posted to the What's Up Neighbor app

"You have a boyfriend?" My brother looked exactly as he had working on his first science fair project, a thing involving polymers that had been beyond me even back then, but I'd never forgotten Brandon's wide-eyed wonder and joy at the discovery. Apparently, the idea that I might date was equally as astonishing, even to the genius.

"Something like that," I hedged because this was not exactly how I'd pictured introductions going. Even if the dating part shocked him, Brandon had known perfectly well that I was gay, so it was more Gideon's reaction that was giving me pause. His expression was a mirror of Brandon's, only with a touch more horror, like this boyfriend business was a surprise to him as well. Exactly what did he think we were doing here? But I couldn't exactly ask him that with him halfway across the house. "Gideon is…"

"The neighbor," he supplied helpfully as he left the kitchen to come into the living room.

"I was going to say *new.*" Neighbor. As if. The guy had been legit happy when he thought I'd elevated him to friend. I wasn't so scary and grumpy that he'd assumed I'd try to pass him off as a mere acquaintance, was I? I knew Gideon by now. He was only saying *neighbor* to try to spare himself the pain of me saying it first, but hurting him was the absolute last thing I wanted to do.

"Oh." Gideon shut his mouth in a hurry, but the corners twitched like he might be pleased and was trying to hide it.

Brandon had no such issue hiding his feelings because he was grinning like we were the best entertainment he'd had in months. "So your new boyfriend is the old neighbor. Wait. The one who's always blocking the drive? I thought—"

"Look at that tree!" Elaine said too brightly, striding into the living room. She was a lot smaller than Brandon, but she knew how to command a room. Or at least my brother, as he dropped their bags in the foyer and followed her into the living room, much better at heeling than Jim even.

"I should have known you were seeing someone." Brandon wasn't done laughing as his gaze swept over the living room. The tree twinkled in the corner, the new couch commanded center stage with its Christmas pillows, and the mantle looked like a magazine shoot. Even the TV we'd dragged up from the basement had a bow. "No way could you pull off all this decorating yourself. I wasn't aware you even knew what fake snow was."

"Flocking," I corrected.

"Pardon?" Brandon narrowed his eyes, and even Elaine blinked.

The back of my neck heated. "Fake snow. That's what it's called."

"Is it now?" Brandon wasn't even trying to disguise how much fun he was having at this point, but proving I hadn't raised him completely in a barn, he stuck out a hand. "Hi, Gideon."

Further introductions were made with handshakes all around, and then the four of us stood there, more than a little awkward, no one speaking or moving to sit.

"Do I smell cookies?" Elaine asked at last.

"Yeah, we were almost to the decorating part. But even naked, they're tasty." Um. What had just come out of my mouth? Maybe I needed to give up on speaking altogether. "Um. Plain. I mean plain."

"I knew what you meant." Elaine had a gentle laugh. "And I want to help. My parents never let me help the housekeeper. They said I got in the way, especially at holidays."

"Well, here you can absolutely help." Gideon gave her a dazzling smile, recovering much of his usual charm as he led her to the kitchen.

"You haven't seen the unspeakable things she's done to refrigerated chocolate chip cookie dough," Brandon warned as we followed. "There's a reason every takeout service driver in our zip code knows our names."

"You're not any better." Elaine rolled her eyes at Brandon as she took a seat at one of the stools on the side of the island. "You're the one who's forgotten that hard-boiled eggs require water. More than once."

"Guilty." Not looking particularly repentant, Brandon swiped a snowflake from the rack and broke it in half to share with Elaine.

"Luckily, the icing recipe involves neither the stove nor any eggs, so I think we're safe." Gideon flipped the cookbook open to the part that showed how to decorate the cookies.

"Hey. This cookbook looks familiar." Squinting, Brandon peered around Gideon to examine the red binder more closely.

"You remember?" I asked softly, something sharp pinching deep in my chest.

"Yeah." He nodded slowly. "Plaid cover. The metal rings make a clicking noise if you spin them too fast. Mom would tell me to leave it alone."

"Me too. She had to reinforce her favorite pages with clear tape. This is one Gideon found at some antique sale, but hers had this same cover. Same brand."

"I remember." Brandon had a far-off look in his eyes as he petted the book. "Her Santa ones were my favorite."

"Mine were the stars." My voice came out all gruff. I always forgot there were things he did remember. He'd been at that in-between age, where much of his before memories were fuzzy, but then he'd surprise me with something he did remember.

"With yellow icing." A smile crept across Brandon's face like remembering all this pleased him. Which was good. Last thing I wanted was for his throat to feel as raw as mine. I'd keep all the chest pangs to myself. We should have made cookies years earlier. I was always the one who couldn't easily talk about our parents, not him.

"Aw. I bet you were such a cute kid." Elaine gazed adoringly at Brandon before turning to me. "Do you have pictures?"

"Not many," I said honestly, but then her face fell, and I had to backtrack. "I mean, a few. School ones and such."

"Paul was late to the digital revolution," Brandon

teased. More like I'd been too broke for a fancy camera and never had much patience for the film kind, but Elaine's expectant expression made me wish I'd taken dozens more.

"Hey, I have an actual smartphone now and everything." My voice came out all defensive, which wasn't how I wanted things to go, so I took a breath to try to let go of my guilt. "After we finish with the cookies, I'll show you what I have."

"I'd like that." Elaine slid one of the makeshift cookie racks closer to her and Brandon as Gideon set out tubes of ready-made icing. He was also stirring up some sort of white glaze in a bowl.

"You must be so tired if you did a red-eye flight." After placing the bowl of icing on the counter, Gideon bustled around, getting cups from the cupboard. Funny how he almost knew my cabinets better than me. Funnier still that I apparently owned four matching Christmas mugs. "Coffee?"

"Please." Elaine accepted a cup with a grateful smile. Gideon was such an effortless host, supplying sugar and creamer in little containers I also hadn't seen before.

"A French press?" Brandon was back to laughing as Gideon poured the coffee. "Did aliens kidnap my actual brother?"

"Gideon doesn't like my coffee. He brought his own."

"I don't blame Gideon one bit. That's the same coffee maker you had ten years ago." Brandon pointed at my white one, which sat next to an equally ancient toaster.

"Guilty." The whole not sounding defensive thing was hard, but Gideon discreetly patting my arm helped. He handed me a coffee, and the strong brew coupled with the distraction of cookie decorating helped me to relax more. Watching Elaine and Brandon was cute, the way they worked together.

"I can slip out when you help them take their luggage up to the guest room," Gideon whispered as he added silver sprinkles to the white glaze I'd spread on a snowflake.

"What? Why?" The sprinkles looked good, and I turned the plate so the other cookie I'd iced could get some. Gideon wasn't making a ton of sense. "You said the cat was fine, so why all this hurry to leave?"

"I don't want to home in on your time with your brother." Ah. Now it made more sense. He was worried about feeling like a fifth wheel. I patted his hand, but he continued to protest, "It's Christmas Eve. It should be a family thing."

"I need you here." I had a feeling that *I want* wasn't going to get me very far with Gideon and his weird sense of nobility, but he couldn't argue with *I need*. And I did. No way could I enjoy myself knowing he was alone over at his house.

"Oh." His mouth made a perfect circle before he nodded. "I suppose I can help."

That wasn't at all what I'd meant, but before I could explain that I needed more than simply his hosting skills, Elaine interrupted, holding up a cookie.

"Gideon, do you have blue icing? This guy wants a blue sweater."

"Absolutely." Gideon passed her the tube of blue. "Your snowman is too cute to eat."

"Elaine always has an eye for detail." Brandon rubbed her shoulder.

"She'll like the soap then," I said absently, which got me two blank stares from Brandon and Elaine.

"Paul and I disagree on the importance of things matching," Gideon swooped in to explain. "I had some fun with the guest bath's decor. You'll see."

"I'm team matchy-matchy." Elaine gave a delicate

laugh as she finished her perfect snowman and set him aside.

"I had too many years with Paul to notice matching. Give me functional." Brandon's gingerbread man-shaped cookie had buttons in some unfortunate places, and I laughed, even though I wasn't sure whether that was a dig at me. Of course, I'd valued functionality. I'd had a kid growing like a weed, too many bills, and not enough time.

Back to decorating, I leaned closer to Gideon to whisper, "See? I need all the help I can get."

"You're doing fine." Gideon didn't even look up from arranging finished cookies on Mom's platter, which he'd washed earlier like he was handling a newborn infant. I had a lot more I wanted to say to him, but my heart was closing off my throat again, so it would have to wait.

"Let's take the cookies and coffee to the living room," Gideon suggested as Brandon and Elaine finished their rack of cookies. Dutifully, we all followed orders and trooped into the living room. I found a seat in one of the side chairs, but Elaine took a moment to more closely examine the tree.

"A train!" She bent to look under the tree and Brandon followed suit. "Oh, I love it."

Gideon shot me an "I told you so" look, and I made a mental note to tell Brandon about Gideon's idea for the ring to be riding on the train.

"Candy canes." Brandon beamed as he snagged one from the coal car as Elaine set the train to chugging around the tree. "You remembered."

"He went through two boxes last year on his own." Elaine's tone was fond before she straightened and started examining the homemade ornaments. "Show me which of these you made."

"Dude." Brandon looked back at me. "You kept my craft stick creations?"

"Um. Yeah." I shifted in my chair, but something strange happened to Brandon's face, a soft expression I wasn't sure I'd seen before.

"Thanks," he said quietly. Huh. Apparently, Gideon had been right there too. He'd been correct about almost everything, and I was going to give him a proper thank you the moment we were alone.

Chapter Twenty-Five
GIDEON

This traffic is worse every year! It took us over ten minutes to reach our own house. Unacceptable! ~Ernest Morrison posted to the What's Up Neighbor app

It was cute the way Paul was so sure he needed me to keep things running smoothly. And I did make a lovely charcuterie board for lunch, but need me? *Nah*. He'd been fine, winning big points with Elaine by producing a faded album with Brandon's school pictures and falling into an easy conversation with Brandon about which college games they were following. He didn't *need* me, but as long as he believed it, I was staying.

"Thought I'd find you here." Paul came up behind me. I'd snuck off to his bedroom to wrap his present to Elaine while the three of them were watching an old Christmas comedy after lunch. She'd talked the guys into a movie instead of a sporting event, and when I'd last seen him, Paul had seemed half-asleep.

But he was wide awake now, holding me close, and I couldn't help my happy sigh.

"Needed to get your wrapping done." I leaned into his hug, folding his arms tighter around me. I might as well enjoy this while I had it.

"It looks nice." Releasing me, he moved so he could touch the present on the bed. "Is that fabric or paper?"

"Fabric. Forgot I brought over some tea towels I never found a purpose for. Makes for an extra-special look, especially when coupled with this velvet ribbon leftover from decorating."

"It does. You're so good at details." He looked at me with enough wonder to make me feel like the grand champion of wrapping.

I wanted to volunteer to handle all his future wrapping needs but wasn't sure if I could play that off as a joke, so I simply nodded. "Thanks."

I was beginning not to know what to make of Paul's praise. I wasn't that extraordinary, simply an organized person with a side of too much free time for shopping. But when he looked at me with his eyes shining and lips parted, I felt truly special.

And when he kissed me, soft and sweet, I almost believed it. This particular kiss was all the sweeter for its unhurried vibe. No mad dash to the bed, simply Paul saying, "thank you" and melting all my circuits in the process.

His tongue met mine, making me reconsider that no-bed stance, but before I could tumble us onto the blanket, a voice made us spring apart.

"Oops. Not the bathroom." Brandon's blush was so deep it was almost purple.

I'd been so wrapped up in the kiss, I hadn't even registered the door opening.

"Second door. Not third." Paul didn't seem particularly embarrassed, unlike me. I sputtered like a teen caught in a cinch by parents, not a forty-something guy totally chill with being discovered kissing his...whatever Paul was. *Something like that*, Paul had said, which wasn't the same as *my boyfriend*, but it also wasn't *not* my boyfriend either. *New.* I was *new*. Fitting because everything felt brand new with Paul, so fresh it was both scary and wonderful in its unfamiliarity.

"Do...uh...you need help with dinner?" Brandon was still blushing. "Not that there's any rush. You can...resume. Or not. None of my business."

I had to laugh because it was nice not being the only flustered one.

"We'll handle dinner." Smiling, Paul waved Brandon away. "I've got Gideon to help."

He had the menu and the recipe in the spreadsheet. He didn't *need* me, but I still straightened my spine, tried to look useful, grateful for the excuse to stay. "Yup. We've got it. You should watch the sequel movie next. It's better than the original."

"Okay." Brandon seemed more than a little relieved to be off the hook for helping. "After dinner, let's walk to see the neighborhood lights."

"Excellent idea." I nodded before I realized I'd essentially invited myself along.

But Paul was nodding too, so I didn't take it back. And dinner went splendidly. Paul and I cooked together like we'd been doing Christmas Eve for years, me chopping, him searing, the sounds of the movie a comforting soundtrack, almost like I'd been here before and would be again.

Dinner conversation was also easy. Because Paul didn't actually need me playing host to ensure things went well, it was nice to simply hang out, no requirement to be quick with a joke. With certain friend circles, I always felt this pressure to perform. Be witty. Be the one with the tastiest dish, the funniest one-liner, earn a repeat invitation.

But here, I felt less like a guest and more part of the group. Elaine told us about Brandon's cooking disasters, and he countered with stories about what Paul made him eat when Paul himself was first learning to cook. Through it all, I let the good feelings swirl around me until my mouth ached from smiling so much.

We had wine with dinner, making my muscles loose and warm before our lights outing. Tired of cookies, we'd lingered over the cheesecake Paul had picked up as per my menu. I did love it when a plan played out perfectly.

"The wine was a nice touch," Paul said as we put on our coats and gloves in the kitchen.

"It was." I nodded, entirely unprepared for his swift cheek kiss.

"Let's go," Brandon called from the front door while my skin was still warm from Paul's lips. Brandon was as eager as a kid expecting Santa in the morning.

"Oh, my goodness! The dog is ready." Elaine laughed as Paul put Jim on her leash. Jim was back in her tracksuit, this time with the addition of some antlers I'd found at the same shop I'd bought her Grinch toy.

I'd walked the neighborhood many times the last few weeks, but I saw it with fresh eyes now. Brandon and Elaine walked slowly, full of awe, noticing little details I'd missed, like the lit ballerina twirling in the Reed's front window or how the snowperson family at the Jordan house all had matching sweaters with a J on them. Cheryl's driveway was packed and lively piano sounds filtered out to the sidewalk. The Clark family's display had piped-in music, and the line of car traffic slowed for gawkers to enjoy their animated figurines moving in time to "Jingle Bells."

"Look! You have reindeer on the roof," Elaine crowed with even more delight than she'd had for Jim's outfit as we turned a corner with a great view of Paul's house.

"So I do." Paul shrugged as if he'd forgotten they were there. "Gideon made me."

"I like Gideon." Brandon clapped me on the shoulder.

"Me too." Elaine linked arms with me. Lowering her voice and slowing her steps, she whispered, "Tell me a picture of Brandon in the lab isn't a ridiculous present for Paul. I'm having second thoughts."

"It's perfect." My chest got tight simply watching Paul and Brandon together ahead of us, both tall and broad-shouldered with the same easy strides. Paul had done so damn much to get Brandon to this point, given up far more than most would have.

"Good." Elaine smiled. "Brandon got him concert tickets to some band he used to play in the truck when taking Brandon to school. There are two tickets, although we both joked he'd give the second one to Jim."

"Also perfect." I kept my voice light. Maybe that would be another post-holiday excuse to see Paul. Or maybe he'd give the other ticket to the human Jim, and that would be that.

"What did you get him?" Elaine asked.

I actually had something, but I hadn't been sure about whether to give it or not. "A surprise."

"Ooh, a private one?" Her eyes danced like the gold lights of the house ahead of us.

"Not that kind." I blushed harder than I would have thought possible.

"Darn." She laughed and swung my arm. "We're both so happy for Paul. Seriously. Brandon worries about him, all alone and broody."

"He does do grumpy well," I agreed as we caught up to him and Brandon, who had slowed to wait for us.

"That house is so sad." Brandon had stopped in front of the Morrisons' house, and Paul was also frowning up at its dark facade.

"Yup." As always, I saw both the current state of the house with the deteriorating exterior and the darkened windows and the past with what had once been every room lit and a huge tree in the front bay window. So many times, I had played the what-if game standing here, deciding what I would do if I'd ended up with the place. I let out a little sigh, and it was Paul, not Elaine, who took my hand and held it fast.

"Tell them about your grandparents," he urged as we resumed walking. I obliged, expecting my wistful mood to continue. But for once, the memories didn't hurt. It felt good to share. The memories were mine, a part of me. I was lucky to have as many as I did. Brandon reacting earlier to the cookbook had reminded me of that. My wealth of special memories were treasures.

"Somehow, even on Christmas morning, my grandfather had a pressed shirt and tie on before coffee." I drew myself up taller into an approximation of my grandpa's perfect posture, and everyone laughed.

"Gee. Who else does that sound like?" Paul squeezed my hand. "Gideon has holiday bow ties. As in multiple. So far, I've counted three plaid, two snowmen, and one gingerbread cookie."

"You've kept track of my ties?"

"It's fun." He grinned at me.

"Okay, you have to wear the cookie one tomorrow," Brandon said as we neared our shared driveway. "I need to see one of these dapper outfits."

"Please," Elaine added with big eyes.

"I…" I stumbled over a graceful exit. Christmas Eve was one thing, but I couldn't simply invite myself to Christmas.

"You need to feed the cat anyway, right? Grab a tie while you're there," Paul ordered. "Then hurry back. Brandon talked me into eggnog before bed."

"I'm sleeping over?" Head tilting, I studied him carefully. Maybe Brandon had been right earlier and an alien had replaced his brother.

"Of course. It's Christmas Eve." Brandon wrinkled his nose like I was missing some obvious point. "Where else would you sleep? Don't feel you need to sneak around on our behalf."

Where else indeed. I blinked.

"Don't you want to be here for Christmas morning?" Elaine made a pouty face, and yes, yes I did, and she didn't even know the real reason why.

"I need you to make sure I don't screw up the apple waffles you made me put on the menu." Paul leaned in, then added in a whisper, "Say yes."

Agreeing was only too easy, especially with Paul right there, warm and delicious-smelling with his lips still against my ear. "Yes."

Chapter Twenty-Six
GIDEON

Way to go, holiday volunteers! A record donation to the community center projects! Many thanks to Gideon for organizing. I, for one, think the temporary traffic hassle was worth it. ~Cheryl Bridges posted to the What's Up Neighbor app

SLEEPING NEXT TO PAUL WITHOUT SEX WAS GOING TO DO me in, especially when he was all good mood and laughter on the way to bed.

"What's so funny?" Still buttoning my pajama shirt, I turned toward Paul, who was chuckling as he had much of the evening. His lack of grumpiness was throwing me off-kilter.

"You have Christmas pajamas." He gestured at my plaid shirt and bottoms, both of which were a couple of years old, purchased for a group holiday vacation.

"So I do." I channeled one of his stock responses to cover my rapidly heating cheeks. I'd felt a little silly packing the pajamas along with clothes for tomorrow after feeding the cat at my place. But Paul had all but ordered me to sleep over, and hell if I could say no. But I still wasn't sure what to make of the laughter.

"You're fucking adorable."

I snorted, not sure I liked the "adorable" label. "Had I known you apparently lack pajamas of all varieties, you too would have Christmas pajamas."

While I had changed clothes, Paul had dug through his dresser, muttering until he'd come up with a faded pair of gray sweatpants. And if I was adorable, he was criminally sexy, especially since he'd yet to put on a shirt. The sweatpants rode low, exposing more of his defined muscles, and there needed to be some sort of regulation against showing off hipbones that bitable on a night when I couldn't do more than look.

"If you slept over more often, you'd get more say in my pajama choices," Paul said easily as he scooped up my jeans from the floor and put them on the chair in the corner. My glasses were already on his nightstand, almost as at home in this room as I was.

"Somehow, when I sleep over, we never make it as far as the pajamas."

"Yup. And I like that." Wrapping me up in a hug, he nuzzled my neck.

"Hey now." I wiggled away before he could get me hard and make my common sense flee. "We can't be starting anything,"

"Why not?" He frowned but didn't seem that deterred as he ran a finger along the neckline of my shirt.

"Your brother is down the hall," I reminded him in an urgent whisper.

"Down the hall. No shared walls." Paul made a dismissive gesture before striding over to lock the door. "And I personally made sure the bed doesn't squeak. I think we've tested it enough times to make sure of that."

"This is true." I could feel myself starting to relent.

"It's Christmas Eve." He resumed kissing my neck, and this time I didn't wiggle away. "Don't people get Christmas Eve wishes?"

"That's your birthday," I corrected with a laugh.

"April seventeenth."

"What?" My mind was all foggy from the heat of his mouth against the back of my neck, but also the wine and spiked eggnog catching up to me.

"My birthday. It's April seventeenth. I'll take my wish in advance if Scrooge here won't give me a Christmas one."

"Hey!" I spun so I could meet his twinkling eyes. Like I could deny this man anything. If anyone deserved a Christmas wish, it was Paul. "You can have a wish."

"Good. It's Christmas Eve, it was a great day, and I get to wake up with you tomorrow. Let me put you to sleep the fun way."

"It was a good day." I looped my arms around his neck. He was right. It was Christmas Eve, and for the first time in a long time, I wasn't by myself. That alone deserved celebrating. Being here felt a little like a dream, like a wish I'd been too scared to make on my own, but if this was what Paul wanted, I wasn't going to hold back. I pressed a soft kiss to his mouth. "We still better be quieter than usual."

"Trust me, I can be plenty quiet. You're the screamer." Smiling, he deftly undid my pajama shirt buttons. "Let's save these for the morning."

"Deal, but I get to pick out something better for you." I finished undressing, making sure not to leave them on the floor.

"I have a rather limited selection of plaid." He wriggled out of his sweatpants, giving me an excellent view of his ass as he put them on the chair next to my pajamas. Turning back to me, he smiled, and for a second, all those cheesy wishes I tried never to make bubbled up.

"I could fix that." I made my voice light, another joke, nothing serious. But in a perfect world, this would be Paul's last Christmas in ratty sweats, and I'd boss him and Jim into matching me next year in some ridiculous print that made for a good photo opportunity. But this wasn't a perfect world, and next year was something I dared not think about, let alone get my hopes up for.

"Ha. I have better uses for you than shopping." He gave me a sinful grin. I supposed that was a win, him wanting me for sex, but part of me wanted him to need me. For planning. For shopping. *Something.* That he didn't was both a joy and a frustration. I loved watching him succeed, but I couldn't help wanting to be needed too.

"Put me to work." I pulled him close for another kiss before he could meet my eyes and see how much I wanted exactly that. He even tasted like Christmas—rum and spice and sweet, a memory in the making—and I couldn't get enough. Our bare torsos met, and we both groaned. The rough rasp of his fuzzy chest countered by the gentleness of his mouth was enough to make me dizzy.

"Bed," he growled as he released me long enough to flip off the lights. I crawled into the bed, but he took a moment to open the window curtains. The Reed's cheerful lights across the street filtered in along with other glimpses of the neighborhood displays farther down the hill.

"Oh, that was a perfect idea." I grinned as he slid in next to me under the covers and gathered me close. "I'm thanking the Reeds for their lights."

"Uh-huh. Put that thank you on the app you all use."

"Sure. Thank you to the Reed family for inspiring Paul to…" I trailed off on a gasp as he lightly bit my shoulder.

"Go on." He licked where he'd bit before dropping kisses on his way back to my neck.

"Thank you. Just that. Thank you." I meant him, not the Reeds, and he seemed to get that as he snuggled up tighter along my back.

"That's my line. You made a great night for Brandon and Elaine."

"You did that. I was just along for the ride." My tone was far more wistful than I'd intended.

"Gideon." Paul's voice went deliciously stern. "It was your plan. You saved our Christmas. Accept the praise."

"All right." Arguing wasn't what I wanted to do right then, not with his hard cock against my ass and his voice all warm in my ear.

"Mmm. I like you all compliant." He kissed the back of my neck, hands roaming all over my front and sides.

"Don't get used to it. And you should let me play too." I tried to turn, but he flexed his arms, locking me against him. Damn. Displays of brute strength had never done it for me before, but apparently, Paul going all he-man on me was my new favorite thing. I sagged against him, letting him have his way and reaping the benefit as he touched and teased.

"I want to be the one to light you up," he whispered. Continuing to nibble my neck, he swept his hands over my chest, thumbs flicking against my nipples.

"You do." Already every nerve ending was singing, simply from being this close to him. He slid one hand lower to stroke my stomach before gripping my cock. Much as I liked the attention, I worried I should be doing more for him. "We can…"

"Quit trying to direct." He nipped my shoulder. "Enjoy. This right here is perfect."

He punctuated his words by grinding against my ass, erection rubbing on me.

"Hard to argue with that," I snickered.

"Tip your head back. Want to kiss you." Licking my ear, he made a happy noise when I complied. His mouth found mine, there in the dark, outside lights dancing over us, and it was indeed perfect. His kiss, hot and urgent. His hand on my cock, sure and strong. His thrusts against me, purposeful and possessive.

"Oh. I like this." I let out a breathy laugh against his lips.

"Don't sound so surprised." He kissed the side of my face before shifting slightly so that his cock rode between my thighs, dragging against my crack and balls in a way that made electricity zoom up my spine with each thrust.

"I'm definitely lit up." I tried to laugh, but it came out more of a moan when he tightened his grip on my cock. "Fuck."

"Shush."

"Oops." I turned my head so I could bury any more noises in the pillow, and we lay like that for several long minutes, him moving against me while stroking my cock with long leisurely pulls. I tried to lie back and let the pleasure gather slowly, but it was all too good, and eventually, I started pushing back against him.

"Gideon," he whispered desperately against my neck. "You're going to get me off."

"Yes. Please." Usually, I'd be the one in control of the pace, and being at his mercy was surprisingly sexy, waiting for him to let go. My cock was desperate for him to speed up his hand, but patience was its own kind of tortuous pleasure.

"You too." And like he'd read my silent pleas, he did

increase his rhythm, thrusts harder, hand faster. "Come on."

"That. Like that," I whispered, my breathing as harsh as his. He added a tighter grip at the top of each stroke, and staying quiet and patient became increasingly impossible. I bit the pillow to keep from moaning, but then he guided my head back for a kiss. His hand was hot on my neck. Possessive. Greedy, the way he kissed me deeply while thrusting faster.

"Yes." And I was his for the taking, moving with him, faster and faster and faster until we were swallowing each other's moans. He seemed hell-bent on getting me off first, but it was only when his thrusts started to stutter that I let his hand take me over the edge. My orgasm went on and on, endless gentle waves as he milked my cock with his hand and gradually slowed his movements. And still, we kissed, trading little gasps and chuckles.

"Beautiful," I sighed as we finally broke apart, sticky and messy and absolutely wonderfully perfect.

"You make me want year-round lights." Paul kissed my shoulder. I hadn't meant the view, hadn't even opened my eyes in several long minutes. Paul might want more Christmas, but I wanted more *him*. I wanted every damn thing he had to give.

Chapter Twenty-Seven
PAUL

Did Santa come to your house? Remember to properly dispose of all boxes and wrapping paper! Trash collection is on the usual day, and let's not make too much extra work for our loyal sanitation workers!
~Cheryl Bridges posted to the What's Up Neighbor app

CHRISTMAS MORNING DAWNED WITH A FRESH LAYER OF snow, and even Jim seemed to understand that today was different, taking care of her business in record time and bounding back up the stairs to where Brandon and Elaine were emerging from the guest room.

"Waffles or presents?" Gideon asked as he too made his way into the hall. He was back in his matching pajamas, every button perfectly straight, no thanks to me who'd tried to lure him back to bed before Jim had had other ideas.

"Breakfast?" Brandon scoffed. "Who would want food first?"

"Says the always-hungry guy who could live on Christmas candy if I let him." Elaine gave him a fast kiss on the cheek. They were in matching thermal pajamas, red and white print with cartoon elves on the shirts. Maybe there were worst fates than plaid.

"Your pajamas are the cutest thing ever." Gideon whipped out his phone to do a picture as Elaine struck a pose. Bossy as ever, he'd dug through my dresser until he found green plaid flannel pants and a gray T-shirt I'd forgotten I owned that had a fir tree on it. The shirt was advertising a local nursery we used for the business, but it had been seasonal enough to satisfy Gideon's critical eye.

We all trooped downstairs, Jim leading the way, making our way to the living room.

"Stockings!" Elaine made a delighted noise like the presents had actually arrived by sleigh. After our walk the night before, we'd all pretended not to notice as one by one, we'd snuck gifts under the tree and trinkets into stockings. Similarly, I'd pretended to stay asleep when Gideon had left the bed in the middle of the night. I'd done my own Santa work while Jim had been outside, and I was rather proud of the fact that I'd thought to tell Gideon to grab a stocking from his place. That had earned me an eye roll, but it was worth it to see all four in a neat row on the mantel.

"Santa came!" Brandon was as happy as Elaine, and the two of them were first to grab their stockings after Elaine took a picture of the mantel. "And see? Candy!"

He swiped the comically oversized candy cane I'd stuck in his stocking and broke off a piece.

"Check yours," I said to Gideon as the other two emptied their stockings in front of them. I wasn't all bouncy like Elaine, but my stomach was strangely fluttery. I hadn't even needed the reminder of an entry on Gideon's spreadsheet to remember to pick up a few things for stockings. It was still his fault, though, how he had me in a Christmas state of mind.

"Hey, he gets cookies." Brandon pointed as Gideon revealed a pack of mini-whoopie pies in a chocolate-and-peppermint combination.

"I can share." Gideon's cheeks were pink as he handed Brandon one of the cookies. "Your brother is obsessed with this new bakery."

"And you got cat treats." Elaine laughed. The bakery had been a special stop, but the cat stuff was because I'd been in the pet aisle for Jim, and the cat on the tuna treat bag looked a little like Gideon's. And maybe I felt guilty that I'd been keeping Gideon from his place so much.

"Butterscotch says thank you," Gideon said primly, but his eyes were pleased.

"Has the cat met Jim yet?" Brandon asked as he absently petted Jim's furry head. She'd flopped down between him and Elaine on the floor in front of the tree. Gideon and I had the couch.

"Oh, that would be a funny picture." Elaine joined the love fest on Jim, rubbing her belly. Jim wasn't going to know what to do when the place went back to only the two of us. And the dog wasn't the only one.

"I'm not sure Butterscotch does dogs." Gideon's voice was light, which made it hard to tell whether he was serious or merely deflecting the matchmaking. Setting his stocking aside, he pointed at Elaine's haul. "Look at your stickers!"

She held up a pack of stickers with various science-based puns and another with famous female scientists. "Brandon knows me well."

"More like Brandon has access to your wish list on that crafting site." He dug around in his own pile to come up with a little envelope. "Cooking lessons. Is that a hint?"

"Yup." Elaine smiled smugly, then held up a figurine

with a huge head from some sci-fi franchise. "Wait. That's what I got you."

"Yeah, you did." Brandon held up his.

"Too cute." Gideon snapped a picture of them holding up their matching figures. "Paul's turn."

I revealed a number of candy items, including some from a California-based company Elaine apparently frequented, as well others I was sure came from Gideon even though he pretended to have had nothing to do with that or Jim's favorite brand of chews showing up. The bottom of my stocking held a joke book and fancy pine soap, which were absolutely from Gideon, who continued to play innocent.

"Presents." Elaine turned her attention to the stack under the tree, starting with a flat envelope she handed to Brandon. "This is from my parents to us both. They said they wanted something packable."

"Weekend in Tahoe!" Brandon seemed happy but not overly impressed by the card, which made me want to hide my own card with the dinner gift certificate. No way could I compete with his potential in-laws.

"That's awesome," I said tightly, earning me a searching look from Gideon.

"And one for you." Elaine handed me a beautifully wrapped box with shiny paper and a matching bow. Gideon was right that she did seem to love details, almost as much as Gideon himself did. The box held a framed picture of Brandon hard at work in his lab with some big model of a molecule next to him. "I wasn't entirely sure what to get you, but the frame seemed so perfect."

The wide frame had a poem off to the side about gratitude for support, more the sort of thing a kid might give a parent at graduation. I had a feeling it was far more her idea than Brandon's, but he was nodding along with

Elaine. "I wanted to name a particle phenomenon for you, but then Elaine showed me that on her craft site, and I decided something for the mantle might be more practical."

"You don't have to name something for me." My neck heated, and I couldn't take my eyes off the picture. He looked so happy. *You did good.* Gideon's pride when we'd talked about Brandon echoed in my ears. I didn't need some flowery poem of thanks, but maybe I had played a tiny role in that smile as he lived his best genius life. My chest went warm and way, way too full.

"I want to see what Gideon got you," Elaine demanded next.

"He didn't..." I started to protest but trailed off as she dumped a heavy box in my lap. It too was expertly wrapped, plaid paper with every line straight and a perfectly aligned red ribbon.

"I think we need to challenge Gideon and Elaine to a wrapping contest," Brandon joked.

"That would be fun," I said absently as I unwrapped the box. Next to me, Gideon looked like he was chewing nails, mouth tense and shoulders stiff. The box I revealed was older, which was curious, but it was the contents that made me legit need to suck in a breath.

"Oh. Wow. They match the cookie platter." Elaine was first to speak, pointing at the set of dessert plates and mugs, all with the same Rockwell pattern as the platter.

"I have a friend who's amazing at tracking down antique dishes." Gideon sounded uncertain, voice soft. "I hope it's okay. I didn't want to overstep."

"It's perfect," Brandon spoke when I still couldn't. "I never knew it was part of a set."

"It was." My tongue was three times as thick as normal. That too-full feeling in my chest had intensified, a balloon stretched to the limit, lifting me up and alarming me both. "Thank you." I swallowed hard, needing to get myself under control. "There's one for you, but I'm not sure it's gonna top this."

"You didn't have to get me anything." Gideon gave me a stern look as Elaine handed him my gift. My wrapping job was nothing compared to either of theirs, snowflake paper that had been in a half-off bin near the register, but Gideon didn't seem to mind, slowly unwrapping the box. He started laughing before he finished removing the paper. "Boots!"

"Dude." Brandon made a rude noise. "You got your boyfriend work boots?"

"Next year, send me a text," Elaine suggested, gentler than Brandon but no less concerned. "I can help you out."

"They're perfect." Gideon beamed at me before turning to the other two. "It's an inside joke. He doesn't approve of my footwear choice for roof work."

"Figured they might come in handy for taking everything back down."

"They will." His smile dimmed a little. Heck. What had I said wrong? But before I could apologize, Elaine continued in her amateur Santa role, giving Brandon a box to open. It contained a complicated LEGO set for the same fandom as their matching figurines. He made all sorts of happy noises as he posed with the box before giving her a long kiss.

"Your turn." Brandon pointed at Elaine.

"Mine?" She looked under the tree where the stack had dwindled to only a few remaining gifts.

"Better check the Christmas train." Brandon snagged the remote for the train, starting it going, but instead of the crackly Christmas carol it had played previously, a popular pop ballad accompanied the train around the tree.

"Oh my gosh." Elaine's smile widened. "It's playing our song."

"Sorry, Paul." Brandon spared a sheepish look in my direction. "I might have temporarily reprogrammed your train."

"It's fine," I said right as Elaine discovered the small box riding in one of the freight cars. The jewelry store had wrapped it in gold paper with a shiny bow as Brandon had requested, and it looked impressive in Elaine's palm.

"Ooh." She touched the bow with a delicate finger, expression cautious like the box might suddenly transform into a puppy if she wasn't careful.

"Open it," Brandon urged. She complied, but so slowly that I bet Brandon died a million little deaths waiting for her to reveal the ring. Her eyes went wide as she sucked in a breath.

"Is this…?"

"Elaine, will you marry me?" Brandon's voice went wobbly. They were both already sitting, but he moved to more of a kneeling position in front of her. "You're the best thing to ever happen to me, and I want to spend forever telling you how lucky I am to have found you."

Her mouth made a perfect circle, but no sound came out. And she held the position so long it went from comical to worrying. This wasn't the ready yes I'd expected, and even Gideon looked worried, leaning forward. He'd been snapping pictures on his phone, but he paused, mouth clamping shut like he was working to not speak. I shared the impulse because I was tempted to prod Elaine into an answer, but at the same time, there was nothing to do but wait.

Jim nosed at her hand, and she glanced down as Brandon made a sound that was somewhere between a cough and moan. Fuck. He was about to get his heart broken, and there was nothing I could do about it. All my years of looking out for him, and I still didn't have magical powers to keep him from pain. I hadn't felt this helpless in years. Next to me, Gideon scooted closer, grabbed my hand.

"Elaine?" Brandon finally asked in a strangled tone.

"Oops." Folding forward, she released a giddy laugh. "Yes. Of course, yes."

The entire room exhaled, relief sweeping through the space so swiftly, I swore the tree branches swayed. My eyes were burning. That never happened. Ever. Gideon squeezed my hand.

"You sure?" Brandon's voice was soft as fake snow.

"Yes. Sorry. I've played this out in my head so many times…" She was still laughing, a sort of near-hysterical giggle. "Funny. I never expected to be so dumbstruck that I couldn't speak. That wasn't in any of my fantasies. But yes. I'm absolutely a yes."

"Oh, thank God." Brandon embraced her, more him collapsing against her than a hug even, and she kissed the top of his head.

"I was always a yes. From day one."

"I didn't want to assume…" He trailed off, still breathing hard.

"Oh, don't get me wrong. I love the train and the ring. I definitely wanted a proposal. But I was always going to say yes, even if you'd gone the jumbotron at a sporting event route."

"Paul talked me out of the flash mob." Brandon finally managed a laugh of his own.

"Good. I'm glad." She kissed him again, and Gideon snapped another few pictures of them.

"Congratulations." He grinned at them. "Ready for some celebratory breakfast?"

"Waffles are supposed to top that?" I joined the laughter. Laughter helped. I had too many feels still, and I didn't like the overwhelming emotions one bit. "Better lower the expectations for my cooking."

"But you have Gideon." Elaine's eyes danced. "I trust the waffles to be spectacular."

"This is true." Left to my own devices, we'd be having pancakes from a boxed mix, but he elevated my game, made everything that much more special. And I was so, so glad he'd been here with me to witness the proposal. I had no idea how to start processing everything rattling around in my brain, let alone put together the sort of pretty thank-you speech Gideon undoubtedly deserved. I settled for kissing his cheek, hoping like hell he'd understand even if words failed me.

Chapter Twenty-Eight
GIDEON

We surprised Dad with a new recliner! The old one is at the bottom of our drive with a FREE sign on it! First come, first served! ~Jean Clark posted to the What's Up Neighbor app

"Maybe these waffles truly are magical." Elaine helped herself to a third. The four of us were sitting at the kitchen island, feast spread out before us.

"It's the dried cranberries plus the apples," I said lightly, knowing perfectly well it was the excitement of the day. Paul could have served boiled shoe, and it would have been memorable and equally appreciated by the glowing newly-engaged couple. I doubted either of them tasted a thing. Brandon had packed away a stunning amount of bacon, but he too seemed lit from within. And relieved. Probably that most of all, the way he kept smiling to himself like he'd narrowly avoided some terrible fate.

"The real maple syrup was a nice touch. Let Gideon menu plan more often." He bumped Paul's shoulder before grinning at me. "Paul never met a generic knockoff he didn't love."

"Paul is impressive with a budget. Fake syrup probably meant more science fairs for you." I kept my voice easy, but I gave Brandon a pointed look. He was a great guy and no doubt as smart as advertised, but he was also remarkably clueless to all Paul had given up for him. The photo from Elaine had been thoughtful, but a few lines of poetry weren't the same as truly appreciating Paul's sacrifices on a meaningful level.

"Oh. Yeah." Brandon at least had the grace to blush. "Things were tight before Paul got his first house especially. The apartment was so teeny that even that little tree of ours seemed huge. Paul tried though. Every year, we'd drive around for hours looking at lights. I dragged Elaine out last year to see the lights in the suburbs near the university, but it wasn't the same."

"What? No stack of candy canes and cheap hot chocolate to keep you company in the back seat?" Paul teased, but his mouth was tight. I hoped he wasn't irked at my prodding Brandon, but it had needed saying. He'd done so much, and my heart broke every time I pictured him and Brandon alone for Christmas, Paul doing the best he could. Brandon damn well better name a phenomenon for him. He deserved it.

"Elaine lets me have extra marshmallows. But I mean it. I missed this."

"Don't go getting sappy," Paul ordered. "We all know you're not trading in all that sunshine."

Brandon glanced at Elaine. "You never know."

"I know it's a tight market for professors, but you both aren't going to have a problem finding offers." Paul sounded so resigned that it was a good thing he was out of arm's reach from me because the man needed a good shaking.

"You—" Brandon started, but Elaine tapped her lips, and he changed directions. "We'll see."

He shrugged, but now I was curious. Paul needed to simply tell them he wanted them to job hunt on this coast. But, of course, he wouldn't. Stubborn man.

"Is it weird that I totally want to go out and get a big stack of wedding magazines?" Elaine asked in a clear bid to change the topic.

"You're going to be a bridezilla." Leaving his seat next to Paul, Brandon stood behind her and rubbed her shoulder. "You can even drag me to one of those wedding showcase events back home. I don't mind. Just remember to say I do."

"I will." She smiled brightly. "I won't keep you waiting again. Promise. I'll write my vows on cue cards."

"You better." Brandon kissed the side of her head, dopey grin still firmly in place. They were so in love it hurt, and those few moments when I'd thought she'd been about to say no had been terrifying. It would have crushed Brandon's whole world. Honestly, his bravery was admirable.

Putting one's heart on the line was a risk worse than skydiving if you asked me. No thank you. Even secondhand, the terror had been palpable. But then she'd said yes, and he'd smiled, and maybe, for an instant, I had wanted...*something*. I still wasn't sure, only that Paul's hand in mine had been the only thing keeping me from shattering from the emotional jolt. Even now, I felt rather fragile, a coffee cup repaired too many times. Not to be trusted.

"You should use the song Brandon made the train play at the wedding." Trying to distance myself from my muddled thoughts, I started clearing away the breakfast dishes and packaging up the leftover food.

"Yes!" Elaine beamed at me as she took a stack of plates to the sink. "You're the best with details."

"You're the one who can see discrepancies in subatomic particles," I teased as I wrapped up the leftover waffles.

"I don't know what sort of dress I want yet, but I can't wait to wear those earrings." Elaine touched Paul's shoulder lightly as she scooped up the syrup container.

"You don't have to wear them for the wedding." Paul's cheeks turned ruddy, and he looked down at his hands.

"I want to. Something old. Something new. Something borrowed. Something blue." She counted off the old saying on her fingers. "The pearls will be good luck. Thank you, again."

She'd said it earlier when Paul had given her the box, getting misty eyes and waving her hands in front of her face, but I wasn't sure Paul believed her that his gesture meant a great deal.

"I'm happy for you both," he said stiffly, then gave a rusty laugh like he was making a herculean effort to push off any weighty thoughts about his mom. "I don't suppose I can tell you to elope?"

"Absolutely no fun in that." Elaine laughed. "But I do plan to keep it small."

"You're not getting out of the speech-writing or the suit-wearing." Brandon had a stern stare for Paul.

"Speech?" Paul blinked.

"Haven't you been to many weddings?" Elaine's eyes narrowed.

"The best man always does a toast." Brandon used a slow voice like Paul might need some extra time to catch up. "And there's no one else I'd want to ask."

Swallowing audibly, Paul nodded. "I'd be honored."

"Good." Brandon clapped him on the shoulder, giving

a hearty laugh, exactly like Paul when he was trying not to get overly emotional. "Even if your version of a bachelor party is probably going to involve a sporting event."

"Better that than my taste in strippers," Paul deadpanned.

"True." Brandon laughed so hard his eyes shined. "And you'll survive the tux. I promise nothing too out there."

"If Gideon can wear a bow tie, so can you," Elaine tittered.

Oh. She was undoubtedly assuming I'd be Paul's plus one, which I most assuredly had not been counting on. Letting me join in on Christmas was one thing. A cross country wedding was another beast entirely, but in that instant, I saw how easy it would be to offer my help. Tux wearing and toast making and fancy dinner rules. I could easily wrangle another six months out of that sort of usefulness.

Too easily. How much more would it hurt to part after the wedding when I wasn't needed anymore?

"It's not hard," I said, biting back the offer of help. If Paul asked, I might still say yes. I didn't trust myself to turn him down, but I could at least make him ask, not invite myself along.

"See?" Brandon swiped the last piece of bacon from the tray before I could put it in a plastic bag. "Dressing up is easy. And if you want, we can try for fall when you're less in the middle of your busy season than at graduation."

"Don't choose a date on my account." Paul waved away the concern as he stood and grabbed a sponge to wipe down the counter while Elaine finished loading the dishwasher. "Elaine's parents likely have even more crowded schedules."

"My mother." Elaine shuddered. "I better have date,

venue, and dress picked before they're back stateside. She'll have me in a tiara and ruffles if I'm not careful."

"You'd look cute in a tiara," Brandon said loyally.

"Ha. You'd like me in anything." She patted his face with soapy fingers. "You should watch a Christmas Day game with your brother while I browse wedding websites on my phone."

Ah. This was where I'd need to retreat, finally head home. I shut the fridge with a decisive click, last of the leftovers stowed. I'd already put the box with my new boots near my shoes and coat. The boots had been such a *Paul* gift. Other people might simply say, "Be careful" or "I don't want you to fall," but Paul actually went out and did something to try to ensure my safety. And spare him having to admit he cared about my neck. I loved the boots, even if they were a reminder that tomorrow I'd start packing the season away and everything would go back to normal. I sighed softly to myself.

But right when I would have grabbed my shoes, Paul tugged me toward the living room. "Come on. I know you hate sports, but you can make fun of their uniforms or something while we relax before we have to start the roast."

"Oh." Apparently, I was staying for Christmas dinner. I should speak up, give a polite excuse, but when I opened my mouth, what came out was, "All right. I'm good at potato peeling."

"So I've heard," he said easily as he arranged us on the couch after Elaine took over one of the chairs, Brandon sprawling at her feet with a cushion, dog next to him. They sure were a cute couple. Must be nice to have that sort of devotion.

Paul's arms came around me as he shifted around until he arrived at a satisfactory position, holding me against his side as he used the remote to find a basketball game. He kept right on holding me as he and Brandon made a friendly bet. Every so often, Elaine would ask his opinion on flowers or mine on colors, and it was unbearably cozy, the four of us hanging out like this was an everyday occurrence.

I needed to go home and soon, but I seemed rooted to the couch, tangled up in Paul's limbs and my own reluctance. All I could do was soak the moment up, let the good feelings add to my personal memory bank. *This.* This right here was both the happiest and most wistful I'd ever been. I might not survive Paul Frost.

Chapter Twenty-Nine
PAUL

Temperatures are dropping! Expect a record low tonight! Better watch those pipes, hope nothing freezes! ~Tim Frisk posted to the What's Up Neighbor app

SOMETHING WAS WRONG WITH GIDEON. OR MAYBE NOT *wrong*. But definitely off. I studied him across the table as we tucked into dessert. The peppermint stick ice cream with homemade hot fudge had been one of his contributions to the menu, but he kept taking slow, almost disinterested bites.

He'd seemed quiet all afternoon, less animated than usual, less quick with a laugh, and even less bossy. The bossy thing was the most concerning, honestly. The other two probably didn't notice any difference because Gideon had preened when they'd admired his bow tie after we all finally got dressed after brunch. He'd smiled and let them talk him into assisting with assembling Brandon's new LEGO project, and he'd been helpful as ever after that, bustling around my kitchen for the dinner assembly.

He'd produced a mountain of peeled potatoes with a smile, but I hadn't been able to shake the feeling that something was off. Gideon was normally a bright light, cutting through any darkness, a warm glow that couldn't be denied. And today, it was like someone had put a shade over his inner lamp. Still there, but dimmer. I wanted him to tell me what the matter was, but every time we caught a slow moment together, something kept getting in the way. Elaine with a question. The oven timer. Jim needing outside. His phone dinging with Christmas messages from friends and relatives he didn't seem inclined to answer.

"Maybe I want an ice cream bar at the wedding reception." Elaine swiped more hot fudge for her ice cream from the bowl Gideon had set on the table. He'd performed some sort of culinary magic involving my microwave and chocolate chips. Damn, but I loved how he could elevate the ordinary. It was a unique skill set I hadn't properly appreciated before him.

"The wedding needs cake, but we could do ice cream at the rehearsal dinner." Brandon took seconds of the ice cream himself. "And a waffle bar at the morning-after breakfast."

"Oh, I love that." Elaine beamed at him. "The ice cream will fit the whole fun theme of the Friday night dinner and the costumes."

"Costumes?" I suppressed a groan. Somehow the two of them had evolved over the course of the afternoon from a "small, intimate" ceremony and reception to an entire weekend extravaganza of events and obligations.

"Cosplay. All our friends are into different fandoms, so we thought it would be fun to ask people to come to the rehearsal dinner as their favorite characters. The pictures will be so fun," Elaine enthused, scooping up more ice cream to add to the river of hot fudge in her bowl. "This is going to be the best weekend ever."

"Since you love photos so much, you totally need to do a photo booth with props and backgrounds," Gideon suggested. "I've been to a couple of weddings with those. You'll love having those pictures to add to your albums."

"So smart!" Elaine saluted him with her spoon. And he was smart. Thank God one of us knew all the wedding traditions and rules. Brandon really should have asked one of his genius friends to be best man. I was likely to stick out like a grease stain on a linen tablecloth, but he wanted me there, so I'd for damn sure do my best.

"You'll have to tell me what costume to get."

"Sure thing," Brandon said easily. I'd meant Gideon, but this worked too. As long as I wasn't left to my own devices.

"I'd pay good money to see Gideon as Frodo and Paul as Aragorn." Elaine was giggling so hard she had to set her spoon down.

"I...uh..." I didn't want to admit that I wasn't entirely sure who those characters were.

"Keep it simple. Batman and Superman." Brandon joined Elaine in snickering, but Gideon stayed quiet. Maybe he didn't like the meddling, or maybe he too lacked comic book aspirations.

"I'll figure something out." I made my voice stern because I didn't need them making Gideon uncomfortable. And hell, if Gideon was anti-costume, so much the better for me.

"Okay, okay." Elaine was still laughing. "I haven't even settled on my final colors. We've got time."

"Not too much time," Brandon protested. "No long engagements."

"Don't want me getting away?" she teased as Gideon started collecting our empty bowls.

"Nope." Brandon gave her a loud kiss before we all trooped to the kitchen to start cleaning up from dinner. We made a good team, the four of us. Elaine made an art form out of loading the dishwasher, Gideon was the expert leftover packer, I enjoyed scrubbing, and Brandon was the comic relief.

"You should take the cat some beef scraps as a peace offering for us keeping you all day," Elaine said to Gideon as he sliced up the rest of the roast.

"Maybe I'll do that after we finish cleaning up." Gideon sounded weary. "I should probably get back in any event."

Huh. Perhaps that was the issue. We had monopolized him for the better part of two days. Despite being such an extrovert, he might be the kind of person who needed alone time to recharge his batteries. God knew I usually was. Preferring to be alone with Gideon was something new, and I could certainly understand needing a break from all this togetherness without taking it personally.

Heck, if Gideon did go home, I was likely to escape to my basement with Jim myself. This had easily been the best holiday I'd ever had, but it was still a ton of talking for a guy as used to his own company as I was.

"Take as much meat as you want." I handed him some plastic storage bags. "Potatoes too. We've got potatoes for days."

"All right." He nodded sharply. "You can turn leftovers into potato pancakes as well. I'll text you the recipe."

"Thanks." I licked my lips, not sure what to make of this new formality between us. "And thank you for everything today. I couldn't have done it without you."

"Yes, you could." His tone was kind as he patted my arm, but there remained a strange stiffness about him.

"Well, I'm glad I didn't have to try," I said stubbornly, trying to meet his gaze, but he was already hustling away to take the remaining leftovers to the fridge. "I meant what I said last night. You saved our Christmas."

"Good." He exhaled hard as he headed over to where his shoes were stashed. "Think you'll need help taking all the decor down?"

"Nah. You've already done so much." I certainly didn't want to take advantage of him, especially with him seeming so tired. "Your work is complete, Boss," I joked, but he didn't smile. "Seriously, I've got Brandon for help. We'll follow your schematic for putting everything away, and after watching Elaine with the dishwasher, I think she can handle the tree ornaments."

"Yeah. She can. I've got my own house to put to rights. That'll likely take most of the day tomorrow."

"Okay." I'd been preparing to come up with some cooking emergency or outing that required him, but I didn't want to keep him from his plans.

"Well. Goodnight." Shoes on, he straightened back up, his presents and leftovers in his arms.

"You got all that? I could help you carry." And I could also stay long enough for another make-out session on his couch, but he was already shaking his head even before I could get a heated look in.

"Nah. I've got it."

"All right." I went in for a clumsy kiss, his armload between us. Couldn't kiss him the way I truly wanted with Elaine and Brandon still lingering in the kitchen, which was probably for the best as Gideon didn't seem in much of a kissing mood. "Thank you again."

"Anytime." He gave me a sad smile before slipping out into the frigid night. A weird emptiness settled over me as the door clicked shut. I couldn't shake the feeling that I'd said exactly the wrong thing, and hell if I knew how to fix it.

Chapter Thirty
GIDEON

Does anyone have any spare rock salt? We're out, and I need to get out early in the morning! ~Cheryl Bridges posted to the What's Up Neighbor app

"Did you miss me?" Predictably, the cat didn't answer, although Butterscotch did nose at the tuna treats Paul had put in my stocking. I'd lined up the treats on the large cat tree in my office where Butterscotch tended to hang out. He didn't seem to care much that I hadn't been around. He'd been happy enough to come when I set out fresh food and water, and he tolerated some head scratches now, but otherwise, he stayed aloof as ever.

I'd adopted him around the time I bought my house, thinking I was giving a home to an animal who needed me, but Butterscotch needed precious little beyond food and his robotic litter box emptied.

Maybe there was a lesson there. The things I was so sure needed me really were self-sufficient. And okay, Paul wasn't a grouchy cat, but the feeling that he was merely indulging me lingered. I still wasn't sure whether I'd invited myself along for their Christmas or whether he'd kept me around out of pity. Regardless, I wasn't going to insert myself in the rest of Brandon's visit, nor was I about to offer wedding help. Especially not without Paul *asking*.

Because, like with the cat, Paul might not need me, but I sure as hell needed him, and I hated that feeling. The trudge over to my house had never seemed longer or colder. He'd packed me off with leftovers and a hearty thanks for my help, and I shouldn't have felt so empty, but I did.

This sucks. I took myself and my morose mood back downstairs, where the sight of my tree made everything worse. Was I ever going to see my decorations again without immediately thinking of Paul and that hot-as-fuck make-out session in front of my tree?

My phone buzzed in my pocket, and it spoke to how desperate I was for distraction that I pulled it out. It was Lori, not one of my parents with our semi-annual stilted greeting, so I went ahead and answered, making my tone as cheery as I could.

"Hey there. How goes Florida?"

"Good." Lori's voice was warm and welcome. "Kids are having a blast. Tomorrow is Disney."

"Wow. They must be bouncing off the walls. Surprised you had a minute to call me." I smiled to myself. Most of my relatives hadn't bothered to do more than text this year, so it was nice Lori had thought of me. "You must have been missing my superior mashed potato skills at dinner."

"Oh, you." She laughed. "We ordered the whole dinner in advance as takeout. No cooking for anyone, but I'll always have time for you. You know you're family to us, even if we're not together this year."

"Thanks." My tree twinkled in front of me, memories less sharp now.

"And I want to hear all about your day. But don't let me forget that I'm also calling about a little favor."

"Oh?" I should have known. And as usual, I was happy to be of service, but I couldn't help my small sigh. It would have been nice had she been calling simply to check on me. "How can I help?"

"I saw on the news how cold it's going to get there. Can you stop by tomorrow, check our faucets and basement, make sure nothing burst or froze?"

"Absolutely." I nodded to my empty living room. The wind had already been howling when I'd made my way home. No snow, but a bitter chill.

"Thank you. You're the best." There was a clicking sound on her end. Probably a pen as she crossed that item off her to-do list. "I figured you'd be heading out to the clearance sales anyway."

"Maybe not this year." I flopped onto my couch. I couldn't think of one item I needed or wanted that might be at a store, and even the thrill of a bargain held no appeal.

"What? No shopping?" Lori scoffed. "Where is the real Gideon?"

"Here. I'm fine." My voice didn't sound the finest, but maybe if I said it enough times, I'd start believing it. "I just need to focus on packing everything away."

"Ooh." She drew the word out all knowingly, but there was a certain long-standing sympathy there too. "Your annual post-holiday slump. Happens every year."

"Yeah." That wasn't it either, but it was easier to agree than to explain my jumbled-up thoughts. And I did always get down after the holidays were through and the dark winter marched on with spring seeming so far off, but my current mood wasn't the sort of thing light therapy or other self-care could cure.

"Leave the decorations up," Lori advised, voice gentle. "They make you happy. You can wait through New Year's, at least."

"Nah. Better get them packed up. No sense in drawing it out." An image of Paul popped into my head. That was why I'd returned home rather than linger after the cleaning was through. Walking away was going to hurt regardless, but better to get it over with, and certainly better than having to wait for them to start dropping subtle hints.

"It's Christmas decorations, Gideon. Not a tax extension." Lori gave a long-suffering chuckle, the sort only someone who'd known me this long and well could get away with. "And you're a grown adult. If you want to eke out a little more joy from the season, do it. There will be time enough to put things away, and if you leave the lights up, well, you'll hardly be the only one."

"Yeah." I agreed because it was easier than arguing, but inside, my mind was whirring. Should I have grabbed a little more happiness with Paul? Stored up a few more good memories? Hell, maybe I should have volunteered wedding help after all. Maybe Lori was right, and it would be better to have more nice times to look back on. There'd be plenty of time to part awkwardly later.

"Worried about the neighbors complaining?" Lori interrupted my musing, and I had to blink a couple of times, come back to the present conversation.

"What?" I shook my head. "Oh. The lights. No."

"Ah. I think I understand now." Lori's tone was warmer now, more conspiratorial. "You struck out with the hot neighbor? Didn't have the right silver-fox bait after all?"

"My…bait is just fine, thank you very much." I bristled, sitting up straighter, spine stiffening like the cat when I offended his dignity. "I'll have you know I had a delightful Christmas with him and his family."

Oops. I hadn't meant to reveal that.

"Then why so glum, sweetie? Go jump his bones until your post-Christmas funk passes."

"Not that simple," I countered. But maybe it was. We hadn't parted *badly*. Paul had certainly been affectionate enough all day. I could probably wheedle a booty call out of him without much effort. Put another delicious encounter in my memory bank. But every time I thought about texting him, my fists clenched into tight balls.

Lori sighed heavily. "You've never met a problem you couldn't overthink."

"I'm not even sure there is a problem," I admitted. If Paul would be happy enough to oblige me with sex, and I had the perfect excuse of the wedding to stick around and offer continuing help, maybe this pining for something more truly was ridiculous. The cat had made his way downstairs at last and prowled along the back of the couch, undoubtedly on the hunt for more treats, but he evaded my hand when I tried to give him a pat.

"See? There you go. Go lay out some more fox bait," Lori ordered lightly as more voices sounded on her end, typical evening chaos with the kids. "I've got to go, but I'm cheering for you. And I'm here if you need to talk more. I know all about your post-Christmas crash. You can call me."

"I'm fine." Somehow my repetition hadn't worked yet. I still wasn't fine. "You have fun at Disney tomorrow."

"We will. Take care, sweetie."

We ended the call, and I hauled myself up off the couch. I had an unopened carton of eggnog and a liquor cabinet calling my name, but when I arrived in the kitchen, a peculiar scraping sound distracted me. I went to the window where I discovered Paul in our shared driveway with a shovel and a huge bag of rock salt. As I watched, he salted not only his own walk but mine too.

Huh. Had he done that previously and I'd never noticed? Or had something changed to make him think he needed to take care of me? Perversely, I wasn't sure I liked that. Him taking care of me was perilously close to more pity. If I was Lori, I'd say he was making sure the path between us was clear, a sweet, very Paul gesture to ensure I didn't fall en route to a hookup.

But my phone was devoid of messages. No request for a booty call. No suggestion of plans for tomorrow or the next day. Maybe he truly was like the cat and didn't need me nearly as much as I needed him. And that sobering thought was what kept me anchored to the spot in front of the window, keeping me from going to him.

A braver man would call out to him, offer him a hot beverage to warm up, let things inevitably turn sexy from there. A truly courageous person would try *talking* to Paul. I wasn't brave. Not like that. But I wanted to be.

Chapter Thirty-One

PAUL

Hopefully, this is the last night of bad traffic around here. Can't wait for the lights to come down and things to return to normal. ~Ernest Morrison posted to the What's Up Neighbor app

"I MADE HOT CHOCOLATE." ELAINE HAD A STEAMING MUG on the counter for me after I removed my boots and coat.

"Thanks." I wrapped my hands around the warm mug. Even having worn gloves, my fingers were still half-frozen. "Cold out there."

"Surprised you didn't go next door to warm up." Tittering, she took a seat on one of the island stools, leaving me to follow suit.

"Me too." There had been a moment where I'd been sure I saw his shadow in his window, but he hadn't called out, and I hadn't gone over and knocked. "I think he needed some alone time. He seemed tired after dinner."

"You're wearing him out." Her eyes were sly as she took a sip of her cocoa.

"Maybe." I didn't regret the sex one bit, but maybe I

had been keeping him up late and away from his own bed more than I should have. That was what had kept me from going to him. If he needed some time to recharge, the least I could do was give it to him. I glanced around the kitchen, surprised Elaine's constant shadow was nowhere to be seen. "Where's Brandon?"

"Taking a hot shower to warm up." She pointed toward the stairs. "He says his body isn't used to this kind of cold anymore."

"I'll turn up the thermostat."

"You can do that, but honestly, he probably wanted the escape." She rolled her shoulders from side to side. "Like Gideon. Too many hours of socializing, and besides, he always does his best thinking in the shower."

"He always did love baths when he was little." I smiled at the memory of the hours he'd spent in the tub in the apartment, me sitting in the doorway, trying to make sense of one of the textbooks for my community college business classes, and him babbling about some interesting scientific tidbit.

"He's so lucky he had you." Elaine's smile was even warmer than the hot chocolate and made the back of my neck heat.

"Thanks."

"Was it terribly hard?" She touched my arm. "Doing it all on your own?"

"N—" I started the same lie I told everyone, but then I remembered Gideon and our pact to be honest about when things sucked. Maybe there wasn't virtue in pretending. "Yeah. It wasn't easy. But it was worth it. He's worth it."

A weird creeping sensation raced up my spine. Here I was being honest with Elaine, but had I been truly honest with Gideon? The chilly work outside hadn't chased away the feeling I'd had ever since Gideon had left that I'd screwed up somehow. I hadn't told him I liked it better when he was here, had pretended to be perfectly fine with him leaving. Maybe that hadn't been the best course of action.

"I know. Brandon's so worth it." She patted the back of my hand before glancing over at the neat stack of her presents on the edge of the island. She slid the jewelry case closer to herself, tracing the embossed saying on the top. "Thank you for trusting me with his heart."

"Take good care of it," I said gruffly as my brain whirred. I'd agreed with Gideon that the line on the jewelry case was perfect, but had I truly understood the words? The L-word was big and scary, and I couldn't think too hard about it or my pulse sped up to alarming levels. But I also couldn't deny that I cared about Gideon. And I hated that I couldn't say for certain that I'd taken good care of his heart. I wasn't sure exactly what Gideon needed—space or reassurance, or whatever—but I hadn't spent a ton of time trying to figure out those needs either.

"I'll take care of Brandon. Don't worry." Elaine's eyes were still on the case, dreamy and faraway. She was undoubtedly lost in another wedding daydream, but I wasn't entirely sure wanting a white dress was the same thing as wanting Brandon, specifically.

"If you're not sure…"

"I am." Meeting my gaze, she leaned forward. "I know I scared him by not answering quickly. But it wasn't because I didn't want him. Rather, I want this so much. I've played the moment out in my head so many times. I knew it was coming, but then it was actually *here*, and I was overwhelmed."

"You knew?" My mouth pursed.

"Well, I didn't know for sure it would be this trip." She

made a vague gesture with her hand. "But we've spent the last few years dreaming and scheming together. I certainly dropped enough hints. And before you say it, yeah, I could have been the one to ask him."

"But where's the fun in that?" I guessed. She and Brandon did seem to have a lot of fun together. A big wedding was hardly my own definition of a good time, but planning it as a couple sure did seem to make them happy.

Happy. Was I doing enough of the things that made Gideon happy? Not simply folding him into my life, but was I giving Gideon room to be Gideon?

"Exactly." Elaine nodded. "I was curious as to what he might do for a proposal. The daydreaming about possibilities was fun. And to be frank, he's often in the lab for long hours. We both are. I'm pretty sure he goes days without remembering I exist."

"I'm sure he remembers you exist," I protested even as my chest twinged. Fuck. It really was easy to take someone for granted, wasn't it?

"Ha. When he's wrestling with a problem in his head, he's been known to forget pants. But I'm the same way. We bump around for weeks at a time without remembering to tell each other how much we care."

Huh. I'd been operating on the assumption that Gideon had had the same realization as me, that we were accidentally dating. I'd let my own dislike of awkward conversations keep me from putting into words that which I'd presumed was obvious.

"I guess I can see how that might happen."

"Exactly. I know it's terribly cliché, but I wanted to know I meant so much to him." Blushing, Elaine glanced away. "I was always going to say yes, but the asking, that mattered, if that makes sense."

"It does," I agreed slowly. Damn it, why did everything

come back to communication skills I wasn't sure I had? But I couldn't argue with her point. Speaking up mattered.

"I'm sure it seems like I'm one roll of tulle away from going full-on bridezilla, but really, the joint project of wedding planning is going to be fun." Her eyes sparkled as she made an excited gesture. "And incorporating all his favorite things like costumes, that's how I show him I care too. Because I do."

"I know." My tone came out more growly than I'd intended, so I worked to soften it. "He's lucky to have you."

"Eh." She shrugged. "We're lucky to have each other."

"Yeah." My voice sounded as far away as my thoughts. *Luck.* So much of my life had been defined by bad luck, an act of fate that changed everything, but there had also been plenty of good luck along the way. Maybe I wasn't always the best at seeing those lucky things. *Like Gideon.*

"Do I smell hot chocolate?" Brandon came bounding down the stairs.

"Right here. I'll heat your cup back up." Leaving her stool, Elaine put a mug for Brandon in the microwave. "How was the shower?"

"Excellent. I think I came up with the perfect concluding paragraph for my dissertation." Brandon bounced on his feet, holiday slippers slapping against the hardwoods. "And some neat ideas for wedding favors."

"We are not handing out lightsabers." Elain gave him a stern look.

"Darn." He slumped onto the stool next to me but then brightened. "Commemorative towels?"

"*Brandon.*" She added to her death glare with a wrinkled nose and pursed lips.

"You two need to come with a geek culture dictionary," I grumbled.

"Didn't you pay attention to any of the movies I made you sit through?" Brandon asked with a laugh.

"I was usually multitasking. Bills. Homework for my business classes. Bids for clients," I admitted, looking down at my empty mug. "Never enough hours in the day."

I wasn't sure that being busy was enough of an excuse for not paying attention to the things Brandon found important, but he nodded. "Yeah. I remember now. Your business literally started at the kitchen table."

"It did." My jaw tensed. Damn it. What had I missed those years I was working every waking minute? And what about now? Had I failed to pay close enough attention again? What had I missed with Gideon? And more importantly, how could I make it right again?

"Hey. Don't sweat it." Brandon clapped me on the shoulder. "You showed up when it counted. That's what really matters."

Showed up. That was it. A sharp bolt of clarity raced through me, and I knew exactly what I had to do.

Chapter Thirty-Two
GIDEON

※

I'm so glad Boxing Day is a Saturday this year. Don't forget to support our local small businesses if you're out and about! ~Molly Reed posted to the What's Up Neighbor app

THE KNOCKING AT MY DOOR WOKE ME UP. AFTER MY second ill-advised eggnog the night before, I had turned off my alarm, but apparently, the universe didn't want me sleeping in. Grabbing my phone off the nightstand, I swiped my doorbell app, expecting to see a package delivery, but instead, there was Paul, holding two coffee cups and looking decidedly uncomfortable,

Grabbing my robe and slippers, I hurried to the door while shoving my glasses on my face.

"Paul?" I opened the door wide, which was a mistake because outside even the air was crusty, the sort of cold where it hurt to take a full breath. "Get in here."

"Gladly." Paul was at least bundled up for the weather with a coat, gloves, hat, and boots. But even with all that, he still shivered as I ushered him in.

"What's wrong?" I asked as I shut the door. "It's not even seven yet."

"Aren't you getting ready?" He frowned, gaze sweeping over my plaid robe and fuzzy slippers and undoubtedly bleary eyes. "I brought the coffee."

"Ready?" I felt like we were in a play I no longer knew the lines to. Heck, I wasn't sure I knew which act we were in with everything seeming far off-script. I did, however, accept one of the paper cups. "You got coffee out? You always drink yours at home."

A rosy flush spread across his already pink-from-the-cold cheeks. "Yeah, well, you don't like my brew, and it's so cold, I figured you'd need it for the drive."

"Drive?" I blinked again. What was I missing here? Maybe I'd had more to drink than I'd thought if I couldn't follow Paul's usually straightforward train of thought at all. "Maybe you should come sit down so I can let the caffeine start working on my brain."

After removing his boots and coat, he followed me to my kitchen table, where I took several bracing sips of the coffee. And still couldn't quite figure out what Paul was up to. "Did we have plans?"

"Well…not exactly. But the after-Christmas sales…you said you always go?" His face sagged. "I wanted to catch you before you went. I figured you'd already be up with a list of where to go and in which order."

"I wasn't in the mood this year," I admitted before I took another drink of my coffee, which was vaguely minty. Apparently, Paul had paid attention to the times I'd ordered peppermint mochas around him. "I turned off my alarm. Too much eggnog last night."

"Yeah? You should have come back over." He waggled his eyebrows at me, but his eyes remained uncertain. "I have sleep cures that don't involve hangovers."

"You shoveled my walk." I looked out the kitchen window at the frozen side yard and my bone-dry path to the garage. "Salted it too."

"I did." Voice matter-of-fact, he stretched his arms. "Didn't want you slipping if you headed out early before I could come over."

"You came to go shopping with me?" I tilted my head, considering this very un-Paul-like development.

"I thought I might." A muscle in his cheek twitched. "Get a head start on next year. You can tell me what all I might need."

"Because you want my help with next Christmas?"

"No." Paul licked his lips as he darted his gaze everywhere but at me. "I mean, yes. Damn it. This is why I'm not good with words. I want *you* for next Christmas. The help is a bonus."

"Oh." My nervous system jolted as if the barista had snuck an extra quad shot in my coffee. Paul wanted *me*. And to go shopping. But me. He wanted *me*. I dug my fingers into my thigh. Yup. Definitely awake. But there had to be a catch. "And between now and then?"

Paul nodded solemnly. "There's a lot of holidays I've been ignoring. I want you for all those too. Figured I might start by letting you talk me into the right kind of glasses for champagne for New Year's. And last year you did some sort of heart wreath on the door for February. The easter bunny cutouts, those might startle Jim, but you can probably twist my arm into some spring flowers for my place."

"You noticed my changing decorations?" My eyebrows shot up so high that the stretch was just short of painful.

"I notice a lot." He shrugged, all his shoulder muscles rippling. "Maybe not as much as you and your eye for detail."

"Oh, you'd be surprised what I miss," I said dryly.

Apparently, I'd missed him deciding he wanted to keep me around. And true, he hadn't ever *said* he wanted to end things after Christmas. I'd just assumed because he hadn't said otherwise either. But looking back, I could see any number of clues that perhaps he hadn't had one foot out the door after all.

"Maybe if I spoke up more, you wouldn't need to play detective." Doing an excellent mind-reading job yet again, Paul gave a sheepish smile.

"So you're saying you'll need my help for all the occasions between now and next Christmas?" I needed him to spell things out for me because I still wasn't entirely sure what he was after. "Is this because you're worried about the wedding?"

"Nope. Elaine's as bossy as you." He chuckled as Butterscotch landed on the table between us. He gave the cat an idle pat. "She'll tell me what to wear, and I can probably muddle through which fork to use when. But I need *you*, Gideon. Just you. Even if you wear sweats and hang out on my ugly couch and take a year or two off from decorating."

I made an undignified noise. "Or two?"

"That's not me putting out an end date." He made a dismissive gesture before scratching between the cat's ears. "Just doubting you can last forty-eight hours, let alone twelve or more months without decorating, shopping, organizing, or scheming."

"I am good at schemes." My tone was all pleased before a new thought paraded through my addled brain. "Maybe too good."

"What?" He wrinkled up his face as if I were the one being confusing when he was the one who'd tossed me on a roller coaster without a seat belt with all these revelations.

"I really did want to save your Christmas." My mouth

twisted as I tried to find the right words. Paul wasn't the only one who had a hard time speaking up. "But I also kinda wanted in your pants. I think I might have tricked you into keeping me around."

Paul blinked, then blinked again. "Well. Can you keep on tricking me?"

"Pardon?"

"First, I'm not sure you noticed, but outside of letting you boss me around, I'm a tough guy." He offered another crooked smile. "Not a pushover. No one's weaseling their way into my life if I don't want it. If you trapped me, I wanted to be caught."

"*Oh.*" I considered this, recalibrating how I'd framed the events of the last month. "So, you want me to keep inviting myself along?"

"Well, ideally, I'll get better at doing the inviting." He reached for my hand. The tremble in his fingers made my chest clench. Paul nervous and tentative was new. And that it was because of me, well that was enough to make my own hand shake against his. "But yes. Keep showing up. I want you to."

"Is that what this morning is about?" I asked. His presence was finally starting to make some sense. "You showing up? Inviting yourself shopping?"

"It seemed important to you. I can show up for you too. Maybe I'm not as good at knowing when and how to help as you, but I want to try."

"You do help. You knew I didn't want to be alone on Christmas. And maybe you felt sorry for me—"

"It's not pity." He squeezed my hand. "Trust me, I hate pity more than anyone. I wanted you there. For me. Because you being there makes everything better. I told you. I need *you.*"

Oh. He had said that, hadn't he? Lori was right, I truly

was dense. Or maybe, more to the point, I was so bogged down by old fears that I hadn't let myself hope for what I wanted most.

"I need you too," I admitted softly. The words, they hurt, jagged little things, but once they were out, I could exhale. Perhaps trying to ignore that need for weeks hadn't been my wisest choice. "Maybe you're the one who saved *my* Christmas."

"Can't it be both?" He rubbed his thumb against my palm. "We rescued each other. And now we don't have to be alone for any of the other nine zillion holidays you celebrate."

My laugh sounded a lot like Elaine's had the day before, closer to a hysterical giggle than a normal chuckle. But it was either laugh or give in to the rising urge to weep. "You don't have to suddenly embrace shopping and seasonal decor."

"I would. For you." He held my gaze, eyes as serious as I'd seen them. And not grumpy serious either. Solemn. Like he wasn't kidding about wanting me around. Another giddy laugh escaped my chest even as he continued, "Making you happy, that's important. So if bargain hunting makes you happy, let's go."

"Hmm." I made a noncommittal noise. Laughter wasn't the only escape valve for dealing with emotional overload. I glanced in the direction of my stairs before peering again at the frozen world outside.

"Gideon," Paul groaned. "Stop looking like you're trying to decide between hauling me back to bed upstairs with you and the shopping trip."

Busted. My laugh this time was free and easy. "Can I have both?"

"You can." Giving me a lusty grin, he jerked his head toward the stairs. "Maybe bed first?"

"You're on." Abandoning my coffee, I hustled away from the table, him close behind me. Outside, the temperatures were reaching record lows, but in here, things were about to get mighty toasty.

Chapter Thirty-Three
PAUL

Our lights are a hopeless tangle. Does anyone have good light storage tips? I'd ask our local Holiday expert, but he's not answering his messages! ~ Penny Jordan posted to the What's Up Neighbor app

I WAS SO HAPPY TO BE BACK ON DECENT FOOTING WITH Gideon that I almost forgot I'd never been upstairs at his place. We passed a room with an enormous cat tree and enough computer equipment to power a small space station, but I didn't slow down until we were in Gideon's room. Like the rest of the place, it was very finished in feel. Mulberry walls, big four-poster bed, matching dresser and nightstands, and extremely Gideon decor.

"Your bedding is plaid." I'd been about to grab him for a kiss, but I had to stop and laugh. His bedding matched some of his ties and his Christmas pajamas and had smart piping along the edges. "I love it."

"Happy to amuse you." Gideon shut the door behind us. "Making sure the cat doesn't come investigating. Are your guests going to notice you're gone?"

"Nope." I pulled him to me. "I saw to Jim before I went for the coffee, and Elaine and Brandon have plans for a brunch with friends from Brandon's undergrad program. I'm all yours."

"Good." He looped his arms around my neck as I fiddled with the double knot in his robe belt.

"At first, I thought your robe was ridiculously stuffy. But now..." I trailed off as I finally got the knot free and could use both ends of the belt to draw him even closer against me.

"And now?"

"Now it gives me ideas." Lowering my head, I nipped at his neck while holding tight to the belt, but Gideon frowned.

"Is that why we never did this sooner? You thought I was too uptight?"

Busted. Damn it. I didn't want to lose this mood and easy peace between us, but I couldn't lie either. "I was wrong. Honestly, your genius exterior is a little intimidating. Plus, I didn't realize how enjoyable your bossiness could be or how much fun I'd have unwrapping you. I definitely underestimated you for far too long. I'm sorry."

"I'm hardly that scary," Gideon scoffed, not looking at all reassured. "And I *can* be casual. I own jeans."

"Don't change, Gideon." I dropped the belt so I could cup his face instead. My stomach cramped. I hated that I'd hurt him. "Not for me. Keep the robe. And the slippers. And the drawer of bow ties. I love them."

"Really?" He narrowed his eyes, but a small smile teased the corners of his mouth.

"Yeah." I kissed him then because I was better at action than words, which I seemed to keep screwing up. Either I said the wrong thing or not enough things or had bad timing, but kissing, that I could get right. His cheeks were scratchy with morning stubble, but his lips were soft. I sank into the kiss, holding him close, trying to engrave all these confusing feelings of mine onto his soul.

I tried to tell him with my mouth that I'd do better to find the right words. He deserved that. And maybe I couldn't write him poetry, but I could put it into my touch, my lips, my very breath. He tasted familiar, like a memory I hadn't known I'd had until our first kiss. Funny how I'd avoided him for so long when now I felt like I'd known him forever.

"I'm not the only one too bundled up." Releasing a breathy sigh, he shoved at my shirts. "How many layers do you have on anyway?"

"Too many." Laughing, I pulled off my undershirt, thermal shirt, and overshirt all at once. Because he wasn't the only one with quirks, I set my clothes on a low chaise near the foot of the bed as we both stripped. I was careful with my pants, remembering what I had in my pocket. Later. I wasn't slowing down now for more talking, and maybe later I'd have finally found the right words.

"That's much better." Naked, he tugged me back to face him so he could give a rather possessive kiss. Perhaps we still had some things to work out, but the return of his bossy ways was reassuring. If he wanted to claim me, I'd happily let him. Heck, he could slap one of his color-coded labels on me. I was all his, and I tried to tell him that with my lips as the kiss built and built, one turning into ten turning into both of us panting. "Bed. Now."

He gently pushed me onto the mattress, and I readily scrambled to the center so there was room for him. I stretched out against the pillows, fisting my cock and giving it several slow strokes as Gideon took his sweet time joining me.

"See?" I asked as he retrieved condoms and lube from

the nightstand. My cock pulsed harder as the items landed next to me on the bed. "I like you bossy plenty."

"I don't always have to be in charge." Gideon wriggled in next to me, on his side, and when I turned toward him, he used my momentum to pull me on top of him. He looked up with such wonder and adoration that my breath caught. Damn. My luck had indeed changed for the better, and I was going to do my damnedest to appreciate him.

"Keep looking at me like that and you can have whatever you'd like." My voice was gruff as I swept my hands down his sides. "Be in charge. Or not. Whatever does it for you."

"You. You do it for me." He kissed me hungrily, strong arms holding me tighter against him. He smelled warm and cozy, scent as familiar as his taste and equally as good at driving me out of my mind. Wrapping his legs around my hips, he shifted until our cocks dragged past each other, a slow grind with each kiss.

"Now." His voice was breathless and husky. "Want you in me."

"Like this?" I asked, moving back slightly to give him room to move if he wanted. We'd only ever done this with him on top of me, which I loved, him riding me hard and fast, but I was happy enough to change it up.

"Yeah." He licked his lips as he reached for the lube. "Let me…"

"Do it." I slid back into more of a kneeling position so he had space to pull his legs back and use his hand to lube himself up. He was more aggressive than I would have been, going right to two fingers and thrusting them deep as he moaned low and urgent. "Fuck. You're the hottest thing I've ever seen."

I made quick work of the condom, then slowed down, enjoying his show, tracing his rim with a fingertip, brushing against his hand as he worked himself open. He must have liked that because he made a desperate noise.

"You're plenty hot too. Come here." Spreading his legs wider, he tilted his ass up, a clear offering. So fucking hot. And such a gift. Somehow I knew he didn't do it this way very often, and his trust in me was every bit as sexy as his lewd display. I didn't want to ever let him down again, and I had to swallow hard as I moved into position.

"This good?" I went for slow, shallow thrusts, trying not to rush, both for him but also for me. I wanted to memorize this moment, how good he felt, hot and slick against my cock, and how soft and open his expression was. He hissed out a breath even as he pushed up to take more of my cock.

"Fuck. So much more than good. Intense." Breathing hard, he met my thrusts until I was deep as I could get, thighs brushing his ass. I held his hips, searching for the angle that had him chanting my name. "Paul. There. Right there."

Shutting his eyes, he stretched, torso rippling as he clutched at the sheets. He was tight and perfect and so sexy letting go like this that my pulse pounded, muscles tensing. Needing to get him closer to coming and fast, I grabbed one of his hands and moved it to his cock.

"Let me watch you."

"Want you to touch me too." Linking our hands together, he thrust up into our shared grip. Sharing his pleasure like this was almost more intense than being inside him, and inside him was pretty damn amazing. He moved restlessly, body straining. "Need more."

"Yeah." I sped up my thrusts, meeting his motions until we were moving in perfect sync, him urging me on by wrapping one of his legs around me. "That's it. Take what you need."

"Faster," he demanded through clenched teeth. He was letting me set the pace, but every bossy command of his pushed me higher and higher. I loved how there was zero guessing in bed with Gideon. When he wanted more, he simply took it, and fuck if that wasn't enough to have me right up on the edge.

"Fuck. Gideon."

"More." His back bowed, body arching up, cock going harder in my grip.

"You're killing me," I groaned even as I obeyed. For him, I'd gladly suffer any number of endings, if only for the chance to see him like this, body splayed out, every muscle straining toward me, head tipping back like he was waiting. Waiting for me.

I fucked harder and faster, going deep, both of us moaning with every thrust until he stiffened. "There. Oh. There. Paul."

He shot so hard the first rope of come hit his shoulder, torso curving up like he couldn't get enough of me, couldn't take me deep enough, like he wanted every last bit of me. That need, as much as the sight of his climax and the way his body clenched around my cock pushed me over, hips thrusting frantically until I too was coming.

"Yes. Yes." The pleasure was so intense it was a sweet pain, making me shout, helpless to do anything other than shudder over and over until I collapsed next to him. We were both sweaty and breathless, and I couldn't do anything other than kiss him over and over. His forehead. His cheek. His parted lips. The pulse in his neck, racing as hard as my own.

He laughed, undoubtedly at my ridiculousness. "Wow. This is how I want to spend every Boxing Day from now on."

"You've got it," I groaned. I liked the sound of "from

now on." Gideon not eyeing the door was a decided improvement, and maybe he'd start believing me that I wasn't going anywhere either. "But tell me your shopping plans aren't going to require me to move anytime in the next five years."

"All this and shopping too?" A wide smile broke across his face, the sort of sun that could chase away the fiercest of cold snaps. "I'm a lucky guy."

"Me too." Wonder raced through me. He was wrong. I was the lucky one, and I could only hope he kept giving me the chance to show him. For once, I was seizing my good luck fast, not letting go, greedily hoarding every damn second with him.

Chapter Thirty-Four
GIDEON

Lights question answered! Now, what to do with the giant nativity set my mother-in-law bestowed on us? ~Penny Jordan posted to the What's Up Neighbor app

"Think there are still bargains to be had?" Naked, Paul stretched in my bed, a gorgeous display that almost tempted me right back to bed before he added, "Guess I better see to poor Jim before we go."

"Poor Jim." I made a sympathetic noise as I toweled off. We'd dozed together for a while, then I'd snuck out of bed while he snoozed to take a fast shower. "And yes, we'll find some deals. I don't mind picked-over shelves either. I'll take the nap with you any day."

"Me too." Sitting up, he offered me a soft smile. "That was really nice. Thank you."

I started to bristle at the gratitude for something that had been a mutual pleasure, but then I reconsidered, chewing the inside of my cheek as I reasoned this out.

"When you say thank you, do you mean it like *job well done* or more like *that was awesome?*"

Paul frowned as if I were as dense as Lori thought. "Is that what you assumed all Christmas? That your job was finished and I didn't need you anymore? Like thank you as shorthand for goodbye?"

"Maybe," I hedged as I pulled on clothes.

"No, I'm not through with you." Leaving the bed, he hugged me from behind, hindering my ability to get dressed, but that was okay. The warm feeling in my chest was worth it, particularly when he put his lips near my ear. "Not by a long shot."

"Oh."

"I say thank you a lot to everyone." His tone shifted to something more solemn. "Not just you. You only get so many chances in life to say it."

Oh. Of course, Paul more than anyone else would know the value of not waiting to tell people how much you appreciated them. And this was his way of saying I mattered to him. I understood now, and I sank into his embrace, head falling against his shoulder.

"Feels like I should be the one thanking you," I admitted as he squeezed me closer, his husky laugh in my ear saying he thought I meant orgasms. "And not just for the sex. But everything else. Thank you."

"You're welcome." He kissed my ear before releasing me. "That reminds me. I have something for you." Scooping his jeans off the chaise, he dug around in the pocket before coming up with two cuff links. "For your collection."

He gestured at the clear case on top of my dresser where I kept my grandfather's cuff links along with some others I'd found over the years. But somehow, I knew these were more than a flea market find, and I accepted them with a hushed reverence. They were a simple set but heavy, chunky silver steel with a crosshatch pattern.

"Where are they from?" I asked as I gazed down at my palm.

"My attic." He too was staring at the pair. "I found them when I was looking for the earrings for Elaine. I don't know exactly who they belonged to as I only saw Dad in a shirt with buttons a handful of times, but Mom kept them with her jewelry."

"I can't accept these." An almost physically painful level of regret laced my words. "Brandon will want them for the wedding."

Paul shook his head. "I asked. He doesn't. Too fiddly for him. I told him I wanted you to have them. I trust you to keep them safe for me."

I sucked in a breath. Once, a million years ago, I'd proposed to Lori because that was what all our friends were doing. Get a ring. Have a nice dinner. Pop the question. But in this moment, these humble pieces of steel felt far more significant and life-altering. And I wasn't so dense that I couldn't understand Paul's subtext here. He wanted me to keep his heart safe. And I would.

"Thank you," I whispered. "I'll keep them safe."

Forever. I didn't add the word, but I felt it deep in my bones. I wasn't letting the gift that was Paul's heart go. I carefully put the set in my box right next to the ones my grandfather had worn on his wedding day.

"I wish I had something as significant to give you." My mouth twisted.

"The dishes you found, those were pretty special," Paul said as he finished dressing. "But you gave me something even more important."

"Oh?"

"You gave me back the season. I didn't even realize

how low I'd sunk until you pulled me back out of the pit. Not dreading the holiday, that's something."

"Pun intended?" I laughed.

"Pun definitely intended." He captured me in a fast, joyful kiss, and I wasn't sure I'd ever been this happy. Like him, I hadn't realized how badly I'd wanted exactly this until I had it, and now, I was going to cling to it with everything I had.

Chapter Thirty-Five
PAUL

❧

Good luck to everyone on the road this weekend. Need a ride to the airport? Skip the ride-sharing app. Text me. Looking for a little extra work to pay down the coming credit card avalanche! ~Molly Reed posted to the What's Up Neighbor app

"You win," Elaine crowed with obvious delight at Gideon's victory with the board game he'd brought over from his place. The well-worn box and his experienced play had made his victory predictable but no less fun to watch.

"Again." Brandon let out a low groan. Okay, watching Gideon win had been fun for *me*. Maybe not Mr. Ultra Competitive. "Next time, we're bringing our favorite game. Then I'll stand more of a chance."

"My poor genius." Elaine wrapped an arm around him. She and Brandon were on one side of the table, Gideon and I the other, the game perfectly placed in the center like the table had been waiting for a night exactly like this. Brandon swiped the last cracker from a board of snacks Gideon had set out, and Elaine laughed more. "Tell Paul you need a gaming rematch as your bachelor party."

"Paul probably already has Dodgers tickets." Brandon made a dismissive gesture with his cracker. It was a long, thin gourmet variety that Gideon had picked up on our shopping trip. The festive snack board was another purchase, and this cozy game night was well worth the purchases.

"You have to tell me a date first," I reminded him.

"Our graduation is May. And trying to do it the same weekend is probably a recipe for disaster."

"Probably," I agreed easily. The last two days had been all about wedding debates, and I was more than ready for some concrete details I could plan around. "Pick your date. I'll have the human Jim to mind things. I'm not going to miss your big day."

"So we're thinking last weekend in July." Elaine leaned forward, all excitement and glowing eyes. "That should beat whatever school schedules we're dealing with and Gideon's start of the term rush too."

"Me?" Gideon made a startled noise.

"You are coming, right?" Brandon frowned around the last of his cracker. "I doubt Paul gets on a plane without you."

"Oh, and say you'll come to graduation if you don't have a work thing yourself that weekend," Elaine added, reaching across to pat Gideon's hand. "You might have to rescue us all from Brandon's cooking."

"Hey now! I'm taking lessons."

"Yes, and we all have lots of faith in you." Elaine gave him a kiss on the cheek. "But I still want Gideon to come."

Next to me, Gideon stayed tense. "Uh..."

Did he not want to come? We hadn't exactly discussed it, but...*oh*. We hadn't talked. That was it.

"Maybe I didn't ask yet? Gideon, will you come to the wedding with me? And graduation too if you can swing it."

He nodded slowly. "I suppose I can help you with the tux."

"I don't want you to come for *help*." I needed Gideon to get it through his head that I wanted *him*, not his impressive organizational skills. "I want you to come because Brandon's right, I don't want to go without you. You belong there. With me."

"Aww." Elaine's expression went all soft before she prodded the still-silent Gideon. "If you don't say yes…"

Gideon startled like he was just waking up. "Yes." He blinked, then smiled. "Yes, I'll come."

"Good." Brandon took a sip of his wine, a warm and fruity number Gideon had pulled from the back of his pantry. "Grumpy Paul was going to be no fun."

"I don't know." Putting an arm around me, Gideon gave a knowing look. "I kind of like him grumpy."

"You say that now." The tips of my ears were hot. I liked this version of Gideon a lot, more affectionate and playful since our big talk.

"And you say you like me how I am," he countered with a kiss on my temple. "I don't want you changing either."

He was wrong there. I had changed. And I liked it, liked *me* more now, liked the easiness in my step and the hopefulness in my heart. "I'm sure I can still manage enough crankiness to keep you happy."

"You guys are one more long look away from me telling you to get a room," Brandon complained with a fake indignant expression.

I shrugged. "It's my house."

"So it is." Brandon mimicked my shrug and tone both.

"You do a good impression of Paul." Gideon laughed and shook his head.

"I should." Brandon chuckled as well, then turned surprisingly serious. "I had enough practice. I'm always saying everything important, I learned from my big brother."

"Hey, who's getting sappy now?" I had to glance away at Jim in her dog bed before he could see how much the compliment moved me.

"But it's true." Brandon's chair squeaked as he scooted closer to the table. "You taught me everything I needed to know."

Warmth started at my toes, snaked up my back and neck, and made my scalp itch. "I think you have a stack of physics textbooks saying otherwise."

"That's not the important stuff," Brandon scoffed, not letting me deflect like usual. "You taught me what mattered."

"Thanks. I tried," I admitted, then added softly, "You taught me too."

"But it wasn't easy." He held my gaze when I would have looked away again. And the denial was right there on the tip of my tongue, but I remembered my kitchen chat with Elaine and all my talks with Gideon.

"No. It wasn't." Maybe shielding him from that fact hadn't been as much of a kindness as I'd always thought. Maybe he deserved to know some of the truth.

"And it wasn't easy when I moved away, was it?" He frowned like he was puzzling something out for the first time.

"It was f—" I started to lie, then Gideon tapped me with his foot under the table. *Oh. Right.* I was trying to be truthful here. "It wasn't...pleasant. I miss you. But you've got a life to be proud of now. And I'm proud of you. And jealous of the sunshine."

I added the last bit to make him laugh, but he stayed strangely somber. "Maybe I like snow..."

He glanced over at Elaine, who nodded sharply. "Oh, go ahead and tell him."

"We were waiting until we had definitive news, but Elaine's a finalist for a professorship at Stanton Anthony." Brandon beamed, pride lacing every word. "Tenure track. Great research opportunity."

Here. The local college, which, yes, was practically an Ivy, but *here*? My pulse pounded.

"You want to leave the West Coast?"

"We do." Elaine nodded at the same time as Brandon. "We want to be near family."

"But yours..."

"Travels the globe." She rolled her shoulders before refilling her wineglass. "A flight to Philly isn't going to stop my folks. And Brandon misses you too."

"Yup. And eventually, we want to make you an uncle." Brandon's grin reached new levels of wide. "Can't have you miles and miles away."

"No rush on that." My voice came out too gruff. Brandon? A dad? Damn. I wasn't sure I'd ever be ready for that. But them starting a family here, where I could see... that seemed like almost too much to hope for. "But you'll need a job too."

"I'm working on it. I've got a bunch of applications in. Everywhere in commuting distance from here. Something will turn up for me too."

"He's being modest." Elaine bumped his shoulder. "He's already being wooed by some private-sector jobs nearby, and I'm expecting him to get more than a couple of finalist nods for local professorships after the first of the year."

My jaw dropped open. This might really be happening. "Wow."

"Good wow?" Brandon's eyes narrowed. And this was where I should be unselfish, tell them to stay on the coast where they were likely to be happier, but instead, I nodded. Honest. I was trying to be more honest.

"Yeah. Good wow." I swallowed hard, trying to collect the right words. "I don't... You shouldn't make this choice because of me. I love the idea of you here, but I don't want you giving up your sunshine and West Coast living."

"Paul." Brandon gave me a stern look. "You gave up two decades of your life for me. I can shovel a little snow."

My eyes burned, and all I could do was nod. Under the table, Gideon grabbed my hand, laced our fingers together.

"And when it gets to be too cold, Elaine and I will escape to an island." Brandon laughed like he knew I was struggling to keep my composure. "Maybe drag you along."

"I'd pay to see Paul in swim trunks." Gideon offered me a gentle smile.

"See?" Elaine's grin hadn't wavered. "It'll all work out."

"Yeah." I exhaled hard and clung to Gideon's hand like it was the one thing keeping me from drowning. I managed a rough nod for Brandon and Elaine. "Thank you."

"No, thank you." Brandon continued to hold my gaze, his brown eyes way more solemn than usual. I'd told Gideon that I said thank you because I didn't want to miss my chance. Maybe Brandon was doing the same thing. I'd do it all over again, fight to keep him, make all the same sacrifices, and more, and I'd do it without any thanks. But still, him saying it mattered.

Under the table, Gideon squeezed my hand. Funny how "thank you" came so easily to me while other words were so big and scary. I could thank Gideon later, tell him how much it meant to me that he'd given Brandon and me this time together, that he'd helped me make Brandon's dream come true. But thank you wasn't entirely accurate either. I didn't merely appreciate Gideon. And he deserved to know the truth in my heart.

Chapter Thirty-Six
GIDEON

It's my annual New Year's Eve party! All are welcome, families especially! Parking is likely to be tight, so bundle up! See you soon!
~Cheryl Bridges posted to the What's Up Neighbor app

"Tell me we get to leave soon." Paul ambled up next to me right as Penny Jordan left to go chase after one of her kids.

"It's not midnight yet." I pretended to care about staying. Cheryl's party with its loaded buffet table and lively conversation was fun, way more fun with someone by my side than in prior years, but all it took was one heated look from Paul, and I was already calculating exactly how many steps to our driveway.

"I know." Paul threw an arm around me, apparently caring naught for the neighborhood gossip mill. "But I'm old and grumpy and watching you from across the room has me wanting a more private...toast."

"That could maybe be arranged." It was just us, Brandon and Elaine having flown back to California on the twenty-ninth. "Maybe I can tell Cheryl we're worried about Jim in case anyone sets off fireworks at midnight."

"Yes, think of my poor dog and not my d—*Hello*, Molly." Paul went from lecherous to upstanding citizen in three seconds as Molly Reed joined us.

"Hi, Paul. And Gideon. Paul, I just had to tell you how much the kids loved your reindeer this year. What a welcome addition to the neighborhood. Will they be returning next year?"

I waited for Paul's answer almost as eagerly as Molly. He'd said he wanted me to still be around next Christmas. He'd even indulged me in the shopping. But I was still working on believing that cranky Paul Frost truly wanted a future with the Holiday guy. Paul, however, had no such issue, giving Molly a lazy nod.

"Likely." He jerked his head in my direction. "Gideon will undoubtedly make sure I get the reindeer up on time and that they're not lonely. He talked me into snowmen—snow*people*—for the front yard next year too."

I'd found that on clearance and added it to the cart, mainly because it had complicated wiring. Paul would need me to hook it to his main lighting scheme. Insurance. He said he wanted *me*, not my help, but that didn't mean I wouldn't have my talents at the ready.

"Go, Gideon." Molly winked at me, and my cheeks heated.

"Thanks."

"I don't think the little kids are going to make it to midnight." She sighed as a pack of like six kids under eight came barreling through the room.

"Or the big ones." Paul gave me a meaningful look.

"We're thinking of heading out early as well," I added quickly, skin going from warm to supernova.

"Leaving? The party's just getting started!" Cheryl

breezed by with a tray of triangle-shaped pastries. But right as she reached us, her attention was diverted by the herd of kids discovering her new couch. "Oh! Savannah, honey, the couch isn't a trampoline."

"I don't think she'll notice if you sneak out," Molly said in a stage whisper as Cheryl whirled away to go deal with the kids. "Go on, make a break for it while you can."

"Come on," I said to Paul, heading for the spare bedroom that had been turned into a coat room for the party. "Let's find our coats."

Laughing, we dodged a clump of teens hanging out in the corner of the coatroom, phones out and bored expressions firmly in place. Heading out into the night, I pulled my coat more securely around me because the cold snap from earlier in the week had continued. "Wow. It's cold."

"I know." Paul huffed out a breath, little puffs visible against the frigid night air. "How did I let you talk me into walking?"

"Because it's good for you, old man." I bumped his shoulder.

"Ha." Chuckling, he sped up his steps, not quite a jog but zooming ahead of me. "I'll show you old."

"Wait up." I did jog to catch up but then abruptly came to a halt at the corner. The Morrison house was more lit up than usual, but it was the two large shipping containers out front that truly interested me. "Paul. Look."

"Huh." He returned to my side, his head tilting. "Two of those pod things. People only usually get those if they're moving…"

"Exactly." Pulse quickening, I stepped closer to the perimeter of their yard, using the flashlight on my phone to search.

"What *are* you doing?" Paul trailed after me.

"Looking for a sign," I muttered. And the Morrisons

potentially moving after all this time was definitely a sign from the universe, but I meant more the literal kind. A real estate one like the post I discovered to the left of the driveway. "Aha! Found it. They're really moving."

"*Finally.*" Paul watched as I plucked a sheet of paper from the clear plastic holder on the side of the sign. "How much?"

It was typical neighborly curiosity to want to know the asking price, but my chest felt unreasonably tight as I scanned the paper, which extolled the square footage and period-appropriate details. "Oh."

"What?" Paul peered over my shoulder. "That's not that awful. Market keeps going up around here. Your place will fetch more than you think if you want to try for it."

"I should." Several decades' worth of wistfulness laced my voice. The mortgage wasn't the only issue. The place was going to need a huge cash infusion to bring out its potential. And repairs I didn't know the most about, like rooves and windows. Teenage me hadn't thought in practical terms when dreaming about the day the place could be mine. "But it needs a lot of work."

"I could help with that." Putting an arm around me, Paul pulled me closer.

"You could?" I was still caught up in my head, the intersection of years of dreaming and practical realities of what I'd even *do* with such a big house when I rattled around inside my existing one.

Going stiff, he made an indignant noise. "You still think I'm only in this thing for your decorating help?"

"No." I bit my lip hard because that wasn't precisely true. "I mean, maybe, but I'm working on believing you want to be with me as a relationship thing, not simply friends doing each other favors and falling into bed thing."

"That was fun." He kissed right below the brim of my

hat. "But I'm too old for casual. And I want you to get this house. Let me help you make your dreams come true."

A sound somewhere between gasp and moan escaped my throat. I wasn't sure anyone had ever said anything that nice to me before, and I had no idea how to reply.

"I love you, Gideon." Paul's rough whisper hung between us, warm words cutting through arctic air.

"It's so soon." Like him, I was whispering, terrified that if I spoke too loudly, I'd discover this was all a dream.

Next to me, he shrugged before tugging me closer. "And yet not nearly soon enough."

"True." It had been a whirlwind month for sure, but in other ways, this moment had been years in the making. And I couldn't deny the truth in my own heart. "I love you too. Maybe it's not too soon. But it's still scary."

"Terrifying." He gave a strained chuckle. "I wanted to tell you all week. Couldn't find the right words."

"I think you just did." I stretched to kiss his cheek. "You said you want to make my dreams come true. You really want to help me work on this house?"

"Yeah. I mean, I've got years in construction know-how itching for a project like this. There's only so much I can do to my place. But more than that, I want to see the inside of this house, and I want you to tell me stories about your grandparents. And I want to hear all your design specifications for everything."

"I've got a few ideas."

"I know you do." He laughed knowingly. "A project like this where I don't have to make all the decisions on my own, that sounds nice."

"My very own contractor I could boss around certainly has its appeal." The wind whipped around us, but my insides had never been toastier. Paul kissed my head again before moving toward the For Sale sign and removing all the white papers from the box. "What are you doing?"

"Shh." He put a finger to his lips. "You don't need a bidding war. Call first thing. Heck, text tonight. A lot of realtors don't sleep or take New Year's off."

"You're really serious about doing this." I shook my head. His eyes were gleaming and the spring in his step as he returned to my side certainly looked genuine.

"I'm all in, Gideon." Standing in front of me, fist full of papers, he gazed deep into my eyes. "I don't know how else to tell you. I don't care about it being too soon or moving too fast. Life is short."

"I know." I reached out to cup his face with my gloved hand. "I'm in too. I'm terrified. I worry this will slip away. But I'm in."

"It's not going to slip away if we both hold it tight." He leaned into my hand, the pressure of his chin a welcome reminder this wasn't a dream. This was real life, and I couldn't let this chance pass me by simply because I was scared.

"Let's go for it." Dropping my hand, I strode away from him, each step seeming to carry me closer to the real dream, which was him. The exact details were murky, but that was okay. There would be time enough to work out questions like who would live where and when. What mattered most was a future together. But the house sure would be nice, so to that end, I quickly stashed the For Sale sign behind an overgrown hedge.

"That's rather devious." Paul grinned at me.

"I love you." I said the words stronger now, more definitively. If Paul, who had been through so much, could find his way back to hope and be this brave, then so could I.

"Good." He kissed me soundly on the mouth before resuming our trek toward our houses. "It's freezing. You better love me enough to warm me up before you start in with your list-making."

"This project is going to need a new spreadsheet." My voice was teasing, but my growing enthusiasm also shone through. "Maybe multiple ones. With colors."

"Gideon…" Paul warned.

"But the list can wait." I took his hand as we neared our driveway and swung it. "First things first."

"Gideon?" Paul used my hand to pull me flush against him.

"Yeah?" I was breathless from a lot more than the cold.

"I really can't wait to see your plan. I mean it. I want all your dreams to come true."

"Our plan," I corrected him. "If you're all in on doing it together, it needs to be *our* plan. Not just mine. Not just you doing me a favor. Or me bossing you around. Both of us. Together. Our plan."

"I like that." His voice was as soft as his expression as he claimed me for a tender kiss unlike any that had come before it. More than the meeting of lips, this was a promise. Behind us, our houses sparkled, lights still up. Tomorrow, we'd finally get around to taking the decorations down. Or not. We had a future to plan.

Chapter Thirty-Seven
PAUL

It's that time of year again! Make sure you see Gideon about our lighting theme of Home for the Holidays and to get on the schedule for manning the donations tent. And we're trying to beat the snow! Contact Paul Frost about next weekend's cleanup effort for the green space. We got a donation of donuts, so come hungry! ~Cheryl Bridges posted to the What's Up Neighbor App

"Hark the herald angels sing..." Music filtered out of the open bedroom window. I paused, lighting hooks in one hand, roll of clear lights in the other, feet straddling two sections of roof.

"Gideon." I made my voice stern as I moved closer to the flat section where he was securing the reindeer. "Did you turn the stereo on in our room?"

"We *are* hanging decorations," he pointed out, tone all reasonable. "It seemed fitting."

"It's not even December first." I still had a belly full of Thanksgiving leftovers, and we hadn't seen a single snowflake this fall.

"I wanted a head start."

"I know." I groaned, pretending like I hadn't been equally amenable to the idea of using the unseasonable warmth to get the outside work done. "I'm on the roof because you couldn't wait. But you're making me listen to Christmas carols too?"

"Yup." He gave me the sort of smile that usually ensured he got whatever the heck he wanted, everything from trendy gray cabinetry to butter-colored bathroom walls to me on my back and both of us sweaty. "I've already picked a movie out for later while we decorate the trees."

"There better be explosions. Wait. You said trees. Plural." I gave him a hard stare.

"Well, yes." He at least had the grace to look sheepish. "Yours from last year for the front room. My tabletop one for the foyer and—"

"Why, oh, why am I not surprised there's an *and* involved?"

"This red foil one for our room fell into my cart. It matches our hunter-green walls. I couldn't help it."

"Likely story." I shook my head, but I couldn't keep up the fake ire any longer. Even though it had been several months, I still liked the sound of *our room* too much not to grin. My whole life, I'd never shared a room with another person, never knew how much I wanted to or how complete my life would feel waking up next to him with Jim in her dog bed across the room and the cat hanging out on the window seat. *Our room.* I could live with any number of trees as long as Gideon never stopped calling it that.

But apparently, he wasn't done because he gave a sly grin. "And the dining room is so big…"

"Four trees?" I collapsed down next to his perch, setting aside my armful of lights. "I really must love you."

"You must," he agreed happily. He seemed to believe me more these days. The more I said it, the more readily he said it back, and the lighter he seemed with fewer questions about whether I really wanted to be here with him. Like I'd prefer being anywhere else. Silly man. I slung an arm around him as he continued, "I'm doing one entirely with a toy theme."

"Brandon and Elaine aren't expecting yet." Not that I asked my brother these things, but I doubted they were even trying, what with Elaine settling into a new job with a full course load at Stanton Anthony and Brandon doing a post-doc in a lab at a different university, supervising research I didn't entirely understand, but was proud of, nonetheless. They still had a newlywed glow about them, which I loved seeing. I'd seldom been as nervous as I had been making their wedding toast, but I'd only needed to look to Gideon to settle down and make my speech. He'd made the wedding weekend infinitely more tolerable, but of the two of us, he was definitely looking more forward to playing uncles.

"It's not for them." Gideon waved his hand far too dismissively for his precarious position up here on the roof. "For you. You like vintage toys."

Oh. Even now, a year into this thing together, Gideon could still blow me away with his thoughtfulness. He saw things I wasn't sure anyone else ever had.

"You noticed? Heck, I'm not sure *I* noticed, but I guess you're right. I do like the train."

"Of course, I'm right. And you'll see. You'll love this scheme."

"I love you," I said to make him beam that much

wider. "And yes, I'll love your trees, plural. But can we compromise on the movie?"

"Sure. Be a Scrooge." He laughed, but his eyes were twinkling. "Miss the guy from that cop drama you like as a lumberjack fake dating a shopkeeper. A male shopkeeper."

"All right, all right. Twist my arm. Guess we better support quality content like gay lumberjacks."

"I knew you'd see it my way." His voice was so smug that I had to give him a fast kiss, rooftop location be damned.

"I usually do." I held him closer against me. "After all, you've got me doing lights on three houses this year."

"Ours was a given. And do you trust your brother on a roof?" He pointed in the direction of our old houses. When I'd told Gideon that I wanted to make his dreams for his grandparents' house come true, I hadn't been entirely sure what would become of my place. But then Brandon had called, all excited because Elaine got the job, and I'd known. All that work I'd put into the house, all the hours, all the time spent trying not to miss him. It was simply meant to be.

Like Gideon and I. Brandon and I had come to an easy deal on a sale, and now he and Elaine were happily settled in with more photos on the walls than I'd ever thought possible and a steady stream of takeout delivery vehicles in the driveway.

"Brandon? On a roof?" I shuddered at the thought. "He's one brilliant idea away from disaster. No, you're right. You and I handling their outside decorations simply makes sense."

"And the Curry-Williams are new." He gestured at his old house. "We need to be neighborly. When Shelia said they'd only ever had apartments before this, I had to volunteer."

"You had to," I agreed because Gideon's attachment to our new neighbors was super cute. I knew full well he'd turned down two higher offers simply because he was drawn to the two-mom household with their flock of adopted kids. "The kids deserve some fun lights."

"They do." Gideon's eyes went wide like Jim eyeing a treat.

"Gideon, don't look at me like that."

"Like what?" He was all pretend innocence.

"I know perfectly well how many empty bedrooms we have."

"Butterscotch can share," he wheedled. "He ignores his cat tree these days anyway."

Gideon's cranky cat had surprised all of us by taking to Jim like he'd been waiting his whole feline life for a best friend. Now he spent most of his days napping with her on her various dog beds, saving up energy to terrorize us at night with a new level of playfulness. He was like a new cat, which was only fitting since I spent a lot of time feeling like a new human myself.

"How about we get married before you start handing out bedrooms?"

"Oh, all right." He sighed then turned his face toward mine. He frowned, nose wrinkling, and tilted his head. "Wait. You're serious."

Angling my body in the direction of our window, I pressed the remote in my pocket. "Deck the Halls" abruptly switched to a song we'd danced to at Brandon's wedding, one he'd declared his favorite sappy thing ever, even as I'd teased him. But I'd also filed that bit of information away.

"I might have tinkered with your playlist. And your schematic." I hit the other remote in my pocket, this one for the lights I'd strung earlier on the porch roof directly below us. A golden heart glowed as my heart started to thump.

"You planned this?" Gideon's voice was full of wonder.

"I did," I said gruffly. Our rooftop position made kneeling a bit dicey, so I settled for grabbing his hand. "Gideon, will you marry me?"

"Oh." A glow slowly spread across his face as his lips parted. "But I was going to ask you."

"So you were." Somehow, I managed to keep my voice from wavering even as I wanted to pump my fist.

"My method involved 'The Twelve Days of Christmas.'" He pretended to pout, but he remained lit up brighter than the lights beneath us.

"I had to preempt the flash mob."

"A few neighbors does not a flash mob make." He waved his free hand. I held tighter to his other one, both to keep him from flying off the roof and to cover the tremor that raced through me.

"Gideon…"

"I'll have to cancel the reservation for the geese."

"Gideon." My voice came out thin and crackly. "You still haven't answered me."

"You mean my yes wasn't clear?" He blinked like I was missing something obvious.

"Maybe I need to hear it," I admitted. Gideon wasn't the only one with fears. Sometimes I woke up in the middle of the night, him snuggled against me, and I couldn't believe how lucky I'd gotten. I kept expecting him to realize he could do far better, but apparently, he'd chosen me, and now I wanted to hold him to it. I wasn't letting him go.

"Yes." He released a giddy giggle that made him sound far younger. "A thousand times yes. We can even elope."

"No, we can't." I glowered at him.

"Sure, people would object, but they can deal." The setting sun overhead had nothing on the wattage of Gideon's smile.

"You deserve a wedding." After seeing him help with Brandon and Elaine's big day, I'd been convinced he needed an occasion of his own. "After all, we're almost done putting the house to rights. You need another big project to fuss over."

"Maybe a small one?" He smiled slyly and his eyes flashed like his brain was already firing off ideas. "The renovated community center could clean up nicely."

"It could." Thanks to Gideon's tireless fundraising, the community center had more than met its goal, and Gideon kept crowing about how the new programming had the neighborhood more connected than ever before. I knew better though. It was all Gideon who had worked his magic over the neighborhood. And me. Most especially me.

"Would Valentine's be too cliché?"

"It would be perfect. Whatever holiday you want."

"You. Luckily, I love you, bad puns and all." Still beaming, he kissed my cheek. "Thank you."

"No, thank *you*. I mean it, Gideon. You saved me." I honestly wasn't sure I could ever fully tell Gideon how much he meant to me. I tried. But there simply weren't words for what it felt like having my heart returned to my chest, rediscovering that I hadn't lost my capacity for joy after all.

"You saved you." He cupped my face. "But maybe I brought the garland."

"You brought the *you*." I met his kiss eagerly, not caring which of the neighbors might notice. Let them. Heck, maybe someone would snap a picture, put it on that app Gideon loved so much.

As the first snowflakes of the season fluttered down

around us, I wanted everyone to see. I wanted Gideon to see most of all how much he mattered to me. I wasn't ever going to stop giving thanks for my favorite Holiday.

DEAR READERS,

I hope you loved Gideon and Paul and their love story. If you would like even more holiday romance goodness, I have a special thank you for you. MUST BE SANTA is a FREE 13,000 word short story set in my BETTER NOT POUT universe and stars two orphans in search of the perfect dads. It's low angst holiday fun with one of my fan-favorite couples! Click here for your copy!

Making plans for the new year? Iâ€™m so excited to share that 2022 will have a new series from me centered around a group of former SEALs working as bodyguards. TOUGH LUCK will kick things off in March 22 & you can preorder now. While you wait for TOUGH LUCK, why not try the Rainbow Cove series? You can find the series page here!

Want ficlets, contests, and updates on other favorite characters? Make sure you're in my Facebook fan group, Annabeth's Angels, for all the latest news, contests, and freebies. And newsletter subscribers always get the latest news on releases, freebies, and more! Subscribe here.

Want even more books? Be sure and check out my other series and single title books! Thank you so much for all your reviews, likes, shares, social media posts, and other support! I love my readers!

Love,
Annabeth

Acknowledgements

Evergreen Park is a fictional suburb of Philadelphia and draws from the rich history of suburbs in the greater Philadelphia area. Many thanks to the resources and people who aided in my research about the area. The college where Gideon works is also fictional with credit to my mom for the name. Paul's sweet dog, Jim, was inspired by my Bernese Mountain dog loving reader, Jane Henriksen Baird. Any resemblance to real places, people, pets, or events is entirely coincidental.

Lauren Dombrowski did the cover illustration, and their vision helped bring the whole book to life. I'm so grateful for their talent. Cate Ashwood added the typography, and her cover and graphics talent is always so appreciated.

Huge thanks as well to my amazing beta readers. The amazing author Becca Seymour helped me go deeper on the emotions for the story. Melinda Rueter always provides the exact support I need. Layla Noureddine is always so insightful and pushes me to do better by the characters I love so much. Abbie Nicole did an amazing edit for me as well. Abbie's early support for this book was absolutely invaluable as well.

Thank you too for all my author friends and various Facebook and Discord groups for cheering me on with sprints and other support. I'm so proud of this finished book. My family puts up with my crazy hours, and I love them for their understanding. Writing and publishing is a journey, and I'm so grateful to everyone who has helped me along that journey.

Finally, my Facebook group, Annabeth's Angels, has been so supportive of this project, and I treasure all my readers. Thank you to everyone who has reviewed, tweeted, shared, and cheered me on—your support is priceless

Also by Annabeth Albert

Amazon Author Page
Many titles in audio and also available from other retailers!

Rainbow Cove series
Trust with a Chaser

Tender with a Twist

Lumber Jacked

Hope on the Rocks

#Gaymers series
Status Update

Beta Test

Connection Error

Out of Uniform series
Off Base

At Attention

On Point

Wheels Up

Squared Away

Tight Quarters

Rough Terrain

Frozen Hearts series
Arctic Sun

Arctic Wild

Arctic Heat

Hotshots series

Burn Zone

High Heat

Feel the Fire

Up in Smoke

Shore Leave series

Sailor Proof

Sink or Swim (February 2022)

Perfect Harmony series

Treble Maker

Love Me Tenor

All Note Long

Portland Heat series

Served Hot

Baked Fresh

Delivered Fast

Knit Tight

Wrapped Together

Danced Close

True Colors series

Conventionally Yours

Out of Character

Single Titles

Better Not Pout

Resilient Heart

Winning Bracket

Save the Date

Level Up

Mr. Right Now

Sergeant Delicious

Cup of Joe

Featherbed

About the Author

Annabeth Albert grew up sneaking romance novels under the bed covers. Now, she devours all subgenres of romance out in the open—no flashlights required! When she's not adding to her keeper shelf, she's a multi-published Pacific Northwest romance writer.

Emotionally complex, sexy, and funny stories are her favorites both to read and to write. Fans of quirky, Oregon-set books as well as those who enjoy heroes in uniform will want to check out her many fan-favorite and critically acclaimed series. Many titles are also in audio! Her fan group Annabeth's Angels on Facebook is the best place for bonus content and more!

Website: www.annabethalbert.com

Contact & Media Info:

- facebook.com/annabethalbert
- twitter.com/AnnabethAlbert
- instagram.com/annabeth_albert
- amazon.com/Annabeth/e/B00LYFFAZK
- bookbub.com/authors/annabeth-albert